THE MURDER LOOP

BEN BARNES

To Danielle and our girls,
Blessed to be among brilliant women

PART 1

LOST AMID THE WRECKAGE

CHAPTER ONE

Try to stay calm, they say.

You told yourself if it ever happened to you, you'd fight with every ounce of frenzied strength you could muster. But your hands are bound with cable ties cutting so tight into your wrists you can't feel your fingers anymore.

Maintain a non-aggressive posture, make no sudden movements.

You're trembling uncontrollably, desperately trying to push down the panic and nausea. If you could just sit up, maybe you could breathe properly. But you're pinioned to the floor of the van, the knees of one of your captors crushing the small of your back.

Talk with your captors in a non-threatening way and try to establish a bond.

A rag smeared with oil and grease is stuffed in your mouth. You'll choke on your own vomit if you don't hyperventilate first from the hood around your head.

Stay alert, alive to your circumstances, and avoid hysteria at all costs.

Every rut the van hits is a red-hot poker to the ribs that were broken in the violence of the abduction. The immediate terror induced a cold sweat. Now there's a warm streak down your front where you've pissed yourself at the thought of what's next.

Maintain hope.

Death won't be merciful. There will be days, weeks of torture first. Even if you could see through the hood, your eyes are blinded with tears. In the past, when you'd thought about dying, you dared to hope it would come gently in your sleep, after a life well lived. Not like this.

Encourage your captors to contact your loved ones.

Your loved ones will never see your face or hear your voice again. No one's coming to the rescue – you know that. The van screeches to a halt and you're dragged out to the ground.

You're too young for a heart attack. But a blowtorch of pain burns through your arms and chest, and you jerk and convulse and vomit at the same time.

Your mind has already gone and your body is following. Delusional, you hear a thud next to you and then the voice of your late mother.

'Hush, darling, sleep now.'

The gun fires.

CHAPTER TWO

'Nobody blames you.'

Kate Cassidy – Cass to the circle of friends and colleagues from whom she'd walked away – woke around 2am, the sleep-induced flashback having struck again.

'Nobody blames you,' he'd said.

For a woman's life, a child left motherless.

And sure, Cass thought, she wasn't technically responsible.

But she knew when she heard those three words that a couple more were left unspoken.

Nobody blames you... as such.

The flashback was a constant in her life – occurring two or three nights a week in the year since that discussion with her former boss. A flashback to the conversation, followed by an image of the accident. The latter being a false memory, of course, because she hadn't been there. But absence didn't absolve her.

She didn't wake sweating, shivering or scared. She woke crushed by guilt.

Her form of nightly penance, one might say.

As if she'd ever forgive herself.

CHAPTER THREE

I t wasn't that Cass had any better plans for Christmas Eve –
she had no plans at all, in fact. She just hadn't expected a
summons for coffee from her soon-to-be boss. Cass wasn't due
to start in Glencale Garda Station until the first week of the new
year, but already knew she had made a mistake by coming home.

Make a change, she'd told herself.

Well, fuck change, fuck my stupidity. What on earth had driven
her to thinking home would be the answer? As if she could
rebuild her life here. If there was anything worth rebuilding.

The venue for coffee was the town's sole five-star hotel,
Glencale House, an imposing nineteenth-century edifice set on a
lush estate. The estate was bordered to the south by Glencale Bay
– a mecca for tourists, sailors and swimmers – and to the north
by the town itself.

As a kid, it had always amazed Cass that a person could finish
something mundane in the town – a trip to the butcher's or
newsagent's, say – and in less than five minutes, walk into a
fantasy land complete with intricate garden maze and fountains,
chandeliers and silver service, and the most exquisite cakes she'd

e know me as Cass, if it's easier.'

'd nickname?'

raining college – some of the lads started it and it

on brought them maturity, I'm sure.'

Or just a low tolerance for the force's laddish culture?

illed Cass's cup without bothering to ask if Cass

Admittedly, it would be rare enough to find a guard

ainline the stuff.

well?'

wouldn't be a guard if she couldn't make such a

on so seemingly benign.

thanks. Looking forward to getting back to work.'

There is literally nothing I'm looking forward to.

onger as a detective?'

for me.'

ake you long to make up your mind.'

detective for the sum total of three months before it all

he events weren't of my choosing. 'I just didn't feel...

suited to it after everything.'

n reflected on the answer, as if weighing the amount

st what she already knew from her sources. 'Are you

ounsellor right now?'

been through trauma – you don't see the need?'

n't my trauma. I took a year out, went through things in

vay.'

gan sucked her teeth, to Cass's immense irritation.

known only one person before you who asked to be

' Finnegan said. 'He felt the extra responsibility was too

r him. A couple of years later, he cracked up completely.

e fucking basket case.'

Christ. Crack up? Basket case? A fucking waterboarding on

s Eve? Had Finnegan not moved on from when she did her

10

---

ever tasted. Not that the locals tended to frequent the hotel in great numbers – when she was growing up, few in the community had the cash to spare. Nor, to be honest, were they altogether sure they would have been welcome anyway – there were certain standards to be maintained, after all.

But her own parents, if not wealthy, had been comfortable – and assured of their place in society – and her mum would periodically take her to Glencale House for a treat – afternoon tea including the pastry chef's personalised version of madeleines, with a layer of jam and a coating of desiccated coconut. Cass generally wasn't one for nostalgia. But God damn, given how things had turned out in her life, coupled with this morning's summons, she could be forgiven for harking back to better times.

She principally blamed herself. All those years ago, her father had given her one overriding piece of advice: *don't join the Guards.* Ideally, he wanted her to be a lawyer or doctor, but would have settled for his only daughter doing just about anything other than following him into the force. When, despite his reservations, she did enlist, he gave her a new piece of advice: *never police your home district.* This, Ted Cassidy knew from personal experience, having spent the latter part of his career as the senior officer in charge of his native County Kerry. 'They'll end up policing you,' he'd said. 'They'll watch your every move and grumble like fuck about anything they don't like.'

She'd ignored that piece of advice too.

Not at first, of course. After basic training, she'd been assigned to Dublin, going on to spend thirteen years in the capital. Moving up the ranks, marrying, buying a house, eventually getting promoted to detective – only for everything to fall apart.

A year-long career break at her own request. Trying to move on, failing, moving back. Reassigned – again at her own request.

7

Home to Kerry, home to Glencale. From the urban east coast to the rural south-west. Going from a suburban station in Dublin that had the highest share of murders, gang violence and drug-related crimes in the country to a station that was predominantly rural in nature.

Glencale and its hinterland boasted a population of fewer than 10,000 people. It would have been ghost-town territory but for the fact that it was blessed by geography, located in a prime perch along one of the country's most glorious coastal routes.

When she was a child, the tourism season had been limited to the spring and summer, with most of the hotels winding up in the autumn and shutting for the winter like an animal in hibernation. But all that had changed in the years since she'd left. Now, as many people flocked to the town around Christmas and New Year's as they did during the summer. Hence, Glencale House was both open and busy this Christmas Eve.

But while unsure of the reason for the meeting, Cass knew why the venue had been chosen – and it wasn't for the cakes. The hotel offered masses of space between tables, unlike the coffee shops and restaurants in town. And although several of the staff were locals, they had been trained to be discreet, and to respect guests' privacy. It was a good place for an introductory meeting, much more inviting than the creaky and crammed Garda station, an old railway office which had seen much better days. Although Cass had heard different things, she decided that Sergeant Nuala Finnegan was clearly a thoughtful sort, not always a given with superior officers.

In previous times, she might have been lifted by the sight of the elegantly decorated Christmas tree in the foyer, the sound of the pianist floating festive standards through the air. Not this time.

She strode into the bar, where Nuala Finnegan was easy to spot in her navy uniform and clip-on tie, leafing through a file at a table already set with coffee for two. Mid-fifties, a bit heavier

than perhaps the gu
expression that brooked
of the community, Finn
club on several occasions
early in her career, she
supposedly honourable in
wife.

Cass knew from her fa
time had managed the incic
wasn't the kind of thing th
these days – properly so, C
was a single one of Finnega
for the act. Hence Finneg
apparently nobody called h
technically inaccurate anyway
had been a nine-iron. Still, fr
knew, Cass was ready to like he

And what would Finnegan ha
woman at least two decades yo
face at risk of looking permanei
whose soul had dissolved in a vat

Stop with the amateur dramatics,
fucking mind-reader. She'll see a wo
hair brushed back in a ponytail, weari
guard – jeans, trekking boots, a North
make-up. In good shape physically b
furrows in the brow that came a dec
nothing unusual in this line of work.

And what will she know?
Everything, if she's any good.

Finnegan put the file aside and stoc
there was no hint of a smile. In ret
served as the first warning.

'Kate?'

'Most peopl
'A schoolya
'From the t
stuck.'
'Qualificati
A bit tart?
Finnegan
liked coffee.
who didn't m
'So, you're
Finnegan
loaded quest
'I'm fine,
First lie.
'But no l
'It wasn'
'Didn't t
I was a
happened.
particularl
Finneg
said again
seeing a c
'No.'
'You'v
'It was
my own
Finne
'I've
demoted
much fo
Comple
Jesus
Christm

own training? Has she completely missed out on the development of more effective and appropriate police standards for developing, mentoring and leading staff?

'I appreciate your concern for my health,' Cass said through gritted teeth, 'but like I said, I'm fine. You have nothing to worry about.' *And fuck your ham-fisted effort to test me.*

'Good,' Finnegan said. 'Because I'm not a counsellor, and Glencale is not a retreat for someone seeking an easier life. I'm under-resourced and can't afford to carry someone. You understand?'

I had a teacher just like this bitch, ending every dressing-down with that patronising question. Every fucking time. 'I wouldn't expect anything less.'

Finnegan did the thing with her teeth a second time, and then lapsed into silence. Whereas in an interrogation room this might have been a tactic designed to pressure the accused – namely Cass – into filling the space, she felt fairly certain in this instance the sergeant was mulling over a decision. But what decision?

Eventually, Finnegan pushed the file towards her and said: 'Read this over the next few days. I want your thoughts on your first day back.'

The file was unlabelled, its plain buff cover giving no hint as to its contents. Finnegan was clearly mindful about prying eyes.

'What is it?' Cass asked.

'An unsolved murder from earlier this year.'

'I'm not a detective anymore.'

'Listen, you might have lost your senses when walking off the detective squad but I assume some of your training stuck and you can still form coherent thoughts. Read the file, form a view, tell me what you think.'

Finnegan stood, her own cup untouched, the meeting suddenly over. 'I'll get the bill,' she said. 'Stay and finish your coffee. Just make sure no one in here sees what's in that.'

Cass was surprised Finnegan didn't finish by asking her if she understood.

But Finnegan was already walking away.

Happy Christmas to you too.

And fuck my life for being stupid enough to come home to this bullshit.

ever tasted. Not that the locals tended to frequent the hotel in great numbers – when she was growing up, few in the community had the cash to spare. Nor, to be honest, were they altogether sure they would have been welcome anyway – there were certain standards to be maintained, after all.

But her own parents, if not wealthy, had been comfortable – and assured of their place in society – and her mum would periodically take her to Glencale House for a treat – afternoon tea including the pastry chef's personalised version of madeleines, with a layer of jam and a coating of desiccated coconut. Cass generally wasn't one for nostalgia. But God damn, given how things had turned out in her life, coupled with this morning's summons, she could be forgiven for harking back to better times.

She principally blamed herself. All those years ago, her father had given her one overriding piece of advice: *don't join the Guards.* Ideally, he wanted her to be a lawyer or doctor, but would have settled for his only daughter doing just about anything other than following him into the force. When, despite his reservations, she did enlist, he gave her a new piece of advice: *never police your home district.* This, Ted Cassidy knew from personal experience, having spent the latter part of his career as the senior officer in charge of his native County Kerry. 'They'll end up policing you,' he'd said. 'They'll watch your every move and grumble like fuck about anything they don't like.'

She'd ignored that piece of advice too.

Not at first, of course. After basic training, she'd been assigned to Dublin, going on to spend thirteen years in the capital. Moving up the ranks, marrying, buying a house, eventually getting promoted to detective – only for everything to fall apart.

A year-long career break at her own request. Trying to move on, failing, moving back. Reassigned – again at her own request.

Home to Kerry, home to Glencale. From the urban east coast to the rural south-west. Going from a suburban station in Dublin that had the highest share of murders, gang violence and drug-related crimes in the country to a station that was predominantly rural in nature.

Glencale and its hinterland boasted a population of fewer than 10,000 people. It would have been ghost-town territory but for the fact that it was blessed by geography, located in a prime perch along one of the country's most glorious coastal routes.

When she was a child, the tourism season had been limited to the spring and summer, with most of the hotels winding up in the autumn and shutting for the winter like an animal in hibernation. But all that had changed in the years since she'd left. Now, as many people flocked to the town around Christmas and New Year's as they did during the summer. Hence, Glencale House was both open and busy this Christmas Eve.

But while unsure of the reason for the meeting, Cass knew why the venue had been chosen – and it wasn't for the cakes. The hotel offered masses of space between tables, unlike the coffee shops and restaurants in town. And although several of the staff were locals, they had been trained to be discreet, and to respect guests' privacy. It was a good place for an introductory meeting, much more inviting than the creaky and crammed Garda station, an old railway office which had seen much better days. Although Cass had heard different things, she decided that Sergeant Nuala Finnegan was clearly a thoughtful sort, not always a given with superior officers.

In previous times, she might have been lifted by the sight of the elegantly decorated Christmas tree in the foyer, the sound of the pianist floating festive standards through the air. Not this time.

She strode into the bar, where Nuala Finnegan was easy to spot in her navy uniform and clip-on tie, leafing through a file at a table already set with coffee for two. Mid-fifties, a bit heavier than perhaps the guidelines would recommend, and an expression that brooked no nonsense. As an upstanding member of the community, Finnegan had been lady captain of the golf club on several occasions. As an upcoming member of the force, early in her career, she'd taken one of her golf clubs to a supposedly honourable individual who had serially abused his wife.

Cass knew from her father that Finnegan's superiors at the time had managed the incident to minimise the fallout to her. It wasn't the kind of thing that management could so easily do these days – properly so, Cass thought. Yet she doubted there was a single one of Finnegan's colleagues who didn't admire her for the act. Hence Finnegan's nickname "Driver", although apparently nobody called her that to her face, and it was technically inaccurate anyway, given the golf club in question had been a nine-iron. Still, from what she saw and what she knew, Cass was ready to like her.

And what would Finnegan have seen and known in return? A woman at least two decades younger than herself, but a gaunt face at risk of looking permanently defeated. A hollow woman whose soul had dissolved in a vat of acidic pain.

Stop with the amateur dramatics, thought Cass. *Finnegan's not a fucking mind-reader. She'll see a woman in her early thirties, blonde hair brushed back in a ponytail, wearing apparel typical of an off-duty guard – jeans, trekking boots, a North Face jacket – and a minimum of make-up. In good shape physically but maybe a bit tired-looking, furrows in the brow that came a decade too soon. In other words, nothing unusual in this line of work.*

And what will she know?

Everything, if she's any good.

Finnegan put the file aside and stood as Cass approached, but there was no hint of a smile. In retrospect, that should have served as the first warning.

'Kate?'

'Most people know me as Cass, if it's easier.'

'A schoolyard nickname?'

'From the training college – some of the lads started it and it stuck.'

'Qualification brought them maturity, I'm sure.'

A bit tart? Or just a low tolerance for the force's laddish culture?

Finnegan filled Cass's cup without bothering to ask if Cass liked coffee. Admittedly, it would be rare enough to find a guard who didn't mainline the stuff.

'So, you're well?'

Finnegan wouldn't be a guard if she couldn't make such a loaded question so seemingly benign.

'I'm fine, thanks. Looking forward to getting back to work.'

First lie. There is literally nothing I'm looking forward to.

'But no longer as a detective?'

'It wasn't for me.'

'Didn't take you long to make up your mind.'

I was a detective for the sum total of three months before it all happened. The events weren't of my choosing. 'I just didn't feel... particularly suited to it after everything.'

Finnegan reflected on the answer, as if weighing the amount said against what she already knew from her sources. 'Are you seeing a counsellor right now?'

'No.'

'You've been through trauma – you don't see the need?'

'It wasn't my trauma. I took a year out, went through things in my own way.'

Finnegan sucked her teeth, to Cass's immense irritation.

'I've known only one person before you who asked to be demoted,' Finnegan said. 'He felt the extra responsibility was too much for him. A couple of years later, he cracked up completely. Complete fucking basket case.'

Jesus Christ. Crack up? Basket case? A fucking waterboarding on Christmas Eve? Had Finnegan not moved on from when she did her

CHAPTER FOUR

There were fresh tyre marks in the shape of eights where teenagers had spun handbrake turns on the narrow road through Killarney National Park. Mason Brady was amused if not quite impressed.

Even if the road twisted its way through the woodland, lakes and mountains, requiring drivers to slow to crawling pace at some points, the park was practically deserted at night. He knew the night-time emptiness first-hand – he'd explored its considerable terrain in the darkness enough times by now. From a quick glance, he could tell the drivers had picked the safer spots, away from the blind turns, where they would see the headlights of approaching cars with plenty of time to spare. So more teenage jinks than high-risk manoeuvres. Still though, they must have frightened the shit out of the deer.

Killarney town was a significant urban centre in comparison to Glencale, and only an hour's scenic drive away. Mason had gone to Killarney because it had a well-stocked camping outlet store, although needless to say, it didn't sell certain of the specialities he would have preferred, such as the military-grade knives to which he was long accustomed. But Brady didn't want to draw Garda attention by being in possession of such specialities anyway, and instead made do with the lethal tools he could acquire through legal means – such as the array of construction knives he'd been using on the renovation project. He'd made one exception, acquiring an unlicensed shotgun as a last resort. The shotgun was well hidden, and Brady considered that it would be a signal failure if he had to use it, though of course he wouldn't hesitate if the circumstances required it.

Killarney town had been busy, as shoppers purchased last-minute gifts and went for Christmas Eve drinks. The national park, by contrast, was devoid of the usual crowds of hikers, day-trippers and cyclists. The inclement weather was no doubt a factor: it had snowed overnight and despite it being mid-afternoon now, there were still pockets of black ice on the more sheltered parts of the route.

While the mountains in these parts were no more than hills compared to what he was used to, their snow-covered peaks looked splendid nonetheless. On a whim, Brady halted the car at one of the more popular viewing spots to savour the scene. He had the place to himself, and as he exited the car and felt the slap of freezing air across his face, he felt content. Alert to the risks he was running, but confident that he had managed them effectively to date.

From his vantage point, he could see clusters of yellow gorse rolling down the mountainside. There were no walking trails in this section, which veered steeply down to the lakes below. In his extensive research, Brady had read that the lakes were up to seventy-five metres deep in some places. Trained as he was to know such things, he understood such depth would work to his advantage. The volume and weight of the water would keep a lot of things hidden deep from view.

While he wouldn't describe any region of the park as

inhospitable – considering some of the environments he'd operated in – it struck him that this particular area was significantly less accessible than others.

It wouldn't be the worst place to bury a body.

But he'd found much better.

CHAPTER FIVE

Over a number of weeks, Cass's parents had repeatedly encouraged her to come over for Christmas lunch, without success. And so on Christmas morning, Cass was by choice alone in her rented apartment in a small estate on the edge of the town, consuming the case file.

Glencale was not without violent crime – there was plenty of it. Drunken brawls that got out of hand, domestic assault, sexual assault and more. Nor did the town's distance from the major cities spare it from occasional drug-related violence. Cass knew her colleagues were currently hunting a marauding gang who had carried out a number of aggravated burglaries on isolated farms across the county over the last few months, terrorising and frequently beating their victims.

But for all that, murder was – thankfully – rare. Cass knew approximate figures without having to look them up. Ireland, in any given year, had about seventy to eighty murders. In a bad year, Kerry, being a rural county, with just a handful of large towns, might account for three or four of them. Glencale might see a murder every three to four years. Which explained the shock in the community when the body of Nabila Fathi had been discovered in woodland halfway up the mountains to the southeast of the town in an area known as the Hag's Loop.

Cass knew instantly that the location of the body would have further troubled locals. For all the town's tourist sheen and sophistication, tradition and superstition died hard. The Loop was named after the mythical crone who controlled the weather, determining the onset of winter and wreaking havoc on those who offended her. Sparsely populated, when the sun shone the Loop was pleasant ground for sightseers and hikers. But when the Hag was angry, the Loop turned eerie: shrouded in mist or bucketed in rain. One minute you could see for miles and a minute later, you'd struggle to make out the pathway in front of you.

Unsurprisingly, all manner of local lore had built up through the centuries – of ancient sacrifices and curses, of animals dying mysteriously, of trails that would swallow you in the mist, never to be seen again. The story went that the crone would wail shortly before the next victim disappeared, a regional version of the banshee tradition.

As a child, the Loop had spooked the hell out of Cass and most of her friends – they didn't need the Bermuda Triangle and its like; the Hag was much more real, immediate and terrifying. And while she had long since left such fears behind, the same couldn't be said for everybody. One section of the Loop was known as the trackway, where a series of indentations in a rock outcrop were said to be the crone's footprints. Preposterous as it may seem, she knew there were farmers on the Loop who wouldn't let their sheep graze anywhere near the trackway, for fear it would bring them bad luck.

The murder of Nabila Fathi would have frightened many in its own right; that her body had been found in the Loop would, no doubt, have added another frisson of fear for some.

Had that been intentional? From the file, Cass got the impression that the original investigation team hadn't given it any thought. In itself, this was not massively surprising given that investigators focused on cold, hard fact.

She read on. As per procedure, a murder incident team had been appointed, headed by a detective inspector from the wider region and drawing on specialist expertise from the Garda criminal investigation and technical bureaux, as well as other units.

In the early days of the investigation, the specialist expertise dominated – members of the technical bureau oversaw crime-scene management, ballistics, mapping, fingerprints and photography; members of the criminal investigation bureau shaped the wider investigation, advising on which leads to follow.

The specialist teams then withdrew either as the technical work was completed or the investigative expertise was required elsewhere, leaving the case in the hands of the local officers. At all times, the detective inspector, as senior investigating officer or SIO, retained responsibility for deciding where to take the investigation. Cass knew the Guards had a good record of detecting murder cases; she also knew the force wasn't perfect, and that there were sometimes major gaps in unsolved cases, where local officers had been too slow to call in national expertise, where crime scenes were badly managed or leads poorly progressed.

But if the investigation team hadn't had time for local superstition, she could see they had clearly been competent and thorough. There was nothing in the job book to suggest otherwise – it had thousands of entries outlining, in the standard chronological order, the tasks undertaken and the leads followed in a bid to solve the case. It and every aspect of the case file pointed to a methodical investigation. The only thing missing was the identity of the killer.

The identity of the victim, by contrast, had taken very little time. Nabila had been reported missing three months before the body was found and officers knew it was her from items found at the scene, before DNA analysis later confirmed as much. A Coptic Christian, Nabila had fled religious persecution in her native Egypt at the age of nineteen, seeking asylum in Ireland. Under the Irish system, she had then spent more than four years in a direct provision centre – whereby the state provided basic accommodation, food and a miniscule weekly payment – until her application was decided upon.

Four fucking years, Cass thought. She was more than familiar with the slow grind of bureaucracy – the Guards had their own shitty version of it – but this system was perverse, a deliberate attempt to discourage others from coming. The state typically contracted out the running of the system to private enterprise – the direct provision centre in Glencale, as well as several others, was run by an investment fund no doubt enjoying excellent returns. The state had finally granted Nabila asylum close to her twenty-fourth birthday. Four months later, just as her world was blossoming, she was dead.

Cass was startled by the buzz of her mobile phone. Work, she supposed, as her parents had already rung earlier, and she wasn't expecting other well-wishers. But when she looked at the screen, she saw a familiar Dublin number: the prison. She treated the call in precisely the same way she had treated all her ex-husband's other attempts to contact her over the previous months – by ignoring it.

All calls to and from the prison, other than ones to a solicitor or counsellor, were recorded, and Cass didn't want recordings of her speaking to Hugh Moran. More than that, she had no desire to speak to him. He had also written repeatedly to her, and again, she knew the chances were the letters had been reviewed by the prison authorities before being posted. In his first such letter, he had pleaded with Cass to use her contacts in the justice system to seek clemency for him. She had saved every letter since, to ensure she had a record in case any trouble arose, but hadn't opened a single one. Cass had no interest in what they said.

Adult prisoners generally got just one call a week. Cass didn't know if the authorities granted any more leeway on Christmas Day, but in any event, she knew Hugh would have tried her first. And she knew what the call meant. He was suffering, crushed mentally by the burden of what he had done, and seized permanently with fear in a hostile and nerve-shredding environment. He needed to hear her voice. To hear that she forgave him, that she understood what he was going through, that it would be all right. That he could – would – make it through.

He can go to hell if he thinks I'm speaking to him today.

Unlike her, Hugh had always needed people, had always needed to be recognised, embraced, applauded, loved. Mere connections wouldn't do; he needed to be bathed in human warmth. There wouldn't be much of that to go around where he was residing for the next seven years. But Cass had no interest in being his saviour.

She recalled another of those times her father had counselled her against joining the Guards. She was more liberal than he was, more prone to seeing the world in grey rather than black and white. Tough on crime – him. Tough on the causes of crime – her.

'Most people in life deserve a second chance,' she'd said.

'Give a second chance to the people I come across on a daily basis and you quickly come to regret it,' her father had replied. 'You've too much empathy, Kate. Keep it for family and friends – it's a lousy attribute in a police officer.'

She had disagreed – of course she had – and by the time she qualified, empathy was in fashion. Which was good at least as far as victims of crime were concerned, because this traditionally had never been the Guards' strong point and slowly it was improving. But she could no longer completely disagree with her father: Cass's years on the force had hardened her, as much as she wished to cling to her core values.

Monsters did exist, and even if they were a small minority, they deserved no mercy. They needed to be gutted – she had no reluctance in saying that. The single worst thing about work was not the bureaucracy, or the draining caseload, or the lack of resources. It was seeing the most twisted offenders serve their time and be released to kill, rape or assault another innocent victim. The case files were littered with such savagery, and society was foolish to believe its practitioners could be rehabilitated.

It wasn't contradictory in Cass's mind to hold that view and still believe the majority of people were inherently decent, tried to do the right thing, and sometimes failed.

She knew what camp Hugh fell into, and it wasn't the minority one. He was the softest of men, a teddy bear. She knew he couldn't live with what he'd done, she knew he was likely to be in the cruellest condition imaginable, she knew what a word of tolerance or forgiveness would mean to him.

Most people in life deserve a second chance...

He'll get it – when he's done his time.

Not now, not from me.

———

Outside the apartment, a handful of children were whizzing around on new bikes they'd got for Christmas. Inside, Cass concluded her study of the case file with a second examination of the crime-scene photographs. Once done, she sighed and rose from the table to sling a frozen pizza and garlic bread in the oven.

She couldn't help but be reminded by this desultory fare of the handful of Christmases when she'd been off duty, and the feasts which Hugh, a gastronome and gifted cook, had conjured up. Multiple courses, and he'd put equal, if not more, effort into the Christmas drinks menu. Champagne for breakfast, claret throughout the day, cocktails to finish off the night. Sugar and spice and all things nice... What had seemed so life-affirming to begin with should have been a warning. But she'd gone fully along with it in those early years, not realising the path he was on.

She glanced at her phone again, knowing he had left a voicemail. Like his letters, she would save it but not listen to it. She didn't doubt the pain he was in; she just had too much of her own to listen to him. Raw, toxic, consuming grief, spreading like an infection through her body, with no antidote she could think of.

Cursing silently, she switched off the oven. As much as she was comfortable with her own company, she wasn't going to allow Hugh to dominate her thoughts for the remainder of the day.

———

The offerings and atmosphere at her parents' house were an immeasurable improvement, and mid-afternoon, she and her father took a long walk to work off some of the calories. There was a pleasant chill in the air as they strolled along the country lanes surrounding the Cassidy homestead.

Cass hadn't sought her father's counsel when moving back to Glencale, nor had she asked him for an advance briefing on Finnegan or her team; if she was going to make mistakes with career choices or colleagues, she wanted them to be her own mistakes.

But she had no difficulty seeking his opinion on cases she was handling, and never had: Ted Cassidy had been a troubleshooter, sent in by senior management to lead the most challenging cases or sharpen up underperforming districts. It was how he had come to police his home county: being put in charge of operations in Kerry at a time in the mid-eighties when the force's reputation there had taken a battering because of its handling of a number of contentious cases.

He was the most experienced officer Cass knew personally, even if he was now retired. His retirement hobbies consisted of hiking the local mountains or re-examining long forgotten unsolved cases – both of which he preferred to the golf course. Hence, he listened keenly as Cass filled him in on Finnegan's request to revisit Nabila Fathi's murder and the details of the file. She was mildly surprised that he knew relatively little of the case, other than what had been in the news.

'Once you're gone, you're gone,' he said. 'The way it should be. The only cases I ever look at are the ancient ones – no longer under active investigation by anybody.'

'I'll bring you up to speed then.'

'Start at the start – every detail.'

So Cass did, explaining that Nabila's body had been found in one of the most isolated parts of the Loop. A farmer had been training an energetic Border collie which had plunged into the pine forest and stayed there, barking ferociously and resisting all orders to heel. The farmer was forced to follow and would spend many years afterwards wishing he hadn't.

'Everything after was by the book. The crime scene was swiftly preserved and a crime-scene coordinator appointed. Incident room was established and the job book opened. A canvass coordinator directed the door-to-doors, although there were obviously few enough houses at which to make inquiries. Friends and acquaintances of Nabila were interviewed – mostly from the direct provision centre and a few from the supermarket where she began working after finally being granted asylum.

'She had no family in Ireland, and there was no suggestion of a partner. Her friends offered little in the way of useful information. They described her as shy, affectionate and loyal –

popular without ever seeming to realise as much. They couldn't think of anybody who would have wanted her dead.'

'Her movements?'

'She was a near-daily attendee at the cathedral – I believe on the basis that it was acceptable to attend a Catholic church if there was none of her own faith nearby. That seemed to be the most regular thing in her life. Nothing else notable, no sudden breaks from the norm.'

'Conflicts at the centre – anything that friends feared to mention?'

'The original team interviewed the management of the centre at length. No conflicts, no trouble, nothing worthy of further pursuit.'

'And at the supermarket?'

'Staff there hadn't known her as long or as well, but said much the same things. Nabila had been excited to have her first job and independence after so many years waiting. She had spoken about doing a night course in accountancy. She hadn't clashed with anybody at work, and no one could think why anybody would have targeted her.'

'It was Harbour Murphy's supermarket, right? He did media interviews at the time she went missing?'

Ted Cassidy was referring to Patrick Murphy, prominent politician and businessman. 'Harbour' was the moniker given to the family generations ago to distinguish them from other local families of the same name – a common practice in these parts since time immemorial – and stemmed from the small mooring near their home a few miles up the coast. Harbour Murphy was what they called in these parts a 'cute hoor' – wily enough to have his hand stuck in seemingly every bit of local business that turned a profit. He'd come from money and turned it into more money, but bought his off-the-peg suits locally and paired them with cheap rubber-sole shoes, working assiduously to give the impression he had no more to spare than the next man.

'Yes,' Cass said. 'Gave media interviews, participated in the searches for her, none of which yielded anything. When her body was discovered three months later, he was interviewed as part of the investigation.'

'And?'

Harbour Murphy had been interviewed but, again, had relatively little to offer. He had personally hired Nabila, been impressed with her work ethic and had 'great hopes' for her. Knowing she was in need of accommodation as well as a job, he had rented her the old flat above the shop. Which, depending on the way you looked at it, may have seemed very charitable, until one realised he was paying her a salary below market rates and charging her rent significantly in excess of what the decrepit flat justified. But it appeared Nabila had been content with the deal, happy to be out on her own and building a future. Nothing more useful had been gleaned from Harbour Murphy.

'Nothing,' Cass answered. 'Nothing obvious, anyway.'

'He's still a bollocks,' Ted Cassidy muttered.

Unlike some of her colleagues in the force, Cass did not disdain politicians, nor was she foolish enough to think they were all the same – she took an interest and recognised the ones who were genuinely interested in progressive policing reform. But from a distance, and probably influenced by her father, she had always thought Harbour Murphy to be something of a crook. Which was why, for reasons she couldn't explain, she'd found herself underlining his name in the file earlier that morning.

Was it just coincidence that Nabila had been killed not while living in the direct provision centre – where many people would have seen her come and go – but shortly after she had moved into a place of her own, where there was nobody to track her movements?

She turned away from Murphy and began describing the victim and the crime scene in detail to her father.

The file photos of Nabila alive showed a timid-looking young woman with black tousled hair and a mole just above her right jawbone. She had the tentative smile of someone accustomed to needing permission to be herself. Cass had briefly imagined that smile widening suddenly and naturally, free of all caution, as Nabila grew comfortable in her new-found freedom. It was a damned sight better to think of her that way than in the grisly crime-scene photos.

Unquestionably murder, even if there was little recognisable left of the victim to examine. The acidic soil that proved so fertile for the pine trees had also accelerated decomposition. But while the body had begun the stage of dry decay – slowly being reduced to bare bones, dried skin and hair – there were sufficient means to determine the cause of death.

'Blunt force trauma from a blow to the back of the head from some kind of cylindrical object, in addition to which the hyoid bone in Nabila's neck was fractured,' Cass said.

'Indicative of strangulation.'

'Yes. The pathologist concluded she'd been hit once to stun her and was then strangled. But not in the woodland. The forensic evidence pointed firmly to the murder having taken place elsewhere, with Nabila's body later dumped.'

'Time of death?'

'Difficult to determine, given the variables involved. The pathologist was assisted by an entomologist. They narrowed it down to the immediate days after Nabila had been reported as missing, but couldn't be more specific.'

'What was she strangled with – any idea?'

'There was a stagnant pool close to where her body had been found, and they discovered a rucksack and scarf there – both identified as Nabila's. The scarf was distinctive – green and black animal print – and was seen as the likely means of strangulation. Nabila's friends at the direct provision centre had clubbed together to buy it for her as a farewell gift when she'd finally been granted asylum.'

'And the water minimised the potential for the rucksack and scarf to yield trace evidence, presumably?'

Cass nodded, for that had been precisely the case, in what had been one of the biggest setbacks to the original investigation. Nonetheless, she felt the murderer had – predictably – made a number of mistakes. Granted, he – and Cass made no apologies for supposing it was a 'he', given it invariably was in such cases – had possessed the wherewithal to dispose of the body in an isolated place, unseen. But it felt a little panicky to not try and bury the body and hide all traces. Discarding the rucksack and scarf in the pool had been another error – the murderer had simply got lucky in the length of time it took to discover the body.

'The forensics of the flat didn't yield anything either,' Cass said. 'The team concluded it wasn't the scene of the murder. So no forensic evidence or leads, and no obvious suspect. The team ran into a dead end.'

'And they were comprehensive?'

'Can't find any reason to say otherwise.'

Cass had looked through every aspect of the file to satisfy herself that nothing obvious was missed. She read back over everything, no matter how big or small, ranging from the house-to-house questionnaires to the transcript of the farmer's emergency call upon discovery of the body. While Cass's time on the detective squad had been brief, every aspect of her training told her the investigation team had done it by the book.

'So what's your guess?'

'I don't have one. It might have been an opportunistic attack by a stranger, but the team found no sign of sexual assault, even if they couldn't be absolutely certain given the lack of bodily fluids and skin tissue. Money had been left in Nabila's rucksack, meaning robbery could probably be discounted too. The team felt, on balance of probabilities, that Nabila had known her killer.

But they got nowhere near to identifying him. I'm not sure what I'm supposed to see that they didn't.'

She sighed audibly, wondering what she could bring to this case that the original team hadn't. She wondered again why Finnegan had thrown it at her, and – if a test – what she was supposed to do to pass it. She didn't care for Finnegan or her expectations, but she did care for her own professionalism. Even after a year out, Cass could feel the familiar clash forming at the back of her mind: a burning desire to set the highest standards; a chronic doubt she would accomplish them.

'Never hurts to get a fresh set of eyes on a case,' her father said.

'I feel like I'm being set up to fail. Like I have a target on my back.'

'And why would they be targeting you?'

'Maybe they want me out – because of Hugh, what happened.'

'Crap,' Ted Cassidy said. 'Your only failure was marrying a failure. His fuck-up meant your personal life crossed over into your professional one. But I see no signs – none – that the force wants you gone. Finnegan has a job to do and needs you to do yours.'

As much as she wanted to be irritated by her father's bluntness, Cass took some comfort in it instead. But she wasn't going to let him off that easily. 'Finnegan and yourself could give a joint TED Talk,' she said.

Her father bit: 'And what would that be now?'

'"How to Infuriate instead of Motivate".'

————

Later that evening, back in the apartment and with the aid of a strong pot of coffee, Cass pored over the case file a second time. Nabila's relatives in Egypt had sought the repatriation of her body; the local community had taken up a collection to cover the costs, aided by a substantial donation from Harbour Murphy.

Cass found herself scribbling another question mark after the politician's name, before returning one final time to the crime-scene photographs, and the contents of Nabila's rucksack. The keys to her flat, attached to a keychain cross. A small black purse containing some coins. A couple of 100-euro notes, found not in the purse but in a hidden compartment in the rucksack, both identically damaged from what appeared to be water erosion.

For a moment, Cass wondered how somebody on a relatively small salary would have such large denominations in her possession, but then guessed that Harbour Murphy possibly paid in cash to evade tax, and she made a mental note to check.

A small make-up bag containing various cosmetics and tampons. A hairbrush and hairbands. Some painkillers, a couple of pens and a phone charger. But no phone – the assumption being that the killer had dumped it elsewhere. A set of prayer beads – but God had not come to her assistance, and Nabila had returned home wrapped in a shroud and placed in a coffin. The last items were a reusable water bottle and a cheap raincoat.

In sum total then: nothing out of the ordinary, no signs of someone who believed her life was in danger – and no pointers towards her killer.

CHAPTER SIX

They looked nothing like him. But Mason Brady knew a mirror image of himself when he encountered it. And from the moment he saw his two fellow Americans walk into the small country store nine miles outside Glencale, he knew they were comfortable inflicting violence.

US tourists were as common as seashells around Glencale and the surrounding region, but the first Friday after Christmas seemed an odd enough day to go sightseeing. And these two were decidedly not holidaymakers. Both wore blue jeans and Guinness-branded sweatshirts, but they looked ill at ease in their chosen costumes. They lacked the casual patter and curiosity of visitors exploring the local landmarks, and Brady, who had popped in for some supplies, pretended to study the store's single wine shelf while monitoring the pair.

Both were late thirties or early forties at most, he guessed. The first, with an appealing crop of sandy hair offset by severely pitted skin, brushed past him to pick up a six-pack from the fridge. The other, with a shaved head and a punch-drunk nose, approached the storekeeper with a smile feigning benevolence and sought directions.

'We're distant relatives of Mr Jeremiah Bannon,' he said with a flourish, 'and we'd love to pay him a visit if we can find his farm.'

Milly Cooper didn't have Brady's experience of encountering brutality and, over her four decades of running this store on the cusp of the Loop, she tended to see the best in people, always willing to help those genuinely in need with some credit until payday. Brady, who had frequented the shop ever since arriving in the Loop, guessed she wouldn't see through the pair.

'The Bridge Bannons, you mean?'

Punch Drunk looked confused. 'I'm sorry, ma'am, I don't quite understand. The "Bridge" Bannons?'

'For the bridge nearest Jer's farm. It's what they're known by locally.'

'I see,' Punch Drunk said, not really seeing at all. 'And can you tell me where we might find them?'

'Well, the bridge is a clue,' Milly responded. 'Go two miles or so up the road towards the Loop, take the first left after the church, after a mile uphill you'll cross a small bridge and Jer's farm is the next gate you'll encounter.' She had to repeat the directions in order for Punch Drunk to take them in.

'Much obliged,' he said, tipping an imaginary hat, as his colleague placed the six-pack on the table and pulled out some cash to pay.

'Is Jer expecting you?' she asked. 'Because he doesn't get many visitors.'

Translation: *he's an old crank and I hope you've given him advance notice because his reaction will be unpredictable otherwise.*

'Yes, we agreed to call on him,' Punch Drunk said.

And yet despite the supposed agreement, they hadn't asked Bridge Bannon for directions.

Brady, who had moved around the store and put a few more things in a basket to avoid suspicion, felt like he was watching a ham actor. The other one, Sandy Hair, stayed mute until finally saying 'Thank you' as he took his change.

'Have a good day now,' Punch Drunk said as both men exited the store.

But chances are Bridge Bannon won't, thought Brady. Then he caught himself, recognising his own paranoia. Just because he was an imposter didn't mean every other stranger was too. Just because he had arrived in Glencale with homicidal intent didn't mean others followed suit. Besides, if these two were intent on harming an elderly farmer in some way, why would they leave a trail by calling into a local store in advance? Brady's mind worked like a sensor light – triggered by the slightest encroachment. But his training could lead him astray occasionally too, he recognised.

Still, training was one thing and instinct was another. And his instinct on these two said something was off.

Milly Cooper's store had an alarm but no CCTV either inside or externally, Brady knew – it was one of the things for which he automatically scanned. Making a rapid decision, he placed the basket on the counter, told Milly he'd left his wallet at home, gently fended off her entreaties to take the supplies and pay later, and slipped out as unobtrusively as he could after the two men.

Sandy Hair was in the driver's seat of a rented SUV and pulling out of the small car park. Brady memorised the licence plate before slipping behind the wheel of his own, considerably less glamorous vehicle – a sixteen-year-old Ford Mondeo which, from the looks of it, had seen much better days.

Brady knew better than to follow the two directly, and instead pulled out of the car park in the opposite direction, knowing there was a nearby side road he could take to double back, wind across the mountainside, and end up in an elevated position from which he could observe Bridge Bannon's farm without being noticed. Upon arriving in the Loop, Brady had spent weeks scouting the area, getting a feel for the terrain and identifying his few neighbours. His knowledge of the area and its people wouldn't have come close to Milly Cooper's, but it would suffice for present purposes.

And what purposes are they? he wondered. *What business is this of mine? What do I care if two hired goons have some beef with a local?* Brady told himself he didn't care. But his sensor light had been triggered, and so the least he could do was check out the cause of it.

———

It took him just a few minutes to drive to his intended lookout above Bridge Bannon's farm. Brady parked the car behind a copse offering excellent cover and, courtesy of a set of M25 high-res binoculars kept in the trunk, a solid vantage point.

He slipped between the trees until he found a satisfactory view, and then focused in. He could see the SUV in the farmyard. No sign of its occupants, however: Punch Drunk and Sandy Hair had clearly gone inside.

Brady scanned the windows, saw nothing, and then turned to the farm sheds with the same result. He settled in, guessing whatever was happening in the house might take some time.

Would he intervene? No: he had no skin in this game and couldn't afford to play the hero. That would draw attention to himself, and he'd come too far for that. So why be here? The spider in the centre of the web wanted to know what caused the vibration – prey or foe. Brady could sense this was a potential disturbance on his territory, and it was best to gauge the potential strength of its shockwaves. In his experience, random unexpected events proved as frequent a cause of failure as poor planning or logistics.

As he waited, he began calculating potential outcomes and his options in each scenario, knowing it might help later. But he didn't get very far, for suddenly Punch Drunk and Sandy Hair reversed out the front door of the farmhouse. They were holding their hands in the air to signify retreat, and a moment later, Brady saw why.

Bridge Bannon, cussed of face, slightly bent in the back and shuffling on arthritic feet, was still spry enough to hold a shotgun. He was roaring but Brady couldn't make out the words, nor what the two Americans were saying in mitigation. But he heard the gunshot cracking the sky.

Punch Drunk and Sandy Hair, knowing it was a warning shot fired over their heads, didn't panic, and for that, went up a little in Brady's professional estimation. They stayed calm enough to choose the wisest course of action, keeping their hands raised until they got back into the SUV and slowly eased out of the yard.

Brady could only guess at the reasons for the drama he'd just witnessed. But there was clearly something of considerable value at stake. And he was pretty sure there would be a sequel.

He just couldn't have guessed it would come so quickly – and the peril it would place him in.

CHAPTER SEVEN

First week back at work for Cass: fielding calls about stray sheep on local roads; setting up checkpoints to detect speeding motorists; stamping passport applications and other paperwork for members of the public; fielding more calls about stray sheep on the roads.

It had been a gentle enough reintroduction, Cass knew. The most serious work of the week had been engaging with the farming associations about measures to improve security for their members. The armed gang carrying out aggravated burglaries had struck four times in the county in a little over six months. In each case, they had inflicted serious injuries on the homeowners, all of whom were elderly and known to keep cash on their properties. Mercifully, the gang hadn't killed anybody yet, but it seemed just a matter of time. All districts had been requested to engage with their respective communities on simple steps to increase personal protection.

'But let's do it subtly,' Finnegan had directed. 'We don't want to stoke fears when this shower of bastards hasn't hit our patch yet.'

Cass didn't associate her superior officer with subtlety. Yet she agreed it was the right approach, and she realised quickly that Finnegan had a deftness for what the force, like so many organisations blindly adopting modern management theory, now called 'outreach and engagement'.

But if Finnegan's management of the community was effective, there were reasons to question the management of her team, Cass thought, and it wasn't just lingering resentment from their first encounter. Finnegan had eight officers reporting to her, working in standard shifts. Like any district, it wasn't enough. Yet on her second day, Cass had walked into the station and seen, in a new colleague, a familiar problem.

At some point in his life, the bottle had got the better of Noel Ryan and now, edging towards retirement age after years of hard drinking, he bore all the signs of it. Thin as a pick, face red, eyes bloodshot, and no amount of toothpaste, mints, deodorant or aftershave could hide the distinct odour of alcohol leaving his body through his breath and sweat rather than his overworked liver. Which was not to say he was drunk on duty: just wishing to be. A functional alcoholic: sober for just about long enough to get through the working day; stuporific by night.

The minute Cass saw him, she thought of her ex-husband, as if she needed more reminders. And immediately and irrationally, without knowing anything about his competence or capabilities, she took an instant dislike to Ryan and his presence on the squad. She knew what tolerating alcoholics could lead to; she'd tolerated her ex-husband for too long, and tragedy had followed.

Nobody blames you... as such.

Ryan's presence would be a daily provocation and Cass already knew she would end up saying something impolitic to Finnegan when the opportunity arose.

At least the others seemed all right – a typically hard-working, diligent bunch who shared the familiar black humour to be found in every station. She'd laughed a bit over the last few days for what felt like the first time in a year. But there was still much more she had to ingest about her colleagues and her new beat. It felt... okay to be back.

The gentle start gave her opportunity to dig into Nabila Fathi's murder. But like any case review, she quickly hit obstacles, such as interviewees no longer being available. She'd visited the direct provision centre to speak to Nabila's closest friend, a fellow asylum-seeker named Maisah Sahraoui, only to learn Maisah had been transferred to a centre in Donegal, more than 400 kilometres away. When she'd asked why, the manager of the Glencale centre had been unable to offer a reason – he'd simply received an order from the state agency responsible for the system to effect Maisah's transfer, and he had done so.

Cass had immediately contacted the Donegal centre and requested to speak to Maisah. Two days had passed without a return call, and she was growing increasingly annoyed. Now, as she sat at her desk and went through some of the other dead ends, she sighed audibly without realising.

'I think you need a sizeable cup of the world's worst coffee – just to show how bad life around here can really get.'

Liam Devine: he'd been an ally from the start and almost made up for Finnegan's verbal assault of an introduction. Married and in his early thirties, Devine had done five years in Glencale, made no bones about his desire to move on, and so was an excellent tour guide, disarmingly shallow and brimming with useful detail. It didn't take a detective to spot the roguish side to Devine, but Cass quite liked that.

'I'll buy,' she said.

———

The ability of her colleagues to find the single worst places for coffee never failed to amuse Cass. In Glencale it was proving no different. A tourist town with a multitude of smashing coffee shops, and still the Guards frequented the one where they used beans as old as Methuselah.

'Horse the sugar in,' Devine said. 'Only way to drink it.'

'You could add a pint glass of whiskey to that stuff and it'd still taste like rubber tyres.'

'That's Noel Ryan's trick,' said Devine with a laugh. 'I don't think he can tell the difference anymore.'

But Cass didn't see anything amusing about it. 'How does everyone tolerate it? He can't possibly be doing his job properly, the rest of you have to pick up the slack, and the reputational risk to the force doesn't even seem to be considered.'

'Finnegan puts up with it, and that's all that counts.'

'But why?' Cass persisted.

'They're friends of old. And Finnegan looks after her friends.' He wasn't laughing anymore, and the flash of anger across his face said more than words ever could.

There was an awkward pause before Devine said: 'Listen, I didn't come here to pick on poor Noel – the fella's harmless and he does a day's work. Something we're all trying to do. How's your case review coming along?'

'Running into brick walls,' she said. 'Two days ago I called to the asylum centre to speak to Nabila's best friend. But she was long gone – transferred to Donegal.'

'Maisah?'

Surprised, Cass asked: 'How do you know her – from the original investigation?'

'Sort of. She used to call to the station every week for months after Nabila's body was found. Asking if there was any update… There never was.'

'You were her contact point?'

'Me? God no. Maisah was smarter than that. Insisted on speaking to Finnegan every week and would wait for hours if she wasn't around. On those shitty plastic chairs in reception – can you imagine? Drove Finnegan nuts.'

An unpleasant suspicion was forming in Cass's mind and, being so new to the station, so new to her colleagues, she hesitated before voicing what felt like a first act of mutiny.

'Do you think Finnegan intervened to have her moved?'

'She didn't have to,' Devine replied.

'What do you mean?'

'Harbour Murphy and herself go a long way back – they're as thick as thieves.'

'Wait – you're saying Murphy intervened politically to get Maisah transferred at Finnegan's request? You know this for a fact?'

'Of course not,' he said. 'But Murphy's a silent investor in the fund that owns the centre. All he had to do was click his fingers and she'd be gone.'

Cass felt nauseous, and it wasn't the coffee. *What the hell was Finnegan doing giving her a case file that had the potential to raise serious questions about her own judgement and integrity? Did she think Cass wouldn't find out?*

Or was Finnegan – despite her father's assurances – trying to provoke some kind of clash that she could use against Cass to get rid of her?

'You look a bit puzzled,' Devine said. 'Everything all right?'

But his words were suddenly extraneous noise, blending into the background with the shouting of orders, the hiss of the coffee machine and the clanking of cups.

I came here to escape the madness. But I've just been plunged back in again.

CHAPTER EIGHT

C ass took to the sea early Saturday morning, alone as was her custom. She'd never been the type to join things and introduce herself – the hangover, perhaps, of growing up a Guard's daughter and people treading warily in her presence. She'd returned home not to be embraced by her community, but simply to retreat from the guilt. It hadn't worked. There wasn't a day when Cass didn't ask herself if she could have done something different, preventative.

There had been a time when Hugh's benders were a one day thing – warm up, get hammered, sleep it off. Then it slipped into two – wake up, start the fire again, keep it lit. She realised at that point there would come a time when two days became three, and then four, until the fire would eventually consume him. She knew she had lost him the day she told him it was the sober Hugh Moran she loved.

'But I hate that fucking guy,' he replied. 'I like the guy I am when I drink.'

She persevered anyway – love gives you little choice. She always thought she'd somehow find a way to rescue him – until the drunken, shambolic shadow of the man she loved got behind the wheel of a car, missed a red light, and ploughed into a mother and child.

So Glencale was a retreat. Since moving back, she had spent a year avoiding people, leaving her apartment as little as possible. And yes, there had been days when she feared she might lose it, when her mental health was perched on a precipice and she felt herself stumbling.

The sea had been her salvation. Glencale bay was a coastal inlet stretching some fifty kilometres from Glencale to the Atlantic Ocean. Provided there were no weather warnings, the bay was generally a safe place for swimmers who were aware of their limitations to take the plunge. In spots, the tides could be deceptive, but these were well signposted.

A few times, on days when her sense of despair was particularly acute, Cass had swum further out than advised, wondering what oblivion might feel like. But she was a strong swimmer, had never got into trouble, and realised subsequently a fundamental truth: she had never put herself at real risk.

Despite her anguish, she would neither completely break down nor experience some flick-of-a-switch recovery. She was built to simply grind on, head down, arching through the water, coming up for air, repeat, repeat, repeat. Self-contained, aware of her own limitations and pushing to no extremes. Resilience, she knew, was one of her core traits, for good or for bad. And on the bad days, the better days, and all the days where she simply endured, the bay invariably called to her, offering its raw and revitalising respite.

But that morning's respite would be very brief indeed: after her cold dip, Cass emerged to dry off and check her voicemail – and got the shocking message there had been another murder.

———

Cass could smell the bleach from the door. After consulting by phone with the assigned SIO, a detective inspector whose arrival from district HQ was awaited, Finnegan had issued instructions to her team. An outer cordon had been established, ensuring that no curious member of the public could come close enough to Bridge Bannon's farm to see anything.

The farmhouse and yard had been designated as the inner cordon. The kitchen was the core crime scene, containing the bloody and bruised body of the elderly farmer. The back door leading directly into the kitchen was designated the sole point of entry and exit to avoid unnecessary contamination, a blue tent erected outside it to prevent photographers with long lenses from snapping the body.

Like a nightclub bouncer, Cass's job was to run security outside the tent, ensuring only those with a strict need to enter the kitchen did so – investigating officers and technical specialists only, each of whom had to be logged.

Cass hadn't actually been in the kitchen herself, hadn't seen the body. A small part of her was almost grateful for the smell of the bleach, recognising that the disinfectant overpowered the sickly sweet, repulsive smell of the decomposing corpse. But without ever having to see the victim's body, the bleach ruled out any suggestion of an accidental killing. Somebody had deliberately intended serious harm to Bridge Bannon, and then had the presence of mind to douse the crime scene afterwards in an attempt to destroy any DNA traces.

The technicians would determine whether it was an amateur or professional effort at evasion, but Cass felt at least some forethought had gone into the murder. Already, the prevailing view among her colleagues was that the burglary gang had struck again, had come prepared, and had decided to leave no more witnesses.

Down at the harbour, she had felt the sun on her back while swimming. But up here, it was, unsurprisingly, a different story.

A low mist had settled over the mountains, and it was distinctly cool. *Sullen weather,* she thought.

Finnegan, dressed in protective overalls and overshoes, emerged from the house, removing her mask and double gloves.

'What does it look like in there?' Cass asked.

'They beat the shit out of him and mashed his head to a pulp, with bars or hammers or something. Ransacked the place while they were at it. Bannon was known to distrust the banks and keep his money at home. My guess is he wouldn't say where the money was and so they kept going. Wouldn't surprise me if the pathologist tells us his heart gave out first.'

'Definitely multiple attackers?' Cass asked.

'The crime-scene boys will tell us that,' Finnegan said. 'But it looks like our gang has escalated from armed robbery and assault to murder.'

It was the straightforward assumption, and likeliest explanation. But Cass wasn't yet convinced. The detective squad didn't like geniuses and was only marginally more tolerant of contrarians. Cass considered herself to be neither – she'd made the squad because she was a plodder, diligent, assembling the jigsaw piece by piece. And she felt several pieces of the puzzle were missing here.

'Did they come close to killing on any of the previous burglaries?' she asked.

'Pretty sure it was a close-run thing in some of the cases,' Finnegan said. 'Just pure luck that somebody wasn't killed previously.'

'But the bleach is new, isn't it? They didn't use it in any of the burglaries before now?'

'They didn't kill anyone before now,' Finnegan said. 'Probably weren't as worried about the burglaries. But knew they'd be facing life sentences for this one if caught.'

'But they'd have had to bring the bleach with them – which

suggests planning, which suggests a change in MO, which is… kind of unusual, isn't it?'

'Not necessarily. A working farm like this – bound to have bleach somewhere.' Finnegan's mobile rang and she took the call and walked off in the direction of her car.

Cass remained in position, knowing she had a good few hours of sentry duty ahead of her. It would be Kearney, the SIO, rather than Finnegan who would assign the duties from here, and Cass knew that, having left the detective squad and returned to the beat, she – and most of the local team – would be assigned the grunt work, including the door-to-doors.

But as with Nabila Fathi's murder, there wouldn't be many doors around here on which to knock, Cass knew – two ruins of old whitewashed cottages for every working farmhouse or renovated family home. And that at least did fit the pattern – because the gang's prior victims all lived in isolated spots and kept cash on their properties.

Maybe it was them after all, she thought. *This isn't the States, where so many murders are never solved. It's Ireland, where at least nine in ten murders* are *solved. And that's because they tend to be straightforward. The killer is usually known to the victim – husband kills wife. Or the killers have form – an organised crime gang gunning down a rival.*

In the end, the facts would determine the case, but the working theory generally proved correct. So Finnegan was probably right.

But as the wind turned and wafted the smell of bleach through the yard once more, Cass instinctively felt something was off with their initial assumptions.

CHAPTER NINE

From the rear of the deconsecrated church high in the Loop, in a position giving him a panoramic view of the valley, Mason Brady spotted the lights, and a jolt of raw panic stabbed him in the chest.

The two Garda cars were moving rapidly, lights flashing but sirens silent, the empty country road not giving them cause to announce their presence.

There was no question about their course: they were proceeding with speed and stealth in Brady's direction.

He forced down the fear and his training kicked in, calculating rough distance and running numbers.

Three minutes to get clear, give or take...

They were close by, and possibly – presumably – coming for him.

He ran inside.

Two minutes, fifty-five seconds...

In the storage room in the chancel, the go-bag was long since packed to facilitate his departure at a moment's notice. Months ago, he had mentally mapped the handful of local back-roads that might be of use. He had practised various escape runs. Evacuate

Glencale, aim for Dublin, hide out in the city, and rely on capable friends to find him the safest route out of the country. More recently, he had come to think it unlikely such a scenario would ever materialise, because at every stage of his labour, he had taken extreme care, worked in the shadows, and hidden all traces. But there was always a risk of detection – and now, it must have materialised.

Two minutes, forty-five seconds...

Closer but still a distance off. Adrenaline surging through his veins and steeling for a fight if required. But flight preferable. He pulled on jeans and an old jumper over his sweat-soaked workout gear.

Two minutes, five seconds...

From the kitchen table, he grabbed his car keys, wallet and phone. But no weapons of any kind. He would only fight if provoked. His goal was to evade the police, not engage in combat with them.

One minute, fifty seconds...

From the storage room, he grabbed the go-bag, and then scanned the front yard before deciding it was safe to exit the house.

One minute, thirty seconds...

He ran to the car and threw everything in, before picking up his binoculars. No panic now, even with the clock working against him.

One minute, ten seconds...

He surveyed the terrain to ensure he was about to take the best exit route.

One minute, three seconds...

And then took a deep breath and exhaled.

Both police cars had turned into Bridge Bannon's farm.

Escape plan stood down.

———

For the next hour, Brady observed the scene through his binoculars, and didn't like what he saw.

His instinct had been right when the two Americans walked into Milly Cooper's store: they would create a disturbance, and bring it close to his door.

It wasn't hard to figure out the gravity of the scene he was observing. No body had been brought out of the house, but the manner in which the cordons had been established, the escalating number of police arriving at the scene, and the protective clothing worn by officers going into the house through a blue tent told him everything he needed to know. The farmer was dead.

The second murder investigation around here in less than a year. The first had posed him no problems – there was nothing to link him to it. By contrast, the farmer's murder – if that's what it was – presented Brady with a serious dilemma. In this sparsely populated area, he was what passed for a 'neighbour' – he knew immediately he would be on the house-to-house inquiry list. He had seen the two Americans – Milly Cooper would vouch for that. So he would have to engage with the very people he had gone to such lengths to avoid – the police.

FUBAR, he mouthed, resorting to the old army slang.

In all the emergency scenarios he had run through, all the escape routes he had devised and practised, he had never planned for something like this.

Fucked up beyond all recognition.

Now he had to figure out how the hell to handle it.

CHAPTER TEN

Eagerness drove Cass into leaving for the station early on Sunday morning, an eagerness she hadn't felt in a considerable time. It was, of course, a somewhat callous emotion in that moment, fuelled as it was by a murder, and the desire to investigate same. But it was more than defensible: the early stages of the investigation were the most critical.

Finnegan knew this too. Some time back, an independent inquiry had criticised the way that Garda rosters and shift patterns could unintentionally impinge on murder investigations. The inquiry gave the example of a case where an investigation team attending a murder on a Sunday had to be replaced the following day, because they were due their day off. Finnegan wasn't going to tolerate such sloppiness; she had issued a clear directive to her own team that leave was cancelled and they were to do everything to support the SIO and assembled detectives.

Cass didn't need the direction. As she walked to the station seized with the case, she passed the supermarket where Nabila Fathi had briefly worked and saw Harbour Murphy's van parked outside. There was no chance of mistaking it, for the livery bore a massive photo of the politician and his contact details. Black hair parted crisply to one side like a well-behaved schoolboy, but the jowly face and red cheeks a sign that the blood pressure tablets had to work overtime to keep the sixty-something-year-old motoring. Murphy had been on her list to contact as a priority in the unsolved case, and Cass decided there was no time like the present. It was a little before 8am and the first daily murder conference in the Bannon case – whereby everybody would assemble in the incident room to go through what they knew and be assigned jobs – wouldn't start until ten.

Fifteen minutes with Harbour Murphy will be time well spent, she thought.

———

Harbour Murphy was unfazed by Cass's unexpected arrival and had no difficulty making time for her.

She quickly realised why: for he assumed she was there to discuss the murder of Bridge Bannon, and was hungry for detail. The Sunday papers were already neatly laid out in their rows and a couple of them had put the murder on the front page, leading with the suggestion that the burglary gang had struck in deadly fashion. But their reports were fairly basic, as the force hadn't said too much publicly in the immediate aftermath of the discovery.

Murphy, by contrast, already seemed to have a good picture of what the Guards knew privately. Local gossip would account for a part of it – word travelled fast in Glencale – but more pertinently, a prominent politician like Murphy would have his contacts in the force, as Cass knew full well.

They were alone in the small stockroom at the back of the store. Murphy had told the staff they were not to be disturbed.

But if he thought such privacy would enable Cass to share confidential information, he was going to be disappointed.

'Any sight yet of those hoors who did it? They've done enough houses now – you must have some lead on them.'

He shares Finnegan's view as to the identity of the culprits. How surprising, she thought. 'The investigation's at an early stage. I wouldn't make any assumptions at this point.'

'I wouldn't be saying that in public now if I were you.'

'Meaning?'

'They've gone from dangerous to deadly. People will be terrified around here, and you're going on about "early stages". They'll want a bit more reassurance you're about to hammer these hoors.'

'Like I said, we're working to identify the person or persons responsible. I really wouldn't jump to conclusions.'

'Sure, didn't they cover the place in bleach? Only professionals would pull that kind of stunt. You've got to nail them to a wall – fast.'

Christ. That information was supposed to be kept solely within the investigation. Cass could feel her anger rising, and tried to contain it, knowing it had never helped her much in the past. 'That information is not public,' she said. 'I'd ask that you not mention it further.'

A curious half-smile broke out on his crimson face, and it wasn't friendly; he wasn't accustomed to being chided. 'You're Ted Cassidy's daughter, aren't you?'

I should have expected this one. 'And?'

'Fine man. Knew the value of public representatives like myself in times like this.'

She'd made a mistake by calling to him on a whim; it was foolish to chase a line of inquiry without sufficient preparation. But she needed to get him back on board – just so that she could, to piss him off again with the questions she'd actually come here to ask.

'I'll pass that on. And of course we'll make it a priority to keep the community informed. But I'm actually here about your former tenant and staff member, Nabila Fathi.'

For a moment, as his brow furrowed in puzzlement, it looked like he had to be reminded who Nabila Fathi was. Then, as it sunk in, the half-smile vanished: she had pissed him off before even getting to the first question.

'This is what you're here about? The day after one of our own has been beaten to death? This is what you want to prioritise? Christ on earth, girl, what are you thinking?'

I'll ignore 'girl'. But 'one of our own'? I've got your number now, Cass thought.

'Nabila Fathi was murdered too. I think you'd agree it is just as important we catch her killer or killers.'

'I couldn't agree more,' he said. 'But ye fucked up that investigation something awful; the killer got off scot-free, and now you're here asking questions about that case instead of prioritising Bridge Bannon's murder. What in the name of Christ are ye up to at all?'

'We're doing our job, Mr Murphy,' she said coolly. 'I thought you'd be willing to assist us in that process.'

Murphy didn't answer. He just shook his head and walked off, leaving Cass standing alone in the storeroom.

'Prick,' she muttered under her breath.

———

Unsurprisingly given the previous day's events, the station was humming with activity when she arrived. Cass headed for the incident room to see who was already gathered and to be brought up to speed on overnight developments.

En route, however, Finnegan appeared and, with a curt flick of her head, beckoned Cass to her office. It had originally been the stationmaster's office, the only remaining evidence of which was a handsome Victorian solid oak wall clock. The renovation to change the property's use from railway station to Garda station had been a crime in itself. The state property agency had thrown all the other historical artefacts and vintage furniture on the scrapheap and replaced them with gunmetal-grey filing cabinets, catalogue desk and chairs and a mounted pinboard now festooned in circulars and notices. Everything functional and grim, the clock being the honourable exception.

That clock's like me, Cass thought. *Out of place.*

Finnegan shut the door and sat behind her desk, beckoning Cass to the chair opposite.

I could have gone to Mass if I needed orders on when to stand and sit.

She noticed that Finnegan had somehow found time – and an available hairdresser on a Sunday morning – to get a blow-dry, and knew the reason why. It would be Finnegan, as the local commanding officer, who'd give the press conference later that day, not the SIO. She clearly wanted to look her best for the cameras.

Priorities.

'Why were you speaking to Harbour Murphy just now?'

Christ. Forget Mass. I've been dragged straight into the confessional box.

'I had some questions for him about Nabila Fathi.' *I'm about to be castigated for my sins.*

'What questions?'

Bless me Sergeant, for stepping on toes. 'He stormed off before I could ask them.'

'What questions?'

Heretical ones. At least in your eyes. 'Just the extent to which he knew Nabila.'

'Isn't that all in the case file?'

It would appear I'm more of a sceptic than the original investigation team. 'I had a few additional questions based on newer information.' *Because maybe that bollocks – to quote my father – has his own secrets to confess.*

'What newer information?'

To hell with another interrogation. 'Did I suddenly become a suspect in the investigation overnight?' Cass asked. She said it neutrally, with no hint of edge. But it served its purpose by stopping Finnegan cold. And then, to Cass's surprise, Finnegan smiled thinly.

An offering of peace?

'I'm told I handle men better than women,' Finnegan said. 'Got lower expectations of the boys. So don't mind me... But I would like to understand the purpose of your visit.'

Cass wasn't exactly mollified. But at least the atmosphere in the room had started to thaw. 'Nabila's friend, Maisah Sahraoui, was moved to an asylum centre in Donegal. I think Harbour Murphy knows why.'

'Why would he know something like that?'

'Because he has a stake in the Glencale direct provision centre. And if he has a stake, he has a say. And I think he used that say to get her moved.'

So that Maisah would no longer bother you. But you know that already, don't you?

Finnegan adopted her most dangerous expression – a neutral one, utterly unreadable to friend or foe. Cass felt as if there was a trapdoor beneath her and Finnegan was debating whether to press the button.

'I wasn't aware Maisah had been moved.'

Pull the other one. You're fooling nobody. 'You didn't notice she was no longer demanding to see you every week?' *Ignorance is not a defence. So no point feigning it.*

Finnegan sucked on her teeth, and didn't answer.

Christ, I'm going to buy a bloody soother for you. 'You knew the rest presumably?' Cass said. 'That he had a stake in the centre?'

'That's no secret,' Finnegan replied. 'It's probably how he came to hire her for the job in his shop.'

'I haven't managed to contact Maisah yet but I'm going to keep trying. I presume that's in order?'

The balance of power had shifted in the confrontation, if that's what it was. Finnegan had been in control, even after Cass shot out the line about being a suspect. But the news of Maisah Sahraoui's departure had changed the atmosphere, and Cass couldn't quite determine why.

Did Finnegan now also suspect something?

And if so, and she was as close to Harbour Murphy as it seemed, would she shut down Cass's lines of inquiry?

'That's fine,' Finnegan said eventually, to Cass's surprise. 'And you can speak to Harbour Murphy again if you want...'

This is unexpected.

'... but your priority is the Bannon murder, and any and all actions the SIO throws at you. Understand? Everything else for now is on hold or side of the desk.'

'Okay. It's probably time I got to the incident room.' *Redeeming the time, because the days are evil.*

'You know, Murphy can be a right old bollocks...'

Exactly what my father said.

'... but he's fairly straight all the same.'

Well, maybe not exactly what he said.

'We did speak to him first time round and he had nothing material to offer,' Finnegan continued. 'I'd be surprised if it were any different this time.'

'He knew about the bleach in the Bannon murder when I spoke to him – he had inside information.'

'Sure, half the town probably knows about the bleach by now.'

'But if someone on the team is talking...'

'Leave it with me. I'll look into it. I'll see you in the incident room shortly.'

Cass didn't see merit in pushing further, and stood to leave. But Finnegan wasn't quite finished. 'When you do get back to the Nabila Fathi file, make sure to keep me briefed.'

Understood would have been the natural response. But it was Cass's turn to nod curtly and go on her way.

CHAPTER ELEVEN

About an hour later, Mason Brady sat in his battered Mondeo across the road from the precinct – or station, in the local lingo – kept the engine running, and ruminated some more.

There were people in the world to whom rest and recovery came easy. He wasn't one of them, hadn't slept overnight, and was far from his best.

The worst time to launch any kind of manoeuvre, defensive or otherwise, he thought.

People in his line of work were supposed to be decisive, and about certain things, he was ruthlessly so – such as killing when required.

And he didn't suffer from the misconception it was somehow dishonourable to shoot somebody in the back. Bullshit. Brady had killed different people in different ways, and knew the fundamental truth: whatever the method, it was easier when your opponent had their back turned, was caught unawares, unable to offer much in the way of resistance. On such matters, he suffered from no hesitation whatsoever.

But when things were less clear-cut, when they demanded

rigorous evaluation and foresight, he could procrastinate with the best of them.

And he was procrastinating now, at the likely cost of increasing the risk to himself.

Not for the first time, he wondered if the procrastination was a symptom. He knew the nightmares probably were. So too, the hyper-vigilance and the extreme fatigue that arose as a consequence. The feeling he had no future. The many days he didn't care if that were suddenly to prove to be the case.

Or maybe the procrastination is just proof I'm the blunt instrument and not the master strategist.

His military career had been about executing missions, not devising them. He drummed his fingers on the steering wheel and calculated, for the umpteenth time, whether it was the safer course of action to walk into the precinct or wait for the police to turn up at his door. He didn't want cops prowling around his house or, worse again, finding any reason to profile him. Equally, though, he knew it might look odd to turn up voluntarily with information, details, descriptions. Most people were not good witnesses. Would they wonder why he was?

From the glove compartment, he took a pill container, flicked it open, and swallowed two benzos he'd brought with him from the States. He couldn't tell if they helped or made things worse, and so used them sparingly. But the simple act of taking a couple usually calmed him a little on the rougher days.

Even the military was teaching mindfulness by the time he'd left, but damned if he was ever going to fall for that psychobabble bullshit. No amount of mindfulness could pull him out of the misery he'd seen; as to the misery he'd inflicted, that didn't haunt him at all.

He shook his head, trying to clear his mind of the negative thoughts.

Focus. You've done what you set out to do. Everything has gone smoothly up to now. This is a speed hump, nothing more. Take it steady and get over it.

The mental siege was lifting, and he finally chose which path to take. He snapped the glove compartment shut, switched the engine off, and took a moment to inspect himself in the visor mirror just to ensure he didn't look as frayed as he felt.

He pushed the visor back up, and that was the moment he realised he had been spotted.

———

Cass emerged from the station following the murder conference with her mind spinning and a list of house-to-house inquiries to make in the Loop. Spinning, because the officers conducting the inch-by-inch search of Bridge Bannon's house had found more than 80,000 euro in cash and another 17,000 in old Irish pound notes in a wall cavity. It wasn't the first or last time that cash would unwisely be kept in a home – but Cass was staggered by the sheer amount of it, and the old man's stubbornness in not even using the banks to change the old pound notes, which were now two decades out of circulation. The money had been well concealed, which was possibly the reason Bridge Bannon was dead. Had it been easier to find, or had the farmer revealed its location, the killer or killers might have left him alive.

The money will do fuck-all for you now.

She pushed the melancholy aside by focusing on the list of inquiries she had to make, all of which would be done by means of the same questionnaire to ensure information was collected in a consistent fashion. She had already settled in her mind on the first house to which to call when she spotted the old Mondeo. The Guards had used this make and model for a number of years and Cass wondered briefly whether it had been a former police car. That was why she eyed up the vehicle – and eyed up Brady in turn.

He was seated, but guessing from his position, he was maybe six foot tall. Trim and tanned from time in the outdoors, with a salt and pepper crew-cut that reminded her of a wolf's fur. But his eyes looked haunted rather than those of a hunter.

There was nothing out of kilter about him; nothing suspicious. She wouldn't have given him a second glance except that he caught her looking – and suddenly his eyes changed. Locked in on her. Sized her up. Almost as if an opponent... or quarry.

A primitive signal sounded in her brain, an early threat warning. Disproportionate response? No. Permanent precaution around people was to be expected when your job necessitated wearing an anti-stab vest on a daily basis.

But something else registered too: on her house-to-house list was an American male in his thirties renovating the old church in the Loop, a couple of miles from Bridge Bannon's farm. She had no description of the American, but instinct told Cass she was looking right at him.

The same American, she recalled from the case file, had been briefly considered by the original team investigating Nabila Fathi's murder, together with all other non-infirm males in the locality. He was ruled out more or less immediately once the team established he'd only arrived in the country two months after her death. As a result, he hadn't been questioned.

Was he looking to speak to the Guards now?

And if so, did she sense some reluctance on his part?

She started walking towards him, and he pushed the car door to get out.

CHAPTER TWELVE

M illy Cooper, owner of the small shop on the road from Glencale to the Loop, was the first person Cass had intended to visit that morning. After news of Bridge Bannon's murder spread, Milly had phoned the station the previous night to say two American visitors had been in the shop asking for the farmer's address. She couldn't remember much else about them, but Cass had been detailed to call to Milly and see if she could jog her memory a little.

But now another American stranger was going one better, verifying Milly Cooper's lead and providing descriptions of the two men. Confirming that they had, indeed, sought directions to Bridge Bannon's farm. And, best of all, offering a licence plate number.

She left the interview room to pass the details to the incident room coordinator without delay, recognising it could be the critical breakthrough.

The burglary gang never killed before, never used bleach to try and cover their tracks. Whoever these Americans are, they sound like a much better bet.

Initially, she hadn't given Brady all that much thought as she took his statement, focusing only on his information and clarifying matters with him as necessary.

But as she returned from the incident room, she found herself wondering: *Who exactly is this guy? How is he sharp enough to give confident, detailed descriptions and recall the car's licence plate? How many randomers can do that?*

And why that shift in the car from passive to on the prowl?

She stopped to get some coffee for them both, taking a minute to mull things over before returning to the incident room. The coffee might serve to keep him talking, now that the formalities were over.

But when she placed it on the table, he thanked her, smiled and then lapsed into silence. Not rudely, just calmly. As if he'd said everything necessary and had nothing left to impart, a ship that had unloaded its cargo and was now waiting patiently at dockside for the green light to depart.

'Thank you again for coming in, Mr Brady. We greatly value information from members of the public.'

'You'll have to call me Brady,' he said. '"Mister" will never stick.'

'You go by your surname?'

'The military goes by surname. It sticks after a while.'

I know the way, she thought. 'The military was where you learned to record licence plates?'

'Some of the places we went, I guess it paid to be observant.'

'It was more than observant; you have an excellent memory.'

Brady returned the compliment with an appealing smile, boyish and confident, no hint of reserve or reticence.

Some people smile and you can see their emotional scars, she thought. *Not this guy.* 'Where did you serve?' she asked.

'Wherever they sent me. Not avoiding your question – it's just sometimes it was kind of hard to distinguish. We weren't exactly there to do the tourist sites.'

'And you're retired now?'

'Honourably discharged. Did my tours, made my contribution, figured it was time for younger models to take over. The knees ain't what they used to be.'

He smiled again, and Cass got the distinct impression he was managing her, even though his answers came without hesitation. He kept eye contact throughout, and seemed at ease in surroundings that would have made other people anxious.

No harm to try and shake him a bit. 'There's just one bit I don't fully understand: if you had suspicions about these two men, why didn't you contact us at the time?'

'I've been asking myself that. I guess a remnant of my old life is mild paranoia. I see suspicious things ten times a day, and note the details, but they're usually nothing. I see a carrier bag on a quiet road, I think improvised device. But in civilian life, it just means some a-hole chucked garbage from their car. I can't go around contacting the authorities every time my nerves twitch.'

Solid enough answer, thought Cass. *Can't fault him on that when I recognise the same professional paranoia.* 'Fair enough,' she said. 'But tell me, what was it specifically about the two that you didn't like?'

'They just didn't fit. Which I guess is pretty ironic coming from me, right? With this accent?'

Which was from where, exactly? Not New York, not Boston, but that was as much as Cass could tell. 'What part of the States are you from?'

'Midwest,' he said. 'And you? Local?'

'Yes. Spent a few years in Dublin before coming back.'

'Couldn't resist the call of home, eh?'

Not exactly. But I noticed that switch in conversation and I'm here to get information out of you, not give it. 'You've been here a while, right – you're doing up Saint Fiachra's church?'

She couldn't say the name without conjuring up long-buried memories of childhood fears – seeing the ruins of the church in the mist, hearing in school the story of the Catholic priest hanged from the bellcote during the seventeenth century Cromwellian conquest of Ireland. Lore had it that on the foulest of nights, the faint sound of the long-gone church bell could be heard above the stormy weather as the cleric's ghost thrashed and swung. There was a reason the church had lain in ruins for decades – nobody in their right mind wanted it.

'That's right. Almost done now. I needed a project.'

'You don't find it a bit isolated up there? It's not exactly midtown Manhattan.'

'You spend enough years sharing bases and barracks and you begin to see the attraction of peace and quiet.'

Cass nodded. She was running out of questions, and couldn't think of subtle ways to seek the information she was really after. Brady wasn't charismatic, exactly, but he had presence – she felt herself warming to his character. But she hadn't forgotten that predatory look she'd briefly seen. It hadn't returned since, but she knew she hadn't imagined it. Was there a touch of chameleon in him?

She got a vague sense Brady was escaping something, but had no grounds to ask what – and besides, lots of foreigners came to Glencale to escape. Wealthy pensioners seeking an idyllic retirement; artists hoping to mine a rich creative seam; students seeking holiday work and adventures. They came to escape family and friends, the rat race and the drudgery of hated jobs, unpaid bills or drug debts, professional or personal failure, persecution or prosecution, and more besides. If Brady was escaping something – provided it wasn't a crime – good luck to him. He wouldn't be the first or last.

After all, Cass thought, *it's precisely what I'm doing myself... But at least I'm not lunatic enough to escape to a haunted ruin in the Loop.*

———

After leaving the precinct, guessing that eyes might still be upon him, Brady decided to act as normally as he could. So he drove to the town mall – or shopping centre as the locals called it – and picked up food, beer and a couple of Sunday newspapers, which would almost certainly go unread. He had dedicated social media alerts set up for the news he needed. Besides which, the performance in the station had required intense focus, and he was now aching for sleep.

As he drove home, he mulled over the events of that morning. To a large extent, he was satisfied.

Yes, he'd been startled after letting his guard drop for a moment in the car before realising the cop was observing him. That had been immensely irritating, and he guessed his instant facial expression had probably been of the 'fight not flight' variety. But he had rapidly adjusted, and everything subsequently had been straightforward enough. He had rehearsed the core of his script and stuck to it, made easier by a simple mantra: tell as much of the truth as you can in order to keep the lies to a minimum. Easier that way.

So he had given her every relevant detail about what he'd seen at the store – what his two fellow countrymen looked like, why he felt they were suspicious, their plate number and more. His descriptions had been full and frank. He had considered giving just a partial number to make his recall seem less notable. But in the end, he'd figured that they would ask about his professional background in any event. Besides, what he ultimately wanted was the cops off his patch. The full plate would help achieve that objective by enabling the cops to do their job more quickly.

His only lie had been when she asked why he failed to report his suspicions. The question was a good one, but also obvious: he had anticipated it and felt his answer sounded plausible. After all, it was rooted in truth. He *was* constantly on watch, because he had to be.

And it was for this reason that he had confined his account to events at the store. Brady didn't know the Guards well enough to understand how they operated, compared with the cops back home, but he trusted the rule was much the same: never volunteer more than you have to. Milly Cooper knew he'd been in the store; he couldn't avoid acknowledging that. But it would have been impossible to explain why he followed his fellow countrymen to Bridge Bannon's farm without the cop raising a series of further questions. Questions he didn't particularly care for.

So you followed them to the farm, is that correct?

Yes.

And watched them from a distance, through binoculars?

Yes.

Did you see the murder?

That wasn't what happened.

So what did you see?

The two men leaving, at gunpoint.

Bridge Bannon pulled a gun on them?

A shotgun, yes.

So you saw these two leave and Bridge Bannon was alive as they did so?

Correct.

Are you in the habit of following people and spying on them?

No, but these two rang all the alarm bells, a goddamned fire department of them.

And yet you still didn't think to ring us?

Maybe I should have, but like I said…

Yes, you can't go around reporting every suspicious thing you see.

Exactly.

Would it surprise you if I said I didn't believe your story?

Yes, because I'm telling the truth.

Funny kind of truth. You get it into your head that these two are trouble, follow them to the farm, and see Bridge Bannon chase them away with a gun. And you still don't think of contacting us?

The old man had handled himself well enough. I figured he was safe – that they wouldn't come back.

And any possibility that you came back?

Come again?

Had you any bad blood with Mr Bannon?

This is insane. I came here to report some information in good faith.

See, the strangest thing in all of this is not immediately reporting what you saw on the farm.

My mistake, I know.

Is there a reason you didn't want to contact us?

Of course not.

Are you hiding something, Mr Brady?

Brady's fine.

Are you hiding something, Mr Brady?

I'll plead the fifth on that.

Yes, some things are better left unsaid, he thought. There was simply no way he could have detailed anything beyond what he'd witnessed at the store.

He was conscious of the slight risk that, by withholding an important piece of information – namely seeing Bridge Bannon very much alive as the two Americans left the farm – he could be steering the investigation in the wrong direction. But he had no doubt the Americans had returned, and had done so without mercy. He'd given the cops a strong lead; now it was up to them to do their job and take care of the rest.

Proactively coming to the precinct had been the right tactic. He'd even earned a compliment about his good memory – a joke if ever there was one, not that the cop would have reason to know.

Truth is my memory is shot through with bullet holes, a thousand of them over the years. They dominate, subjugate all else. Making me an unreliable witness in all but one aspect:

I remember targets.

I remember enemies.

I remember who I killed.

And I remember who I want to kill.

CHAPTER THIRTEEN

M ost detectives Cass knew didn't expect luck to come their way in criminal investigations. But Mason Brady being an unusually observant bystander was, unquestionably, a stroke of good fortune. It took only a short period of time for the investigation team to trace the car to which the licence plate belonged, and it was Liam Devine who came to Cass later that Sunday evening with an update.

'Car rental. The Americans flew into Shannon Airport, picked up the car – SUV, technically – and drove straight down here. One Raymond Russo and one Frank Mangano, both with addresses in Long Island. No red flags with Interpol so we're checking directly with New York and doing a deeper trace on the passports.'

'You think they travelled on false identities?'

'If they have serious records, they'd have struggled to get in.'

'Flights out?' Cass asked.

'Booked to leave Shannon in seventy-two hours.'

'And between now and then?'

'All-points bulletin for the car and its two esteemed occupants. There was no CCTV on Bannon's farm or anywhere nearby that we can locate. But we're pulling in as much CCTV from town as we can find. They're bound to be on it somewhere.'

'You said the car was a rental, right?'

'If you're thinking it might have a tracker fitted, we thought of that,' Devine said. 'Checked with the rental company. No joy.'

Most detectives don't expect luck to come their way in criminal investigations.

'Why travel 3,000 miles across the Atlantic to kill an elderly farmer who, as best we know, never set foot outside Ireland?'

'You know the family?'

Cass shook her head. Glencale might have been a small town but she had been gone a long time, had spent the months since her return in near isolation, and wasn't exactly rooted in the community.

'Bannon was a mean, miserable son-of-a-bitch. Feral. Beat his late wife. Probably beat his kids. Picked fights in whatever pub he walked into. Until he withdrew completely a few years back, and lived practically like a hermit, shutting himself off from everybody.

'Anyway, his daughter – miraculously – is the complete opposite. Sarah Delahunty – her married name – teaches in the small primary school between Glencale and the Loop. Friendly and well liked, community-minded. Lives a mile or so from her father's farm but has had nothing to do with him for years.'

'You know this for sure?'

'Straight from the horse's mouth. Noel Ryan interviewed her yesterday. He's the family liaison officer.'

'Ryan as liaison? You're shitting me. You can smell him fermenting when he walks into a room.'

'Finnegan specifically recommended to the SIO he take on that role,' Devine said. 'Fucking waste of space... Anyway, the daughter isn't the story here. The son is: Peter Bannon. Another fucking waste of space. Came to our attention a few times when he was a teenager for being drunk and disorderly, picking fights in pubs like the father, but no convictions. Mostly cos he lost every fight he started. Skinny runt who didn't have the father's size, strength or sneakiness.'

'And?'

'You're right that Bridge Bannon never stepped off the island. Didn't even have a passport, as far as we can tell. But the son did. He took off to the States a couple of years back.'

'Long Island?'

'You win the prize.'

'Ryan got this from Sarah Delahunty?'

'Ryan got fuck-all from Sarah Delahunty. The guy's a joke. I got this. I remembered Peter had gone to the States. Found his social media profiles in thirty seconds and his location in another thirty. Or his former location, to be exact.'

'Where is he now?'

'I don't know exactly,' Devine said. 'But I do know he returned to Ireland on a flight from JFK three weeks ago.'

'So you think the two Americans were chasing the son – and his father just became collateral damage?'

'That's my guess. They went searching for Peter at the farmhouse; Bridge Bannon probably didn't like the intrusion and things got out of hand.'

'We know for sure they were at the farmhouse? We have no witness yet and I thought the forensics were still a work in progress.'

'Kind of amazing in one way how many visitors a guy gets when he doesn't want any. There were lots of tyre prints in and around the farm. We matched some to Bannon's pickup, tractor, and quad. Others to the postman, oil delivery guy, parish priest. There are a few sets we haven't yet matched to specific vehicles. But one set fit the tyre specification of the make and model of the car rental. The two Americans were there, no doubt about it. Hunting for that runt of a son.'

There was an obvious flaw in that chain of thought, Cass felt.

'If they needed to find the son, why kill the father? In another country where they don't know the terrain? It draws so much attention to them – leaves them with no other option but to lie low or run.'

'That's true,' Devine said. 'But it sounds to me like these guys are muscle, not masterminds. Maybe it was meant to be some kind of message to the son.'

Plausible, thought Cass. *But the team would need something to back it up; otherwise it was purely speculation.*

'Maybe they're still in Glencale then, chasing Peter Bannon.'

'After committing a murder? I doubt it. Those boys are long gone and my guess is the return flights are just a ruse – we'll discover they got out already on some other passports.'

'We should try and find Peter Bannon,' Cass said. 'Regardless of where the two Americans are now, his life could be at risk.'

'Working on it.'

'And Sarah Delahunty spoke of none of this when interviewed?'

'She said her brother was in the States, but wasn't in regular contact with him and hadn't seen him in a couple of years. Ryan didn't push it.'

'You said Sarah Delahunty's house is close to her father's farm – you got the exact address?'

'Yes – you think she has more to tell?'

More than that barely functioning alcoholic would have thought to ask her anyway, she thought. 'Another visit can't hurt. I'll clear it with the SIO. Tomorrow morning?'

'Can't,' Devine said. 'I'm on CCTV duty for my sins. But you should tell her the good news.'

'The good news?'

'There's a wad of cash to add to the inheritance.'

CHAPTER FOURTEEN

It was unseasonably mild the following morning as Cass drove out of Glencale and towards Sarah Delahunty's property.

About five miles outside the town, the main road forked – one route took the driver along the coast, effectively circumnavigating the Loop. The other was a pass directly through it, ascending through the mountains in a series of serpentine curves and hairpin bends until, near the peak, one encountered arguably the Loop's most distinctive feature: a series of hand-hewn rock tunnels. Almost 200 years previously, for reasons of practicality given the troublesome terrain, the road builders had chosen to go through the brows of the last mountains in the range rather than over them, and unknowingly created a tourist attraction in the process.

But Cass was turning off well before the tunnels. There was any number of boreens and byways branching off the pass, including the one that led to Bridge Bannon's farm and, a short distance beyond it, another that led to Sarah Delahunty's house.

As she drove, she reflected on the conversation with Kearney, the SIO, an hour earlier in which she'd sought approval for the visit. Kearney was a veteran detective who came with an excellent reputation both for leading investigations and, unlike Finnegan, trusting his teams.

After a brief discussion, he'd given permission – before closing on a surprising note. 'Sergeant Finnegan tells me you're better than you think,' he said. 'We could do with seeing that on this case.'

She had responded with a lame, 'I'll try.' Now, she wondered what precisely Finnegan had said and the extent to which her superior officer – and possibly everyone in the station – thought Cass to be off the boil. Or overwrought. Or, as Finnegan had implied, a basket case.

Cass had phoned in advance to inform Sarah Delahunty she was coming, and had been told to look for the red steel gate, which would be open. It was easy to find: not many bothered to paint gates around here, especially on working farms. In her mind Cass triangulated the locations so far relevant to the case: Milly Cooper's shop in the valley; turn onto the byway and ascend a few miles into the lower mountains for Bridge Bannon's farm; go east from there for about a mile to Sarah Delahunty's farm and then twist upwards, corkscrewing higher into the mountains, for Mason Brady's church renovation, which, Cass figured, would have unfiltered views across the range.

She had reread the interview notes at the station, and knew that Sarah Delahunty was thirty-eight years of age and hadn't bothered much with her father for the last twenty or so of those. She had concentrated on her own family – an accountant husband, three children aged between six and twelve – and work: her job as a teacher and the stables she and her husband ran, providing lessons during the spring and summer.

There had been relatively little in the notes that seemed of any relevance to the investigation. While it was true to say that family were often suspects and that Delahunty did not seem to care for her father, it was also the case that women, generally, didn't kill in such a violent way. Neither did amateurs have the presence of mind to use bleach to try and erase DNA traces. True, 'at home with my family' wasn't exactly a rock-solid alibi for the night of the murder, but all told, Sarah Delahunty was not a suspect and never would be.

As she drove up the laneway, the stables came first into view, two lengthy and well-maintained buildings running at right angles to the picturesque bungalow that was the family home. In front of the stables, Cass saw three children on horseback, prancing slowly around the gallops, and behind them, giving instructions, Sarah Delahunty.

She was taller than Cass had expected – maybe around five-ten – vigorous and decisive-looking, someone capable of handling small humans and horses and doing so lovingly but tolerating no dissent. She was, Cass thought, quite regal; standing there in jeans, riding boots and jumper in the low winter sun, brown tresses scraped up casually with a wooden hair fork, matching brown eyes that had a warmth and wisdom to them. She looked weary but not broken, as if tired by the daily pressures of life but not particularly grieving the loss of her father. All told, Cass found herself liking Sarah Delahunty instantly, before they had even exchanged a word.

Delahunty gave the children orders to stable the horses and brush their coats, and invited Cass into the kitchen, where a kettle was simmering on the stove and a batch of freshly baked scones lay on a tray on the table. Cass didn't get the impression the cosy domestic scene was pretence for her: she sensed this was a loving home where the family cared for each other. After some small talk about the school and the children while the tea was brewed, Cass got down to business.

'This won't take too long – I can see you've got your hands full. You've been informed, I take it, that your father's body can now be released?'

'Yes, thanks. At least I can finalise the funeral arrangements now. It'll be good to get it over with.'

'Have you wider family? People to notify?'

'Our mother died eleven years ago. It's just me and my brother in terms of immediate family, but Peter went to the States undocumented, so he won't be at the funeral. My father had a couple of older sisters, one living in Galway, the other in Limerick. They're both quite frail now, but I expect my cousins will help them to attend. There'll be some neighbours and acquaintances, I suppose – the usual thing. But if you're asking me whether I expect the funeral home to be packed, probably not. My father was not a popular man, detective.'

'I'm not a detective, and "Cass" is fine. Can you tell me why that was?'

'I told your colleague the other day.'

'I appreciate that, it's just sometimes we need to go over statements again.'

'He was not a nice man, det– Cass. He made home a living hell for my mother and treated my brother like a dog he could kick any time he wanted. He hid some of that in public, but only to an extent. He was no pillar of the community. He won't be missed.'

And if he made your mother's life hell, and treated your brother like a dog, what did he do to you? Cass wondered. *Some bastards deserve to be in the ground.* 'And your brother, I understand he's younger than you?'

'That's right.'

'Have you seen him lately?'

'Peter? We speak a few times a year, WhatsApp each other now and again.'

A non-answer answer. She's given this some thought. But worth probing around the edges first before I startle her. 'Do the names Raymond Russo and Frank Mangano mean anything to you?'

'Are these the two men you suspect killed my father?'

'They're the two Americans who requested directions to your

father's farm. We're seeking to question them, obviously, as persons of interest. Do you recognise the names?'

'I'm afraid not. They mean nothing to me.'

'They're from Long Island, where I believe your brother is based. Do you think Peter might know them?'

'Is there any particular reason he would?'

'That's what we're seeking to establish.'

Sarah Delahunty's answers had been unhesitant to that point, but now she paused, and Cass could tell she was deliberating. Her father hadn't been a pillar of the community but Sarah was; and Cass guessed she placed high value on common decency and honesty. Lying to the Guards, even withholding information, would not come naturally to her.

'Look, I don't know is the honest answer,' she said eventually. 'But I'm sure you know that Peter has had a troubled life. Our father did that to him. Peter struggled to come to terms with his childhood, got into a few scrapes here, and figured America was the answer, as far away from home as he could get. I hoped he'd build a better life for himself there but... he was scarred, I guess. If you're asking me whether it's possible he got into some trouble over there, yes, it is. If you're asking me whether these two men were somehow connected to him, you'd have to ask him that. I can't understand why they'd come all the way over here though.'

'Would it surprise you to know Peter flew into the country in the last three weeks?'

Another long pause. Sarah rose from her chair and went to the kitchen window, from where she could see the stables and her children.

Trying to make a decision, Cass thought.

'No, it wouldn't,' she replied, back turned to Cass. 'He told me he was coming home.'

'You didn't mention this to my colleague.'

'He didn't ask.'

Of course he didn't, Cass thought.

76

'Have you seen Peter since he arrived? Has he been here?'

It had occurred to Cass from the moment she arrived that Peter Bannon could be on the property somewhere. It was certainly big enough to hide a person. She wondered if Sarah was looking to the stables for that reason. But if Peter had fled here seeking a hideout, she couldn't imagine him staying after what had happened to his father. It would have surely been too much of a risk – for him and for Sarah and her family. She wouldn't jeopardise the safety of her three children. And having seen what happened to his father, he wouldn't risk hanging around.

'Yes,' Sarah said, almost in a whisper. 'He arrived a couple of weeks ago. Put on a brave face: said he was tired of America and wanted to come home. Framed it as his decision. But I could tell he was unsettled, scared about something.'

'Did you ask him what?'

'My brother had no one to protect him growing up. I wasn't physically strong enough to stand up to my father and shield Peter. He internalised a lot of his problems. We were close enough that he would eventually tell me, but it could take days, weeks, months, depending on the issue. Which is a long way of saying I don't know exactly what he was running from in America, but I knew he was running from something.'

'So it must have been obvious to you that these two men were looking for Peter, not your father.'

'That was my assumption.'

'It would have been helpful if you had explained this to my colleague.'

'The first time you contacted me – your colleagues, I mean – was to identify the body. I couldn't think straight at that point apart from answering a few basic questions. Then, when Detective Ryan called–'

Ryan wasn't a detective either but Cass let this one pass.

'–I was led to believe you already had a line of inquiry. I assumed it was a burglary gone wrong – there'd been all these break-ins in the county over the last while. And that's what the media was saying too.'

'Yes, and we haven't ruled anything in or out yet. But you can understand why the two Americans would also be persons of interest. And why the information about your brother may have been important.'

'I knew my brother was fleeing something but I thought it was a personal problem. In a million years, I didn't think he'd be chased across the ocean by two thugs and that they'd kill my father.'

Cass couldn't fault the logic and didn't think Sarah was lying. Not about those immediate assumptions at least. But there was still a chance she was holding back about her brother. Cass looked over Sarah's shoulder towards the stables and said softly, 'Where is your brother now, Sarah?'

There was no hesitation this time.

'I don't know. He did come here; he stayed a few days; he took off again.'

'Before or after your father was killed?'

'Before. Why does the timing matter?'

'It's important we have a full picture of everyone's movements.'

'You haven't asked mine.'

'My colleague did.'

'Yes, but you're checking his homework, aren't you?'

Cass felt her face flush, and she silently cursed Noel Ryan and then cursed Finnegan even more for putting them both in this situation.

'It's not like that. Follow-up queries always arise. That's just the nature of a case. I'm asking about your brother's movements to understand the full picture. To be clear, I'm not suggesting he's a person of interest or anything like that.'

'Well, you'd be missing a trick if you were. Because you'd have a better "person of interest" standing right in front of you.'

From reflex, Cass's hand moved to her baton. She kept it there, wondering for a moment if she had fundamentally misread the woman in front of her.

'You'll have to explain that to me, Sarah,' she said. 'Just to ensure I understand fully.'

'I can't call you Cass. Seems way too informal... But I am being totally open with you. I hated his guts. Would happily have killed him years ago if I had the courage. I didn't, of course. But I'm glad he's dead. Now, do you want to ask about my movements?'

'You did the school runs during the afternoon, went shopping with the kids, came home, didn't leave the house again, and your husband can verify as much, correct?'

'Yes.'

Cass relaxed a touch and moved her hand back to a resting position on the table. 'To be clear, Sarah, you're not a person of interest either. Hating someone isn't a crime.'

'Isn't it? I've never hated anyone in this world except my father, and how is that right? And then the thought of Peter – he's just a child no one ever came to rescue. I hate the thought that these men are out there somewhere hunting him.'

'We don't yet know what role, if any, they played,' Cass said. 'If we knew where your brother was, we could ensure his safety. You understand?'

'I don't know where he is.'

'Do you have contact details for him? A mobile number? You said you were in touch through WhatsApp?'

'Through his American mobile, which he left in the States. He doesn't have an Irish one anymore.'

So he's off the grid, thought Cass, *or at least I'm supposed to believe that.*

'Well, if Peter does contact you, or does show up again, we need to speak with him. I trust you can see why that's the case.'

'Of course. For his own safety too.'

'I'll give you my personal mobile. You can ring me at any time, day or night.'

Not really appropriate when Ryan is the liaison officer, but I couldn't care less.

'Thank you.'

'By the way,' Cass said, 'will you also handle your father's affairs – probate and things like that?'

'I presume so. I haven't followed up on that aspect yet. Why?'

'Your father had a lot of money concealed on the property. Euros and old Irish notes. All told, a sum worth more than 100,000 euro.'

It was at that point the youngest child burst through the door laughing, a cocker spaniel chasing at his heels, imploring his mother for chocolate for himself and a biscuit for the dog. It completely disrupted Cass's focus, and, helplessly, she tumbled back into the past, thinking of the boy left motherless by her ex-husband's drunk driving. She wondered if that child would ever be able to run in such a happy, carefree manner.

Sarah ignored her son's specific entreaties and instead put a mound of strawberry jam on one scone and butter on another, in the apparent knowledge that the cocker spaniel would get half, and ushered child and dog out the door again. The sound of the door closing pulled Cass from her trance.

'My husband and I have debts like most people,' Sarah said. 'Inheriting my father's farm would solve a few problems. One hundred thousand euro would solve them even quicker. But as far as I'm concerned, his land can rot and his money can burn. I don't want any of it.'

———

Cass left the farmhouse, trying to hold it together, and drove off as quickly as she could. She had barely made it down the lane and through the gate when she burst into tears. Some triggers were predictable in their timing and nature; others less so. The boy involved in Hugh's crash had survived because his mother had shielded him, taking the brunt of the impact and suffering a fatal brain bleed in the process.

After Hugh's conviction, Cass had sold their house as quickly as possible, and after clearing the small mortgage, requested via her solicitor that the outstanding balance be placed on trust for the child. Cass's solicitor had questioned the wisdom of approaching the family so soon; had delicately suggested that Cass allow an appropriate interval to pass. She hadn't listened, was incapable of hearing anything at that point but the imagined screams of the accident.

Some weeks later, a one-line response came from the boy's father, declining the money. 'You enabled him and you can't buy your absolution.'

In death, Bridge Bannon wouldn't be buying his daughter's absolution either.

His land can rot and his money can burn.

Her chest heaving, her heart breaking, Cass allowed herself to sob for a couple of minutes, knowing from past experience it was better to let it out in private than risk breaking down in public.

His land can rot and his money can burn.

Burn.

Burn.

What's the significance of burning?

In her mind, a red light was flashing. And suddenly, she understood why, seeing a crack of light in the investigation – not in the Bridge Bannon case, but in Nabila Fathi's.

CHAPTER FIFTEEN

Sweeping views, the estate agent had promised. Brady quickly realised that promise came with a proviso: the need to first cut down the old woodland at the back of the church. The woodland grove covered about the width of a football pitch and a quarter of the length.

When Brady moved in, he had chopped a handful of the trees for use in the renovation, and a couple more for firewood. But most of the woodland he'd left intact – because it offered a perfect screen. He could scramble through it with ease and find a position to scan the valley while remaining totally obscured from view. So he got his sweeping views in precisely the way he liked them.

It had been from there, the day Bridge Bannon's body was discovered, that he had seen the patrol cars coming. That spot had been something of a fluke, given Brady had been randomly scanning his surrounds that morning in pauses between interval training, as he was prone to do.

This morning's spot was no such fluke, however. Since returning from the precinct, he had scanned the surrounds every hour, watching the continuing activity on Bannon's farm, watching the cops fan out to other houses across the Loop, presumably completing their door-to-door inquiries.

So it was that he saw Cass drive onto Sarah Delahunty's farm. And as he watched her leave again a little while later, he realised the police and military taught very different skillsets.

Had Brady been leaving the farm, his training would have automatically made him look up to scan the mountain ridges for threats. He would have spotted the slim bellcote, creeping above the grove that hid the rest of the church from view. And he would have wondered whether somebody was watching, even if there was no earthly reason why anybody would be doing so. Old habits and all that...

But as he looked at Cass, he figured the police were trained to be observant, not to perform reconnaissance.

Because Cass didn't look up to scan the mountain ridges as she left. She was wiping her face, as if she'd been crying. Brady couldn't say why – perhaps Sarah Delahunty was particularly grief-stricken and Cass had internalised some of her sorrow; or perhaps Delahunty had criticised the pace of the investigation.

Even if Cass had looked up, she would never have spotted Brady. He was too well versed in his craft to be picked out by a civilian.

But what had he just witnessed? His gut was roaring at him to flee, seeing the police inching closer to his turf, like a wildfire spreading.

But it was too late for that now, he figured. While he felt certain the two Americans had killed Bridge Bannon, he couldn't be absolutely sure of it, because he hadn't witnessed it. If it were established that the Americans were not the killers, the police would have to start over. And who would make a good suspect? Someone living locally, who might know Bannon kept cash on the property, who was capable of inflicting violence, who had, in fact, been trained to kill... To some extent, Brady was surprised the police hadn't grilled him more extensively. Volunteering his information had been the right approach; it was blinding them to his own homicidal criminality.

After so long alone, so focused on the hunt, so ruthless in his objective, sitting across from Cass in the interview room had been loaded with risk and yet... oddly agreeable. He wished he'd been interviewed by somebody else, because this particular cop...

Back home, unmoored after his discharge and divorce, he'd crashed into every one-night stand available. That all changed once Ireland came into focus. In Glencale, he'd been a virtual monk – on a tour of duty once more. He'd figured there would be time afterwards for women, when he was safe from any chance of pursuit, when he could resume the type of life he had once lived. Finding female company in Glencale had never been on his agenda.

But now...

A fucking cop, of all things.

He told himself it would be a wise way of keeping abreast of the investigation. Just in case anything went wrong. But he knew that wasn't the real reason – she had left an impression on him when he'd least expected it. And she hadn't even been trying.

Despite what he was capable of, despite what he had done already, he couldn't see circumstances in which he would pose a threat to her.

But he could see plenty in which she would pose a threat to him.

Different skillsets.

Hers to hunt killers.

His to be one.

But he was prepared.

And if she became a real risk to him, he knew what he would have to do.

CHAPTER SIXTEEN

The image of money burning had sparked in Cass's mind a potential new line of inquiry. There had been two 100-euro notes found in Nabila Fathi's rucksack, both identically damaged. Because the rucksack had been found in a stagnant pool of water, the original investigators had assumed the damage was caused by immersion. But theirs had been a competent investigation, and so they hadn't relied on assumptions.

The notes had been dispatched, together with other items of evidence, to the Forensic Science Laboratory for analysis. Had they been counterfeit notes, it might have offered a lead. The bigger prize, however, would have been DNA evidence. The results, though, had been disappointing: the notes were genuine; and the contents of the rucksack, including the notes, had been too long in the water to yield much in the way of DNA traces. They would offer nothing to assist in building the profile of the killer.

But Cass wasn't interested in fingerprints, hairs or fibres. The damage to the notes – and its precise cause – was what she wanted to re-examine. She had read the case file minutely on Christmas morning, and could recall the salient facts. She was certain, as she replayed them in her head, that she had overlooked the significance of one of those facts. And that the original investigators, despite being thorough, had missed it too.

Sitting at her desk, she pulled out the photographs of the notes and studied them again. She'd done her standard course on counterfeit notes some years back, and knew that euro notes were made from cotton fibre for extra durability, capable of withstanding extremes of temperature and pressure.

Unsurprisingly, therefore, the two notes found in Nabila's rucksack had retained their predominantly green colour, despite the prolonged immersion, but were pockmarked by spots of black, resembling mould. The black spots obscured whatever image was carried on the front of the notes – Cass seemed to recall it was some kind of baroque arch – but other design features remained visible, including the lettering and the signature of the official issuer of the currency. The hologram security patch was still present on both. The black spots were not the only damage: small pieces were missing from the sides of the notes, as if an animal had chewed around the edges – or an attempt had been made to burn them. Cass imagined somebody waving a lighter beneath the notes, for reasons unknown.

She turned to the forensic report to reread what it said about the actual cause of the damage: prolonged exposure to water and traces of a detergent or similar cleaning agent, undetermined. So no fire, but why the cleaning agent? The presence of diatoms – a form of microscopic algae – on the notes had enabled the experts to approximate the length of time the rucksack had been submerged, and closely matched the estimated range for time of death. In other words, after murdering her, the killer had dumped the rucksack before fleeing the scene.

But from what Cass could see in the case file, nobody had asked further questions about the cleaning agent. Which, in one sense, was understandable. The forensics report had merely pointed to its presence as a scientific fact; it hadn't offered a hypothesis. And right now, there was probably someone somewhere in the country stuffing a pair of jeans into a washing machine and forgetting they had left notes in their pocket. Compared with some of the substances found on banknotes when tested – cocaine being a frequent one – detergent seemed pretty innocuous.

But if the explanation wasn't innocuous, then Cass could sense there was something wrong with the sequence. The logical reason for mould-ridden notes to bear the presence of detergent would be because somebody tried to clean the notes *after* they were retrieved from the water. But these notes had borne the presence of the detergent *when* they entered the water. So Nabila – or somebody else – had attempted to clean the notes before her murder. Which meant the notes may already have been damaged in some way, and the immersion in the woodland pool simply degraded them further.

So what? Cass thought. *What does it matter if the notes were damaged elsewhere? And how would I possibly trace them anyway? Wild goose chase probably. But follow the lead to the end. It's worth a few calls… If only because it will allow me to annoy Harbour Murphy again.*

———

When reading the case file the first time, Cass had suspected the politician of being the source of the euro notes, it not being unheard of for an employer – even a national legislator – to pay in cash to evade tax. She was now beginning to doubt that supposition, but there was a simple way of finding out.

She already had her task list for the day on the Bridge Bannon inquiry – but that case was a number one priority, there was a whole team working on it, and they had a solid pair of suspects. Nobody was treating Nabila Fathi's case as a priority any longer; there was nobody working on it aside from Cass, and she wasn't remotely close to identifying a suspect. The team could do without her for an hour and she would make it up by working late.

She had two calls in mind and she started with Harbour Murphy. Famously responsive to calls from his constituents, he answered his mobile on the third ring, and sighed audibly when she identified herself.

Made a friend for life here.

'I'm about to speak on an agriculture debate,' he said. 'You'll have to be quick.'

'I will be,' Cass replied. 'I just wanted to check how you pay your staff.'

'You what now?'

'Nabila Fathi had some cash on her when she died. Large denominations. I'm trying to determine where she got it.'

'From an ATM maybe? How the fuck would I know?'

'Did you pay her in cash? Or any of her colleagues?'

'And if I did, would you report me, huh? Go running to the Revenue? How in the name of Christ would that help Nabila?'

'This is not about the Revenue, Mr Murphy, I assure you. I'm simply trying to trace the origin of the money found in Nabila's rucksack.'

'You know Alan Ormond in CBC Bank?'

'Yes, but I need you to–'

'I pay my staff by electronic transfer. Tenth of every month. Tax, pension payment, social insurance payment, the fucking lot. Go see Alan, tell him you were talking to me; tell him to show you any record of mine that you want to see. Anything.'

He hung up. Which didn't faze Cass in the slightest, because she realised something now: Harbour Murphy had a temper when provoked – a fact which might be of some relevance in the investigation.

As for Alan Ormond, she would accept the invite to pay him a visit – because if anyone knew about damaged cash in circulation, a banker surely would.

———

Rural towns across the country were being stripped of bank branches at a rapid pace with increasing amounts of transactions being done online. Glencale's prominence as a tourist attraction had spared it that fate: the town continued to boast branches of three different national banks, of which CBC was the largest.

While Cass held no personal accounts there, she knew its manager of old: Ormond had been a couple of years ahead of her in school. She remembered him as studious and awkward; he made a good impression on teachers because of his hard work; and virtually none on his fellow students. He'd sooner stare at his shoes than look any of the girls in the eye. Cass would have put money on Ormond moving permanently to Dublin or London and building a more contented life for himself in the anonymity of a big city. She wouldn't have expected him to end up a bank manager in his home town, a position that required its holder to be something of a social animal, actively involved in the community and spearheading local initiatives.

But the Alan Ormond who genially greeted her and welcomed her into his office bore scant resemblance to the reticent teenager. From one glance she knew the sober navy suit was tailored to fit and the pale-blue silk tie had cost a pretty penny too. If the clothes were expensively bland, the smile was all flash: wide and dazzlingly white. But it was his eyes that really surprised her, probably because she had so rarely seen them: lit up from the seemingly genuine pleasure of seeing her.

'It's been far too long, Kate. You'll have some coffee with me?'

He had a machine in his office and gave a brief résumé while popping in pods and making espressos for them both. University in

Cork, joining CBC on its graduate programme, several promotions, appointed branch manager in Glencale three years previously. Married along the way, wife Harry ("for Harriet") a piano teacher and conductor of the town choir; children Danny and Lena excelling, variously, at football, gymnastics and, of course, music. It was gushing but not fake, Cass knew. He had blossomed and his life had blossomed, and she was happy for him. And, to her immense surprise, perhaps even a touch envious of his wife.

'And you? You're keeping well?'

Me? Everyone in this town probably knows about Hugh, she thought. *Let's not.*

'I'm fine, Alan, thank you. But I'm here in a professional capacity. I'm hoping you can help me with something.'

'Of course. It's appalling what happened to Mr Bannon. Absolutely appalling. But if it's an inquiry about accounts, he didn't hold any with us. One of your colleagues already–'

'This is about a different matter.'

'Oh. Well – anything you need.'

Despite Harbour Murphy's invitation, she had no intention of persuading Ormond to let her see the politician's personal banking details. It would be a serious breach of procedure and there was no good reason at this point to seek the information. Instead, she focused on the damaged currency found in Nabila Fathi's rucksack, handing Ormond photos of the two damaged notes.

'These notes are relevant to a separate case I'm looking at,' she said. 'I'm trying to ascertain if any notes like these have been in circulation locally. I thought you might recognise them if so. The damage is quite distinctive.'

'What's the case?' he asked.

'I can't give specifics, I'm afraid.'

'Understood. I was just wondering if it was a robbery or a counterfeit production or something – the kind of things we might be alerted to. Well, the damage is distinctive, as you say.

And more or less identical in both pictures. Burned in some way?'

'Combination of water and chemical damage actually. But I thought the same thing initially.'

'Presumably they're from a batch of notes damaged in the same way?'

'We think so. Do they ring any bells?'

'Afraid not. We get an alert from headquarters if there are stolen or suspicious notes in the system. Money laundering and counterfeit money are both still big business, although a lot of criminal gangs are increasingly focused on cybercrime now. But I can't recall any recent alert about damaged notes, and certainly none like these.'

'You've been here three years – would you remember every alert in that time?'

'I'd remember these, no question. Besides, these are older notes anyway.'

'Why do you say that?'

'The European Central Bank introduced a new series of notes in 2019, called the "Europa" series, across all member states using the euro. These are pre-2019 notes, known as the "First Series". Perfectly legal tender and still in widespread use – but older, like I said. So perhaps the damage was done further back in time than you're thinking?'

'That may be useful,' Cass replied, while struggling to see how it would help her. 'Would your headquarters have a record of all alerts going back over a number of years?'

'Possibly. But if I were you, I wouldn't waste time with us. I'd go straight to the Office of the Currency Comptroller. They handle the euro currency for Ireland, so most of the alerts originate with them. And they're the authority on what is legal tender and what isn't, how badly notes have to be damaged before they're taken out of circulation, and so on. The serial numbers aren't visible in these photographs but if you still have the original notes, perhaps the Currency Comptroller could do something with them – trace the notes and see if they belong to any particular batch that came to their attention.'

'Thank you, Alan. That really is useful.' This time, she could clearly see how the information would assist. She was, however, annoyed not to have already identified the Currency Comptroller as the natural line of inquiry.

Some detective I'd have made.

She thanked him for his time, and he showed her out, with entreaties to come to the family home for dinner on a suitable occasion.

I don't think so. You sound like you have a lovely family but I really don't need any reminders of what I've missed out on.

―――――

Some things in life were certain. Death. Taxes. And the fact that Finnegan would summon Cass to her office any time she had spoken to Harbour Murphy...

She'd had excellent bosses in her time, competent ones, and a couple of inept ones, all and any of whom could be challenging to deal with depending on the circumstance. But none had ever provoked her like Finnegan, and Cass told herself she would not tolerate another inquisition. She hadn't been reared to take shit from people, not even commanding officers...

But to Cass's surprise, it wasn't an inquisition which Finnegan had in mind. It was an assignment.

'Devine is doing a school visit on Thursday. To Saint Al's, the girls' secondary school. I need you to go with him.'

'Two of us stepping away from the investigation? We're still in the early stages.'

'It's an hour, ninety minutes max. It's been scheduled for a long time and I want to give the local community reassurance and one of the ways we can do that is by keeping up our engagement across all sectors, including the schools.'

I've just taken an hour out of my current investigation so it would be hypocritical to argue. But why me? 'Did Devine ask for me?'

'Noel Ryan was scheduled to do it with Devine but is no longer able to. I need you to cover.'

Ryan again. Presumably has an appointment with a barstool. In retrospect, an inquisition would have been less irritating. 'Maybe it's not my place,' Cass said, 'but Noel Ryan seems unable to do a lot of things.'

'Meaning?' There was a sharp edge to Finnegan's voice and Cass heard the warning loud and clear.

But she ploughed on regardless. 'I was married to an alcoholic, as you well know. So I know one when I see one. Noel Ryan shouldn't be on the job.'

'You're completely right,' Finnegan said. 'It's not your place. You can go back to work now.'

'He spoke to Sarah Delahunty and didn't even manage to figure out her brother was back in Ireland.'

'Actually, he did figure that out and was following up accordingly – Devine just got there faster.'

'Well, thank God speed isn't important in a murder investigation.'

'You sound like the fucking reporters now, expecting case closed in twenty-four hours.'

'I'm not criticising the pace of the investigation; I'm criticising Ryan. You know how many murders are committed by family members. That was critical information.'

'Are you telling me you have reason to believe Peter Bannon is a suspect?'

'No, I'm not saying that but–'

'As far as I can see, all relevant leads are being followed and the forensics will tell us more. Kearney's a first-rate SIO. Leave him to do his job.'

'Once again, this isn't about Kearney, or the investigation – it's about Ryan.'

'And I told you already it's not your place. Do I need to say it again? Maybe with a loudspeaker this time?'

'I know the damage alcoholics can cause,' Cass persisted, 'and you're running a huge risk – to the team, to yourself, to the community – by tolerating him.'

'You know fuck-all. And if you ever come in here again and question my judgement, you'll have your own career to worry about, not Noel Ryan's. You understand?'

'I understand bullshit when I see it, and this is bullshit.'

Finnegan stood, face flushed with anger, and for a moment, Cass thought she might jump across the desk and swing for her. Instead, Finnegan clenched her fists and drove them into the desktop, hard enough to make the files, cup and laptop jump in the air.

'Get – the fuck – out of my office and back to work.'

'With pleasure.'

Cass turned and left, banging Finnegan's door as she went. Not her most professional moment, not one she was proud of, but she had her own rage to release.

Had she not been so blinded by that rage, Cass might have registered Finnegan's double-use of the word 'need' in the context of her presence at the school visit. Might have launched her own inquisition of Finnegan to understand precisely what it meant.

And might have avoided a very unpleasant surprise some time later.

CHAPTER SEVENTEEN

B ut as the afternoon progressed, Cass could barely think of 'later'. She could only wonder whether she had any career left after the intemperate showdown with Finnegan. She didn't have to ask herself if she still *wanted* one. It was good to be part of an investigation team again, and she wanted to play whatever part she could in locating Bridge Bannon's killer. More than that, she could see Nabila Fathi's face in her mind, and yearned to make some advance in the case, rather than hand it back to the glacial wilderness of the unsolved pile. Nabila deserved better.

This determination to do right by the victims she found assuring, because a few months back, a few weeks back, she hadn't been at all sure about returning to the force. Now she was at least clear in her own mind that she still wanted to do the job, and for that certainty, she was grateful: the row had served the most unexpected of purposes. Finnegan she would just have to handle – and offer an apology if she didn't choke trying to get the words out.

Her phone call to the Currency Comptroller didn't immediately go as planned. After being routed to the relevant section of the organisation, Cass was informed by a middle manager that he would first have to verify internally that any relevant information could be released. He would also have to verify that he was, indeed, speaking to a member of An Garda Síochána.

A bit officious, Cass thought, but of all places, she supposed, the Currency Comptroller couldn't take chances on being duped or scammed. Rather than her mobile, she provided the station's general number so that the Comptroller could satisfy itself it was dealing with a bona fide guard. She stressed the urgency of her inquiry and requested a return call within twenty-four hours. From past experience in dealing with fellow public agencies, however, and knowing the rigid layers of bureaucracy within them, she knew it might take a week or more.

Which meant she was pleasantly surprised when the front desk routed a call through to her thirty minutes later, and a person identifying himself as Oliver Ashcombe, director of currency, asked her how he might be of assistance.

She described the two notes, the water damage, the eroded edges that looked like burns, and the forensic test results that had shown traces of a cleaning agent. While the serial numbers were not visible in the photographs, they had helpfully been recorded in the file, and Cass relayed these too.

'Can you email the photographs to me?' Ashcombe asked. 'I can look at them while we speak.'

She did so, and about forty seconds later, she heard a ping as he received the email.

'You'll have to bear with me,' he said apologetically. 'The email has come through but our automated systems have removed the photo attachments as suspicious. I'll have to ask our IT department to release them. I'll ring you back as soon as I have them on screen.'

'Can I send them through to your phone instead?'

'I use an office phone – same security system – so no point. Bear with me,' he repeated. 'It might be tomorrow at this stage, but I promise I'll ring you just as soon as I can.'

They laid the first transatlantic cable with fewer problems than this, she thought. *Twenty-first century technology ain't all it's cracked up to be.*

———

She'd done what she could for now on tracing the notes, and, satisfied that the Currency Comptroller would revert, Cass turned back to the Bannon case. She had another call in mind, and searched her phone to see if she still had the mobile number she needed. Once she found it, she did a quick Google search to see if her contact still worked for the FBI. It had been a long time, and no doubt protocol would prevent anything useful emerging from the call, but it was worth a try.

Eight years had passed since Cass had spent a week at Quantico on a ballistics training programme. Eight years since she and Nicole Wilson had exchanged numbers and promised to keep in touch. Six years since Nicole had come to Dublin for a fortnight, staying with Cass and Hugh, and enjoying herself so much she spoke half-seriously about joining the Guards. Two years since she and Cass had last spoken, the latter losing all contact with friends as Hugh went into steep decline.

Wilson answered after what seemed like an age. 'Well now, if this isn't a blast from the past to brighten my day. How the hell are you?'

'It's been way too long, Nicole – my fault entirely.'

'Takes two to tango, sister. How that's charming husband of yours?'

They all remember Hugh, she thought, *male or female. Had the gift of the gab. And when Nicole came to Dublin six years previously, he was still... on the right side of things.* The descent hadn't begun, or at least, Cass hadn't fully noticed it yet. They'd had so much fun that fortnight, Hugh the ringmaster. His forte. Their fault line.

'Hugh's fine, thanks,' Cass lied, because it saved time. 'And you?'

'Really excellent,' she said, 'apart from the succession of assholes I seem to meet in my personal life. We can't all strike it lucky like you. Now, to what do I owe the pleasure?'

'I'd love to say it's a social call but you can probably guess it isn't.'

'You Irish need some help with a case?'

'Something like that. More of an informal request, really.'

'Shoot.'

'We have an active murder – homicide – investigation where I'm currently stationed, in a town called Glencale in the south-west. Two US citizens have been designated as persons of interest. We're going through all the proper procedures, and we're tracking them down this end, as we believe they're still in the country. But I thought maybe–'

'You could see if we had anything on them?'

'Exactly. It might speed things up.'

'Have they been evidentially linked to the crime scene?'

'We're awaiting the full suite of forensics but have enough to believe they were at the scene on the day of the murder.'

'Good enough for me. Give me their names and passport numbers and I'll see what I can do.'

Cass did so, and gave Nicole a brief outline of the facts of the case, including the possibility that the pair were chasing the victim's son across the Atlantic.

'Give me the son's details too – three for the price of two.'

'I appreciate it. I know it's totally out of the blue.'

'What made you think of me?'

'The first transatlantic cable,' Cass replied, and hearing silence from a puzzled counterpart on the other end of the phone, quickly added: 'It's a long story.'

'I'd be glad to hear it some time,' Nicole said with a laugh. 'Let me chase this info first and get back to you. You needed this yesterday, I suppose?'

'Something like that. You know yourself how speed is everything.'

'Long time since I worked a homicide. I'm in public corruption these days. Funny how many of our lawmakers secretly like to break the law.'

I should acquaint you with Harbour Murphy, she thought.

'Some things are universal.'

'Sadly true. I'll get working on these then. Anything else?'

Cass hesitated, because there *was* something else but she knew it was borderline inappropriate, even when using a back channel like this.

No point painting only half the door, Hugh used to say, usually when he was eager to finish whatever bottle was in front of him.

'Actually, one more name, if you don't mind,' Cass said, relaying the details and feeling a twinge of discomfort as she did so.

'Another suspect?'

No, but my curiosity is piqued. 'More to eliminate him from our inquiries,' she lied.

Afterwards, she reflected it wasn't quite true to think that the first transatlantic cable had been laid without issue. Wild seas, formidable depths and snapping cables meant it took five attempts – each of them a Herculean effort – before, in 1858, Valentia Island off the south-west Irish coast was connected to Trinity Bay in Newfoundland. Valentia was less than ninety kilometres from Glencale, and she remembered fondly her school tour to the island. She remembered, too, the first message transmitted: "Glory to God in the highest, and on earth, peace, good will to men."

The American pair hadn't crossed the ocean with good will in their hearts – of that much, Cass was sure. But why they had come in the first place remained unclear. Cass hoped her old friend could fill in some of the puzzle.

And Mason Brady?

If the positions had been reversed, and a counterpart asked Cass to seek background on a person who she subsequently learned was not a suspect, not even a person of interest, she would not have been impressed. Even if sometimes police work demanded it, Cass wasn't, in the main, a fan of trampling on civil liberties.

But if Nicole could rustle up some information about Brady, she would take it, because there was something opaque about him. That predatory look from the car, contrasted with the calm and cordial nature when giving his statement.

He was in control in the station, not me. But I startled him in the car.

So maybe it's time I surprise him again.

CHAPTER EIGHTEEN

At the following morning's conference, Cass deliberately stood closest to the door. Finnegan was seated, and scowling, and Cass hadn't yet summoned sufficient willingness to apologise. The next round – in whatever shape it took – would have to wait. The moment Kearney signalled the conference was at an end, Cass made her exit from the incident room and left the station with equal haste.

This one isn't exactly by the book, so best to act first and use the one apology to cover all sins...

It had been a long time since she'd seen Saint Fiachra's, and teenage memories returned as she drove out once more to the Loop, passed Milly Cooper's shop and took the turn-off that would lead her past Bridge Bannon's farm, up to Sarah Delahunty's house, and beyond it, the old church and graveyard.

Even though the dead didn't scare her, she shivered as she thought of the old tale of the priest hanging from the bell. She wondered if Mason Brady knew the history of the church, and if so, whether the dead held any fears for him. Presumably not, given he was calling the place home. Besides, he'd been trained to put people in graves, not worry about ghosts rising from them.

As she drove, she recalled the church's simple design: the double-height nave formed the core of the building, with a single-height chancel extending from it. Entrance was via a porch to one side of the nave. It had been built at a time when there was a small, mostly self-sufficient community in these parts. Even then, it was the highest building in the Loop, the founding priest believing it was appropriate that people should 'look up' to the church, look up to God.

When she'd last seen it, probably twenty years ago or more, the wooden beams were exposed and rotting and the walls were crumbling. She knew she could expect to see a very different building now but expected there would be something amateur or rough about the renovation. Brady was a soldier, not a craftsman. But from her first glimpse, she was pleasantly surprised. The drystone wall bounding the church had been rebuilt with some care – newly cut red sandstone merging with what was left of the original. What she remembered as an overgrown, rutted narrow drive into the church had been filled and shaped with gravel, which crunched pleasingly beneath the car's wheels. The small garden in front of the church had been cleared of overgrowth and trimmed for winter, with a handful of young trees planted.

As she parked next to his old Mondeo, she could see a bit of the graveyard to the rear of the church, and significant work was evident there too – the gate mended and painted, brambles cut back, and some of the old grave-markers straightened and cleaned. A grove of trees behind it gave windshield and privacy. While to her knowledge the site did not have heritage status, and no archaeological orders would therefore have been imposed, it was clear Brady had treated it with respect.

And that was before she studied the church itself. Again, the walls had been painstakingly restored, the roof repaired and retiled, the arched double-doors in the porch filled, sanded and re-stained. But what caught her eye was what was resting in the nearest window: a tasteful white vase showcasing a green fern.

The fern was wilting, admittedly, but either Brady had a woman in his life or had a surprisingly good eye.

And then, as one of the porch doors opened and he emerged in sweatpants, compression top and sliders, she got the odd sensation yet again that she was missing something. In the station, he'd looked trim and tanned for sure, but had been dressed in a shirt and jeans, giving no real hint to his physique. The compression top, by contrast, revealed toned and tattooed arms and it was immediately clear to her that Brady had maintained a rigorous exercise regime since leaving the military.

Perhaps it was stereotype to assume he'd throw himself into the hard labour of the renovation project but struggle where softer touches were required. Maybe he was one of those "warrior-monk" types the US media had been so fond of eulogising during the Iraq and Afghanistan conflicts. But Cass didn't buy it. There was something here that didn't quite fit. From habit, she sized up every man she encountered, a throwback to her years on the beat when violence could erupt from surprising sources. Most of the time, she fancied her chances, knowing her own training would give her the edge even when her opponent might have natural advantages of height or power. But instinct immediately told her she'd come off second best to Brady. There was something coiled in that calm demeanour.

'Officer, good to see you again. Welcome to my humble quarters.'

'I like what you've done with it,' Cass replied. 'Last time I was up here, it was for teenage drinking parties and ghost stories. Place was in ruins then.'

'It was still in ruins when I got it.'

'You did this all by yourself?'

'Hired local help for the wiring – you need registered guys here, right? And for some of the plumbing, the septic tank and stuff. Everything else, I just took my time with.'

'Where did you learn to do it so well?'

'Our more enlightened leaders always advised it was better to build a road than blow a bridge. Assist communities instead of assaulting them. So I picked up stuff over time.'

'The military renovated a lot of churches in your day?'

He laughed. 'Yeah, maybe I had to improvise. What can I do for you?'

What could *he do for her?*

Cass had travelled with the intention of surprising him, but now that she was here, found herself unsure, wondering what exactly she was hoping to achieve.

He tried but failed to stifle a yawn, and she wondered whether she had woken him, despite it being close to midday. She couldn't help but think of her ex-husband, because in the later years, while she was at work, Hugh had frequently slept well into the afternoon. She wondered if Brady was the boozing type. He didn't look it, though. Tired and drawn, yes, but not hungover.

'Late night?'

'Trouble sleeping once in a while.'

I can identify, she thought. *And if I lived alone here, I'd have trouble sleeping too.* 'Well, this won't take long. Just want to go back over a few details.'

'Please, come inside. I'll brew some coffee and give you the guided tour.'

Like an estate agent selling a property, she thought. It was then that an obvious question struck her: even before stepping across the threshold, it was clear this renovation had needed money. True, Brady had done much of the work himself, which would reduce labour costs, but even still, the materials would have cost a solid five-figure sum. That was on top of the purchase price for the property itself. Where had Brady sourced it?

She made a mental note to check how US military pay and pensions worked. Brady was still a young man, and so, at most she figured, would have clocked up about twenty years of service.

In the Guards, generally speaking, early retirement meant going at fifty, and while twenty years of pension benefits were not to be sniffed at, most people in that situation would still expect to take up some other line of work to supplement their income. It wasn't clear to Cass if Brady worked, and if so, what he did.

Maybe he's just independently wealthy. But how many independently wealthy kids sign up for the military? And if he had that kind of cash, how do you explain the old car? He'd have something much fancier. Maybe he got a lump sum at some point. Or took out a mortgage. Or just managed his money better than I ever could...

Which wasn't a fair reflection on herself. She'd managed her modest salary just fine, and Hugh had a modest trust fund, if that wasn't an oxymoron, as he had come from proper money. They'd had savings, investments and a miniscule mortgage. But his family had gradually tired of his alcoholic antics and the trust fund had tired of the cost of it. And once Hugh had given up on work – or, more accurately, his employers had given up on him – their resources began to dwindle.

She took steps to safeguard their house, ensuring he couldn't attempt to remortgage without her blessing. And when the end came, the house had been all that was left. She wasted no time in selling it. Tried to pass on the proceeds and failed. The money was just sitting in her account now, and Hugh was sitting in prison.

'You coming in?' Brady was still standing at the open door, a querying look on his face.

Cass returned to the present, nodded, and followed him inside.

———

The white vase had not been an aberration. She had expected the interior of the church to be somewhat dark and foreboding, but instead it could have been lifted from a magazine. Seeing the light-filled space she realised the gloomy and smashed stained glass she remembered had been replaced with clear windows. Additionally, a huge chunk of the rear-facing wall had been removed and replaced with sliding patio doors. A further neat trick – not visible from the roadside – was the large triangular skylight installed on the west-facing side of the roof to catch afternoon light. The interior walls were painted white, the old wooden floor had been replaced with subtle grey tiles, and the furniture was in pastel colours to offer contrast.

Again, there was something just a little off about it all – rather than reveal an individual identity, it looked like he'd simply replicated an IKEA showroom by buying its contents outright. But it was done well, nonetheless. The ground floor was now one large living space and kitchen, with the chancel partitioned off, presumably as a spare room or second bedroom. Cass guessed that the main bedroom and bathroom were upstairs on the balcony, which covered roughly a third of the floor area of the nave and where further partition walls subdivided the space.

'What do you think?'

'I think it'd make a much better place for a drinking party now.'

'It gets a pass?'

'It's very impressive,' Cass said, 'and suspiciously tidy.' *I feel like I should remove my shoes rather than soil your pristine floor.*

'No roommates, no children, no pets – makes it easier.'

And no partner either? she wondered. *There isn't a single picture on display – not of parents, not of a loved one, not even a team photo of former military colleagues. Not a memento or hint of personality. Just some generic prints that could have been bought from a catalogue to match the furniture.* Cass's own apartment was utterly devoid of personality too, but she hadn't spent months doing up her place. The church wasn't perfect – the conservationists would no doubt be aghast – but it was pretty polished all the same. This place was all him and yet none of him at the same time. How could that be?

'Bet there's a queue of family and friends wanting to visit when they see what you've done with the place.'

'Not so much. Like I said, I came to Ireland for some space. Figure out the next stage of my life. So it's been pretty much me and the priest.'

She stared at him in mild disbelief.

'Bad joke,' he said quickly. 'The realtor told me the story before we signed the papers. Didn't want me finding out subsequently and complaining. Straight-up lady.'

Estate agent, thought Cass. *No one says realtor around here.* 'It would have deterred a lot of people from buying this place.'

'I'm of little interest to the living, let alone the dead.' He cranked up an expensive-looking barista-style coffee machine and got cups, milk and sugar ready.

Any second now he'll pull some freshly baked sourdough out of the oven and confuse me even more. I can't get a straight read on this guy at all. Home improvements or all-action hero?

Thankfully, though, he didn't – just served Cass her coffee and beckoned for her to take a seat on the first of three stools at the kitchen counter. He took the third, leaving a stool between them as a safe space.

'So is this formal?' he asked. 'Not that it makes a difference – just not sure how these things work with you guys.'

'Routine. Like I said, just wanted to go back over your statement; make sure we missed nothing that might be important later.'

'Are my two fellow countrymen officially suspects now?'

'They're persons of interest, meaning we would like to speak with them.'

'But you haven't found them yet?'

'We're working on it.'

'Airports, ports, that kind of thing?'

'As I said–'

'Got you. There's only so much you can tell me.'

'That I could tell anyone,' she corrected, 'regardless of the assistance they may have provided.'

'Understood. Please, go right ahead.'

She did so, going back over the statement and silently searching for any inconsistencies. There was none. So she decided to widen the search a little.

'Well, that's it for the official questions. Tell me,' she said, as casually as she could muster, 'you mentioned figuring out what's next for you. What do you think that is?'

'Too late to make the NFL,' he said, 'though I'm not sure any man ever gives up on the dream–'

Hugh gave up on his dreams. Drowned them at the bottom of a bottle.

'–I'm looking into college options. Law, maybe. That sound crazy at my age?'

'Not really. They reckon most people will average five or six careers these days.'

'That you too?'

'I'm busy enough,' she replied. 'Haven't really given it much thought. You intend returning to the States to study then?'

'I was thinking of staying here. Maybe rent this place for a little while and go to one of your universities. I really like the look of Trinity College. That Long Room is quite something. Featured in a movie, didn't it?'

Film, she thought. *And I have no earthly idea.* 'Not much of a film buff,' she replied.

This was getting nowhere. Brady was open and hospitable on the surface, and she was incapable of probing beneath it. He clearly liked his privacy: his choice of property emphasised as much.

Loner meet loner, she thought. 'Well, best of luck with the life decisions, and thank you for the coffee. Congratulations on what you've done here. It's very nice.'

He returned the thanks and walked her out in polite silence.

Cass was at the door of the police car when she heard him call after her.

'Say... now that the official part is over, how would you feel about continuing the conversation unofficially sometime?'

Full of surprises, this guy. Admittedly, there was enough to like. Rugged, capable, clearly a bit creative; self-sufficient and self-contained; seemingly normal. So definitely not my type. Not half fucked up or needy enough. I attract the bloody misfits and miscreants, with the world's misanthropes thrown in for good measure.

'I'm afraid it wouldn't really be appropriate,' she said. 'In the middle of an investigation and everything – I'm sure you understand.'

He held his hands up in mock surrender and smiled again. 'There I go again: still thinking I can make the NFL.'

Corny or not, she couldn't help but smile as she got into the car.

———

A mile down the road, her mobile beeped a couple of times to indicate she had missed calls or messages. There were several parts of the Loop that were mobile black spots, and she realised she could add Brady's property to them.

She stopped the car and saw missed calls from the station and a text message from Devine. It was short and sweet. The two Americans had been stopped and detained at Shannon Airport.

Cass's first thought was that they had the break they needed.

Her second was that, if they wrapped up the case quickly, maybe continuing the conversation with Brady might be an option after all...

CHAPTER NINETEEN

Tiredness could get you killed – it had been drilled into Brady since his first week in basic training. That's why go-pills – the military slang for the amphetamine Dexedrine – were so readily available in his old life. They were effective in combatting fatigue and therefore an ally in battle. But once no longer in active service, he'd switched to no-go pills instead to knock him out at night: Ambien or anything stronger he could get his hands on.

But after a while, he realised that nothing would work, because sleeping per se wasn't his problem – it was what happened *when* he slept: the flashbacks, the nightmares, the dread of being surrounded. The scratching sensation on his face, as if steel wool were being dragged across it. Waking up drenched in sweat and, like a child, finding the darkness even worse. The cursed half-second of coming to and being convinced a malign presence was in the room. It was always the fleetest of impressions but shook him for minutes every time, heart hammering and pain shooting up his arms.

He knew his time in the military had left him with PTSD, and guessed that the shooting pains were psychosomatic. But he'd tried and abandoned counselling – not for him. Especially when there were targets to pursue. And so he focused on doing what he could to cope by himself. To avoid the night terrors, he'd come up with the simplest solution he could find: stay awake until dawn and then drift off. It worked, up to a point. And so when the patrol car crunched over the gravel, he'd been asleep, and caught completely off guard by Kate Cassidy. For a second time.

He'd desperately sought to fight back the exhaustion and stay focused during the interview, but it had been tough. Now, he replayed the discussion in his head, probing for any inadvertent slips he may have made. Tiredness could get you killed.

Had it been a mistake to invite her in? It would have seemed antisocial to leave her standing outside. Besides, what was there for her to see? He'd kept one souvenir, that was safely out of sight, and nobody would recognise the significance of it anyway. As for the unlicensed shotgun, that was safely hidden. A sterile site, to the uninitiated. There was nothing on view that would even hint at what he had done, at what he was.

She'd mentioned visitors, and he'd changed the subject, but not so quickly as to be obvious. He'd set this place up as cover, not as a holiday home, and already had too many visitors as it was – a few locals driving by, curious about the church renovation, and the occasional hiker. It had been a mistake to buy it, in retrospect. In the States, you could buy a derelict property in an isolated spot, fix it up, and nobody would care.

He'd failed to realise how truly small and intimate Ireland was in that respect. In the hardware stores in Glencale, they'd ask him how the project was going. A local journalist, not having a phone number or email address for Brady, had posted him her business card, requesting to do a feature about the renovation. He'd ignored it but had to accept the privacy he thought he was buying was heavily qualified. He didn't want anybody seeing the church from the valley and deciding on a whim to drive up. It was one of the reasons he'd kept the screen of trees.

Why had she asked about visitors anyway? Was she trying to form a picture of his habits and contacts? And if so, to what end? Did they doubt his story in some way? Was he, too, a person of interest? She'd hardly tell him if so. But the questions – the official ones at least – had seemed gently probing rather than hostile. She was tough to read and, Brady guessed, tough to shake. That he could admire.

And his answer about why he'd come to Ireland? Largely truthful, again because it was the safest course. He'd come to Glencale for three reasons: he had a target to hunt; he wanted to get his head right; and if he managed both those things, he wanted to figure out what was next. He'd touched on two of the three objectives in his answer, omitting his criminal activity. So that seemed okay.

But the quip about the ghost had been dumb. He had made her recoil and couldn't recover quickly enough. He didn't want to appear weird. But still, probably nothing fatal.

His questions to her about the farmer's murder may have been more of a risk, but he'd needed to try and establish the precise purpose of her visit – and what the cops now knew. He'd made sure to back off as soon as she put up the barriers.

Then her unofficial questions – and his bullshit about Trinity College. It was rehearsed bullshit, though. Dublin was about four hours' drive from Glencale, so an eight-hour return journey. Doable with ease in a single day, but a lot of people would opt for an overnight. So if he told a few people he was thinking of studying there, and he was suddenly absent from Glencale one day, they might think he'd gone to Dublin, exploring his study options. If nothing else, it might give him a head start should he have to flee.

Nothing in her demeanour suggested he'd have to consider such a drastic option anytime soon. But still, best to remain prepared.

So what craziness had momentarily overtaken him in trying to hook up with her?

Better to try and understand why she came up here to see me.

Better to stay close to the investigation.

Better to figure out what action might need to be taken.

Now he realised he was being partially truthful with himself, too.

Because for twenty seconds, he'd let his interest in her show, and in the process, potentially put everything at risk. A moment of weakness, stemming from tiredness.

I'm so fucking tired.

And tiredness could get you killed.

CHAPTER TWENTY

'*Six hours for starters,*' Cass murmured to herself. Then six further hours if authorised by a superintendent. A further twelve if authorised by a chief superintendent. And that was it. Under law, the Guards had twenty-fours in total to question the two Americans before either releasing them or bringing them before court.

When Cass first heard the news that the pair had been located and detained, she envisaged that her colleagues would need every minute of the twenty-four hours to crack them.

She was wrong.

In the event, they needed less than five hours – because in that time, it became abundantly clear the Americans were not Bridge Bannon's killers.

Plenty of investigations had a punch-in-the-gut moment, knocking the air temporarily out of the case team. The trick was to refocus swiftly rather than re-interrogating missteps. The after-action reviews could wait for when the case was solved.

Anyway, Cass didn't think the team had actually taken a misstep: they had simply followed their most promising lead, which they were duty-bound to do. It was just bad luck, rather than poor detective work, that the lead had run into the ground. In any event, Kearney, the SIO, had been careful not to dedicate all his resources to the Americans alone; he had split the investigation team to follow up other aspects of the case at the same time. So the hunt for the burglary gang had continued without interruption, albeit with a smaller number of officers working on that angle than if they had been the chief suspects. Now, given the Americans were out of the picture, the bulk of the team would fall in behind them, and they would seek to make up for valuable lost time.

The news was delivered at the morning murder conference, where the SIO relayed a summary of the previous night's interview. Kearney was meticulous, and so had travelled to Shannon Garda Station himself to ensure that procedure was followed to the letter in interviewing the pair. He had made clear from the first meeting of the investigation team that he wasn't interested in a successful detection, only in a successful conviction.

It wasn't an artificial distinction: in their annual reports, the Guards cited the number of cases they were satisfied they had detected. But detected meant only that the Guards were satisfied they had correctly identified the killer. It didn't necessarily mean the Director of Public Prosecutions would agree there was sufficient evidence against the suspect to launch a prosecution. And even if the director's office did agree, it didn't mean a court of law would convict the accused.

'Detection' figures were, to Cass's mind, tantamount to a fraud on the public; she firmly believed the Guards should report conviction rates and nothing else. She had been grateful, therefore, when Kearney had placed the emphasis on precisely that: getting a conviction. 'We achieve it by doing the right things, by sticking to the rules, by respecting suspects' rights, by ensuring no defence lawyer can pick a single hole in the procedures we've followed. No heavy squad and no heroes on this investigation. By the book and nothing else.' Which was why he had undertaken the two-hour drive to Shannon – to supervise and ensure there was no mishandling of the suspects, no stupid mistakes. And which was why he was able to give a direct account of the interview to the murder conference.

The Americans had been taciturn but not uncooperative. They didn't request a solicitor, which struck their questioners as odd; and they remained composed throughout the interview. They confirmed they were aware of the murder, having heard about it on the radio, but insisted they had no act, hand or part in it. For a significant chunk, the interview went sequentially, as the Guards sought to piece together the pair's movements on the day, hour by hour, and, where necessary, minute by minute. They admitted visiting Bridge Bannon's farm, but insisted he had been alive and well when they left.

Quizzed about the purpose of their visit, they said they were looking to speak with the farmer's son, who had been an acquaintance of theirs in Long Island. When asked why, they said it was a private matter, and no amount of questioning could prise further detail from them. They had expected to find Peter Bannon at the farmhouse; when they didn't, they took their leave. As to the reception they had received from Bridge Bannon, the two insisted it was cordial.

The interviewers said the farmer was not noted for his hospitality; the Americans amended 'cordial' to 'curt'. Pushed further, they acknowledged 'hostile' might be more accurate. But they insisted they had not returned the hostility. Challenged on their initial lie, they said they were simply observing the Irish tradition of not speaking ill of the dead...

And on it went, piece by piece, none of it amounting to an alibi, the interviewers satisfied enough that things were going in the right direction... until suddenly they veered catastrophically off course. Because when they came to the critical three- to six-hour window which the pathologist believed to be the approximate time of death, things fell apart. The Americans had travelled from Glencale to Cork City shortly after leaving the farm, a distance of about 100 kilometres. They had booked into a city-centre hotel, and had dinner in the restaurant. Time-stamped receipts, credit card payments, and CCTV footage from the hotel would all prove as much, they insisted.

While the interview continued, a call was made to the hotel in question where an obliging assistant manager pulled up the relevant details at speed. The pair had indeed booked in that night – two separate rooms. The bookings had been made upon arrival at the hotel rather than in advance, and each man had used his own credit card for the purpose. The credit card details matched. Furthermore, the assistant manager was able to access CCTV footage from the check-in desk at the time of the bookings. Asked to describe the two men seen in the footage, he gave matching descriptions of the pair sitting in the interview room.

While the Guards would, of course, acquire the hotel CCTV and all other relevant sources of information, on the face of it, the Americans seemed to have their alibis.

Possibly the pathologist was wrong about the time of death, which couldn't be ruled out. But it seemed a stretch, and nothing further arose in the interview to give any suggestion that the Americans had been the killers. They provided their mobile phone numbers, and suggested phone-mast triangulation would prove they were nowhere near the farm at time of death. They also volunteered DNA buccal swabs, after which they were released without charge. There was simply nothing to charge them with – not even false passports as originally suspected. Their travel documents were legitimate and, misdemeanours aside, the pair had no criminal records.

Not the kind of result any of the team had expected.

A complete bust.

———

It had been less than thirty-six hours since Cass had spoken with Nicole Wilson, but as soon as the murder conference was over, she rang her old acquaintance again. While Cass doubted the FBI agent had collated much in such a short window, she didn't want to waste any more of her time.

'You can call off the hunt,' she said.

'Your guys not on the watch list anymore?'

'They've been interviewed and released. Pretty solid alibis, unless we have the time of death wrong.'

'That's interesting,' Wilson said, 'because those guys have backgrounds you'll wanna know about.'

'We checked formally. Misdemeanours only.'

'Of course, cos Angelo Scalice isn't going to send two crooks with heavy records to do his business overseas.'

'Who's Angelo Scalice?'

'Mid-level mob boss; runs a bunch of legitimate businesses to launder the proceeds from the illegitimate stuff – drugs, prostitution, trafficking. If he sends someone abroad on a job, it'll be a couple of guys with clean records as you say – he's not stupid. But they'll be professional hoods all the same. And your two, I'm pretty sure, are professional hoods.'

'Which brings us back to the question they wouldn't answer in the interview: why were they chasing Peter Bannon across the ocean?'

'Can't say for sure, but a colleague in the New York office made a few calls for me. Says there's a story doing the rounds in Long Island about an Irish guy working on one of Scalice's construction sites who picked up a bag in an office that didn't belong to him.'

'Drugs?'

'Money. Not a huge amount by their standards – maybe ten, twenty thousand bucks. But not pocket change either.'

'And not the kind of thing they're prepared to let go.'

'Got it in one. I think those two flew to Ireland to tell your boy Bannon that Angelo Scalice wanted his money back.'

'Makes sense. But we still have nothing to pin them to the murder.'

'I guess maybe don't rule them out yet, is what I'm saying. A couple of guys like that, they'd know a few tricks to cover their tracks.'

'That's really good to know, Nicole. Thank you for this information. It will definitely help.'

'Anytime.'

'Listen, I hesitate to ask when you've done so much already but... anything on the other name I gave you?'

'Mason Brady?'

'Yes.'

'He's not accused of any crime, right?'

'That's correct.'

'And not a suspect or a person of interest in any investigation?'

'Also correct.'

'Then I'm a bit more reluctant on that one.'

Wilson lapsed into silence, awaiting proper justification. But Cass didn't have any – not really.

'It's just that he helped with the Bannon investigation and I'm not sure exactly why,' Cass said eventually. 'It's always good to know exactly who we're dealing with in any given case.'

'Well, you're dealing with an upstanding US citizen by the looks of it,' Wilson said. 'Stellar service record, no blemishes, nothing that would give rise to questions.'

'Understood. You think you could share that service record?'

'I'm afraid not, Kate. He hasn't done anything wrong. I can't see any basis – even informally – to share that type of information. You'll have to go through the proper channels for that one.'

'You're right – I totally get it.'

'I'll say this much though: Brady's the opposite of the guys you had in the interrogation room.'

'In what sense?'

'Let me put it this way: If I wanted the likes of Angelo Scalice and his hoods off the street in a hurry, I'd send a team of Mason Bradys.'

———

It now seemed premature to have let the Americans off the hook. From what Nicole Wilson had said about their backgrounds, they were unlikely to have travelled to Ireland seeking a friendly reunion with Peter Bannon.

And what of Mason Brady?

He had been in Glencale for a considerable period of time; his arrival had predated those of Peter Bannon and his two pursuers. But was there some connection she had failed to spot? Why exactly had Brady, with his background, come to Glencale? If it was isolation he was after, his home country, with its vast tracts of wilderness and potential to go truly off-grid, would surely have been better. So had he come to Ireland for a separate reason? Or was his presence merely coincidental? And what, if anything, had Nicole Wilson been hinting at when she drew the contrast between Brady and Scalice's hoods? Was it her way of hinting that there was actually some connection?

Cass couldn't settle any of those questions.

But she knew there was one way of finding at least some answers.

And that was by tracking down Peter Bannon.

CHAPTER TWENTY-ONE

When Cass arrived at work the next day, there was a brown envelope on her desk bearing her name. She recognised the handwriting at once, and her stomach lurched.

Disciplinary notice. Well, fuck her if she can't confront me with it face to face.

Cass was tempted to rip it up, but instead rose from her desk and went to the small kitchenette to make coffee, walking past Finnegan's office as she did so. Cass wanted Finnegan to see her stroll by, to realise the envelope hadn't ruffled her in the slightest. But Finnegan's office was empty, making the gesture of resistance a futile one. Cass continued on nonetheless, and while making her drink, tried to focus on matters at hand.

After first liaising with Kearney to determine the extent to which the team had already dug into Peter Bannon's background and movements, she'd spent much of the previous afternoon on the phone, trying to add what she could to a pretty empty page.

She'd started by ringing Sarah Delahunty, to see if Bannon had been in fresh contact with her. Delahunty said not. Cass took the last Irish mobile number Delahunty had for her brother, and contacted his service provider, seeking to ping the location of the phone. It yielded no result, and as a result, Cass had made a list overnight of the next steps she would take to try and locate Bannon.

She had arrived early with the intention of methodically working through the list before afternoon babysitting duty – undertaking the scheduled school visit with Devine. But try as she might, she could not push thoughts of Finnegan's envelope away. Sighing in frustration, she abandoned the coffee, returned to her desk and slit the envelope open, steeling herself for the contents.

Finnegan had written a total of two sentences.

The first asking for Cass to come see her after the school visit.

The second containing a mobile phone number for Maisah Sahraoui.

Was it some kind of peace offering? She and Finnegan had barely spoken since their blow-up, during which Cass had intimated that Maisah was deliberately transferred from Glencale to a direct provision centre hundreds of kilometres away so as to avoid her asking awkward questions about the lack of progress in Nabila's case. Cass had been unable to reach Maisah at her new location in County Donegal, and the centre manager had been fairly certain she did not own a mobile phone. Now Finnegan had done some of the legwork for her, and procured a mobile number.

Peace offering or managing the process?

Is it possible Finnegan has already spoken to Maisah? Warned her from saying anything to me?

Stop being so paranoid. Take this at face value. It's Finnegan's way of acknowledging what happened to Maisah was wrong, and telling me to keep doing what she originally asked me to do – find Nabila Fathi's killer.

It was a little after 7am – too early to call Maisah, Cass thought. Instead, she switched back to her original plan for the morning – the list of steps to try and find Peter Bannon.

But someone else had started work early that morning and Cass's landline buzzed shortly after 8am. Oliver Ashcombe of the Currency Comptroller's office had eventually managed to access the pictures Cass had sent through – and had an update.

'Your two notes have been on quite the journey. How familiar are you with Benghazi?'

'Not very. Wasn't that where a US consulate was attacked?'

'Well remembered, but the events we're interested in happened a few years later. Around 2017, to be precise. Libya was in the midst of civil war. But even in civil wars, central banks need to keep running. The Libyan central bank has a branch in Benghazi. And in 2017, that branch held a substantial stockpile of 100- and 200-euro notes.'

'How substantial?'

'About 160 million euro, give or take,' Ashcombe replied. 'Needless to say, with the country in turmoil and warlords fighting for territory, that kind of money could fund a lot of empire-building. Men, materiel and so on.'

'Are you telling me some faction robbed some of the money?'

'Not some of it – all of it. Together with 630 million dinar – worth about 120 million euro – and another two million US dollars. They also lifted close to 6,000 silver coins while they were at it.'

'How on earth does that happen? How can you lift that volume of money from a protected building?'

'By taking it over. This wasn't a one-off raid by a small team. Everything valuable in Libya at that point was up for grabs. Oil was the primary target, cash sources not far behind. Different factions fought to control what they could. Benghazi was a hotspot during the civil war, and the branch was a target throughout that time. Eventually, one of the factions seized it and barrelled the money out the front door.'

As Ashcombe spoke, Cass stared intently at the images on her screen of the notes from Nabila's rucksack. 'You're telling me these two notes can be traced back to that stockpile? Presumably through their serial numbers?'

'Serial numbers and sewage,' he stated simply.

'Sewage?'

'Serial numbers are obviously what we use to confirm the origin of any note. In this case, the stolen euro notes belonged to select serial number ranges, so we can trace them back. But we didn't need to see the serial numbers to know these notes were likely to have originated in Benghazi. In addition to the security problems, the branch had an unexplained sewerage problem at some point before the money was taken. The vault was flooded and a significant portion of the money held within it was damaged.'

'And you knew from looking at the pictures I sent you that they had suffered the same kind of damage?'

'I guessed, and the serial numbers confirmed it,' Ashcombe said. 'You had pictures of two notes which looked identically damaged. That's because they were. The two notes were from the same batch.'

'And the cleaning agent?'

'The seizure of the Benghazi branch is still shrouded in mystery, with a lot of differing accounts and conjecture as to precisely what happened, and how it happened. There's a UN Security Council Report that will fill in some of the picture for you – I'll send on a link. But what seems fairly certain is the faction involved distributed the money amongst its top commanders. Two things happened after that. Efforts were made to clean the money, given the sewage damage it had suffered–'

'Hence the cleaning agent,' Cass said.

'Exactly. And secondly, the money – gradually – started showing up around Europe. Individuals walking into central banks across different member states and trying to exchange the damaged notes for new ones. Both in small and large quantities.'

'And the system noticed?'

'We always notice. The European Central Bank and its component national members – including us – share information on matters like these. We investigated the patterns, discovered the origins of these notes, and put out an alert.'

'Which means what exactly?' Cass asked, curious as to the practical effect of such alerts.

'We have strict procedures to counteract money laundering. If someone tries to exchange damaged notes for new ones, and we think those damaged notes were obtained through criminal activity, we are required to refuse the exchange and to retain the notes.'

'How is that legal when you're only working on suspicions?'

'We provide a receipt – effectively an IOU – which will be paid if and when our investigation establishes no link to criminality.'

'Where notes are badly damaged in this way – or any other way – is it only the Currency Comptroller which can exchange them?'

'Yes. It used to be the case that retail banks would accept the money, but only to serve as a kind of intermediary to facilitate the customer – the money would still be sent to us to effect the actual exchange. Given the rise of digital banking and the retail banks' pattern of reducing their high-street presence, most of them won't do that anymore – they'll simply tell an inquiring customer that he or she has to come to us.'

Could it be? Cass wondered. It sounded like the beginning of a breakthrough, and she was almost afraid to ask the next question in case the growing flame was quenched immediately. 'Oliver, did anyone come into your HQ and try to exchange these notes?'

'Yes, several people.'

'Does a person have to present identification when trying to exchange notes?' *Fingers crossed for the right answer.*

'If you want to exchange damaged notes, you have to fill out a form and hand it in with the notes in question. The form requires name, address, date of birth and so on. It also requests you to explain how the notes came to be damaged. Additionally, if the value of exchange is above 200 euro, we request supporting identification, such as a passport or driver's licence. If it's above 1,000 euro, we also request proof that the money is actually yours – supporting documents such as legal papers or bank statements.'

'What happens then?'

'We take the money in, examine it, and if we're satisfied it is genuine and there is no link to criminality or money laundering, we exchange it, paying new money directly into the person's nominated bank account. If, on the other hand, we believe there are grounds to refuse the exchange, we retain the damaged notes and alert the relevant authorities.'

'So you're telling me that if a person tried to exchange notes, you'd have their name, address, date of birth and bank account details on file – at a minimum?' *Please God let the answer be yes.*

'Depending on the length of time that has passed, yes. Under data privacy requirements, we don't retain personal information longer than is strictly necessary.'

'But you surely maintain a list of those who try to exchange suspect notes?'

'Yes, we do.'

'Oliver, was Nabila Fathi one of the names on your list?'

'Can you spell the surname for me?'

She did so, and then spelled out the first name for good measure.

'Let me check.'

This is it – I can sense it.

He paused for a moment to consult whatever records he had to hand.

Somehow Nabila was roped into – or got in the way of – some money-laundering activity and it got her killed.

'No, I'm afraid not,' Ashcombe said eventually. 'There's no mention of that name on my list.'

Should have known. Why would an investigation be easy when it can be hard instead?

She took a moment to reflect on everything Ashcombe had told her so far, and what it could mean.

Somehow the notes had come into Nabila's possession – perhaps before she arrived in Ireland seeking asylum, or possibly after. The notes were real tender, not counterfeit – had she known as much? That seemed like a relevant question in trying to determine what her actions may have been. If Nabila had understood the notes to be legitimate, she may have tried to use them locally, only to be rebuffed because of the extent of the damage. That would have left her with little real alternative but to try and exchange the notes via the Currency Comptroller's office. In which case she would surely have given her real name and address, because she was doing nothing wrong and had nothing to fear.

Then again, it was well documented that asylum-seekers – even when granted refugee status – were, as a general rule, incredibly nervous about interacting with state authorities, often with good reason. So she could have known the notes were legitimate and still felt the need to use a false name. If for any reason she thought they were counterfeit, she would definitely have done so. In a town as small as Glencale, it would have been too great a risk to try and pass off counterfeit large-denomination notes locally, leaving the Currency Comptroller as her only option – and giving her real name and address would have been insane in those circumstances.

All of the above assumed Nabila did actually try to exchange the notes, of course – Cass knew it was possible she had acquired them in the run-up to her death and never had the opportunity to do so, or had had them for some time and was afraid to use them. If that were the case, Cass would have to focus on the source of the notes, and that, she knew, would be a labyrinthine task, a dead-end for sure. They could have come from anywhere.

Who is the patron saint of miracles again? Peter? Jude? Anthony? Whoever it is, I'm praying to you now.

'Could you check if there is anyone on your list with an address in Glencale, or in County Kerry more widely?' Cass asked. 'Woman or man?'

Silence as he consulted the records again. Cass steeled herself for the gates to slam shut on this particular avenue of inquiry.

Good work by me up to a point, she thought, *but ultimately a dead-end.*

'Yes,' he said.

'Yes?'

'Yes, a woman with an address listed as Glencale tried to exchange some of these notes a little over a year ago.'

Nabila Fathi was killed December before last – a little over a year ago.

'What month?'

'December tenth.'

'What was the woman's name?'

'Ezme Khaled. Says here she had about 800 euro to exchange.'

'And the address?'

Oliver Ashcombe proceeded to list the address.

She gave a false name. But it was Nabila. No question. Ordinary people in very pressurised circumstances make mistakes that, in hindsight, appear incredible.

'Does the file say what happened?'

'By that time, we'd had a few cases of people trying to exchange this money. In those cases, we took in the notes on application, retained them, and refused to go through with the exchange until we investigated more fully. We would have followed that approach here except, from what it says on the file, Ms Khaled didn't hand in the notes. She partially completed the application form – name, address, breakdown of notes, and then stopped at the section where the applicant is required to fill out the source of the funds, i.e. the ownership. According to the file, she asked our clerk if she had to fill out every section, and when the clerk said yes, Ms Khaled informed him that she had changed her mind and decided to hold onto the money. The partially completed form was left on the counter, but she left our premises in possession of the notes.'

Something had spooked Nabila. The extent of questions on the form. Or the realisation that the Currency Comptroller wouldn't exchange the damaged notes for physical cash on the spot. Nabila fled, worried that she had been dragged into something that would affect her refugee status. Or that she would get into trouble with someone – someone she was afraid of.

'Oliver, I need one more thing for now, if that's okay. Would your office retain CCTV that long? Would you have footage of who came into and out of HQ on the day?'

'We might be able to go one better,' he said. 'We have a camera over the public counter, for obvious reasons. I'll have to check exactly how long we hold onto footage – but if we have it from back then, we'll have Ezme Khaled on camera.'

'This could be really vital information in an inquiry. Could I press you to–'

'I'll get you an answer today on the length of time we retain CCTV. And if we do have footage, I'll do everything in my power to get it to you within the next twenty-four to forty-eight hours.'

'Much appreciated. And I'd like to see all relevant footage – not just of the public counter, but of Ezme Khaled entering and exiting the building.'

'You'll get everything we have.'

She thanked him and ended the call.

Nabila Fathi was considered by all who knew her to be a kind and decent person, intrinsically shy. At the time she paid her visit to the Currency Comptroller office in Dublin, she had only just been granted asylum after waiting and worrying for four long, arduous years.

How on earth was she persuaded to get caught up in something like this? And did it get her killed?

For the first time since starting back to work in Glencale, Cass was thankful to Finnegan. If anybody might know how and why Nabila had become embroiled in something so murky, her best friend might. And thanks to Finnegan, Cass now had Maisah Sahraoui's mobile number.

Of course, technically speaking, Cass had no confirmation that the woman who had identified herself as Ezme Khaled to the Currency Comptroller was indeed Nabila.

No witnesses. No CCTV footage – not yet, at least. But the address had convinced her.

Nabila Fathi may have given a false name on the day. But she must have realised that if she did hand over the money, the Currency Comptroller would need a verifiable address – somewhere to send the exchanged money to.

And so she'd given her real one…

The flat over Harbour Murphy's shop.

CHAPTER TWENTY-TWO

M aisah Sahraoui's mobile rang out each of the six times Cass attempted to contact her. Eventually, she sent a lengthy text message:

> I've been asked to look again at Nabila's case. I know how much you want to see her killer found. My questions are only about Nabila – not you. Please ring – your help could make a difference.

After hitting send, she wondered briefly whether Maisah had good English, and would be able to read the message. If this didn't work, she would ask one of her colleagues in Donegal to visit the direct provision centre where Maisah was now based and ask for her in person.

'Back to school this afternoon for us,' a voice said suddenly over her shoulder.

'Could do without it,' Cass replied.

'You should wear your old school skirt,' Liam Devine said. 'Bet you'd look great in it.'

'Fuck off, you perv. You'll have to do better than that to wind me up.'

'I'll collect you around two for our date then. We'll sneak a fag around the back of the school shed after.'

He walked away, chuckling to himself. She'd known Devine was fond of himself – he'd lick himself in the mirror, as her mother used to say of his type – but this was the first time he'd made any sexually laced comments. His lame wisecracks didn't bother her – what passed for 'banter' in some of her previous postings in Dublin had been many times worse. She hadn't put Devine down as the type, though, and she groaned inwardly at the thought that even in such a small station as Glencale, she'd have to put up with this shit. Even if Devine meant no harm by it.

———

The rest of the morning she worked through a series of phone calls and social media searches in the hunt for Peter Bannon, but to no avail. She couldn't help but wonder what Sarah Delahunty's phone logs over the last few months might show. But Sarah wasn't a person of interest and, under law, any request to a phone provider could be made only by a chief superintendent or higher rank. Requests couldn't be made on a whim, and Cass knew she'd need good reason before tabling one – reason she didn't have right now.

Nothing for it but to keep shooting in the dark, she thought.

Lunch was a sandwich at her desk and, despite the torrential rain outside, a longing to swim in the sea. At close to two, her phone emitted the familiar beep of a text message. Maisah Sahraoui had broken her silence.

> Ring again but u understand – am afraid. Will do this 4 Nabila.

Cass dialled the number, and Maisah answered on first ring.

'Nabila's murderer you mean,' a voice said, softly-spoken but firm.

'Yes, I'm looking to find the person responsible,' Cass said. 'As per my messages, my name is Officer Kate Cassidy – everyone calls me Cass and you should too. I've been asked to review Nabila's case. I am hoping you can help me.'

'You say "killer" in your message to me. Nabila was not killed in some accident. She was murdered. You see?'

That's told me, Cass thought.

If Maisah was afraid of personal consequences, she wasn't going to let that fear prevent her from standing up for her late friend.

My kind of person. 'Yes, Maisah, you are right. May I call you Maisah? Am I pronouncing your name correctly?' *Bring it back to basics,* thought Cass, *and start over.*

'Yes,' she said, 'and I am sorry for my bluntness. I want everyone to understand she was murdered.'

'But we've always known that, Maisah,' Cass said gently. 'It's why we launched an investigation in the first place.'

'Yes but your fellow officers do not seem interested. Every week I call to the station for updates – to see Sergeant Finnegan – for that I am punished and sent away.'

'Maisah, I wasn't working in Glencale during your time here. I can't speak to the past. I can only tell you that Sergeant Finnegan personally asked me to review the case as a priority. I'm doing that now and, based on some new information received, I have some questions you might be able to help me with. Will you do that?'

'Will it hurt my application – to talk to you?'

'This has nothing to do with your application for asylum, Maisah. For good or for bad, I cannot influence that one way or the other. This is only about Nabila. Nothing else.'

Cass could sense a lifetime of distrusting authority in the pause that followed.

'Okay. I answer your questions for Nabila.'

———

In the car on the way to the school, Devine chuntered on about his glory days as a schoolboy footballer. Cass, who had little time for nostalgia, and even less for the self-aggrandising sort, barely registered a word of it.

She was too engrossed in Nabila Fathi's case, obsessing about the banknotes, wondering how Nabila had come into possession of them. Maisah had answered every question willingly, but in truth had little in the way of valuable information to impart. She painted the same picture of Nabila that Cass already recognised: open-hearted, loyal, reticent. Everything else was mostly a sea of vagueness. One thing about which Maisah had been adamant, however: Nabila had not come to Ireland with any significant sums of money in her possession, damaged or otherwise.

'She has nothing coming here,' Maisah said. 'She gets this money a short time ago. I do not know how.'

Neither did Cass – and that was the problem. If Nabila had come into the money in Ireland, there was no indication in the file of the potential source, and Cass had dug out nothing by way of a lead. The only person who had given her cause for suspicion was Harbour Murphy – but why would an established politician, even a particularly greedy one, risk messing around with dodgy money? It would be an enormous leap to suggest he be questioned over the notes, Cass knew, because there was not one single iota of evidence linking him to them.

The fact that Nabila had given her real address, in the flat over his shop, may have served to increase her suspicions but, in practical terms, signified nothing. Cass's best hope remained that the Currency Comptroller's CCTV footage would throw up something, anything, that would give her the slightest of threads to pull.

She made a mental note to double-check the call logs for Nabila's phone. While the phone itself had never been discovered, the original investigation team had obtained her number from Nabila's friends and pulled the necessary records from her phone provider, before tracing all the calls she made. None of the calls – or the recipients of them – had given rise to suspicion in the original investigation. But Cass now had something the original team didn't: a specific day and date on which Nabila was doing something which – potentially at least – could have been a factor in her death. It would be worth double-checking the call log against that period, especially in the immediate window after she had seemingly panicked and fled the Currency Comptroller's office.

Devine parked and Cass suddenly realised just how long it was since she had been inside the doors of Saint Al's. The old prefabs provided to cater for extra growth in her day had been replaced by a gleaming modern wing to the main building, mixing old and new. She'd neither loved nor hated school; was just glad to leave and get on with her life.

School reunions and the like had never been her thing, and so her toes curled now at the prospect of returning and meeting some of her former teachers, as well as a couple of old school friends who were now on the staff. Granted, it was an important ambassadorial duty: a chance to stand in front of impressionable teenagers and encourage them to follow her lead and join the force. But Cass was not a sales merchant, and had never been. While the job could be rewarding, it could also be stultifying – and soul-destroying, if you let it get to you. So she would focus not on selling the job, but on speaking to the girls' self-interest: encouraging them to avoid the kind of stupid mistakes that could derail a life. That was her plan.

Liam Devine, she later realised with horror, had gone in with an entirely different kind of plan.

It was a fluke she caught it. After the teachers had brought them to the student hall and introduced the pair to their awaiting audience, Cass, as the former pupil, had made some opening remarks – receiving a bouquet of flowers in response, much to her embarrassment. She then handed over to Devine to do the rest of the talking, given he was the main act.

He was at ease with the girls, deploying his easy charm to good effect. It wasn't difficult to see that a few of the girls seemed enticed by him. None of which would have struck her as out of the ordinary – he was precisely the alluring sales merchant that Cass would never be – until the engagement ended and the girls began to file out of the hall. A few lingered to ask individual questions. Cass dealt with a handful and then went to speak with the teachers, leaving Devine to field the last of the queries.

After a couple of minutes, anxious to leave and return to work, she turned back and saw Devine wink and smile at a blonde student as he palmed a piece of paper into her hand.

His cheeks flushed when he realised Cass was looking at him, and then he smiled at her in precisely the same way as with the student.

My charm can overcome, she sensed him thinking.

Cass didn't particularly relish or hate confrontation, just recognised it as something to get through. *But not here. The teachers didn't see it and I won't raise it in front of them. In the car.*

———

'That went well,' Devine said. 'You enjoy being back?'

I should exercise caution here, just in case what I saw was something completely innocuous. But I know it wasn't...

'Good school,' she said. 'Presume your girls will go there.'

'Expect so.'

'What ages are they now?'

'Chloe's nine and Lily is seven.'

'You might be presenting to them at some point so.'

'I hope I'll have passed the baton on then. Promotion or two, or three – or a lottery win!'

And if somebody else came in and hit on one of your daughters when they were sixteen or seventeen, what would you say? What would you do?

She left a long silence and then asked the question.

'What was that piece of paper you gave to the girl at the end?'

'To Alex? Name of a book on forensics. She wants to study it at college.'

A book recommendation – really?

'What's the book – anything I should read?'

'You probably know it already. *Forensic Pathology* by Stafford. The guy who ran the Met lab in London for twenty years.'

He's good, she thought. *Between the school and the car, I gave him a small amount of time to recover his poise, and he not only did so, but came up with something plausible. If I asked Alex, I wonder what her answer would be? But he probably assumes I won't.*

'Why the big interest?' he asked.

'No reason.'

He carried on as if the questions had never arisen, giving no air of a man whose motives had just been challenged. For the rest of the short journey back to the station, he wittered on about music.

Again, Cass tuned out, and wondered whether to say anything to Finnegan. She had always been steadfastly loyal to her colleagues, and nobody in the force liked a rat, but this was different. She'd have to find a way to broach it with Finnegan, even if her superior officer would, if for nothing more than a slightly easier life, look the other way. After all, it wasn't as if Cass had evidence of an offence.

And then it struck her. Finnegan had explicitly requested that Cass come and see her when she arrived back at the station. Finnegan had also ensured it was Cass who went in the place of Noel Ryan. Finnegan had arranged the whole thing on purpose – which could only mean she had her suspicions too.

CHAPTER TWENTY-THREE

'You and I are going for a drink,' Finnegan said tersely when Cass arrived at her office door.

'I'm still on duty.'

'You can sip. Better that than shouting at each other in here.'

They walked in silence to Glencale House, the hotel where Cass had first met Finnegan. In the bar, Finnegan picked a quiet table in a corner, ignoring the 'please wait to be seated' sign, correctly assuming no one would chide her for impertinence. When a waiter came, she ordered a G&T. Cass stuck to coffee.

'Tell me how the school went,' Finnegan said once the waiter had left.

'Tell me how you expected it to go.'

'Christ,' she muttered. 'My teenagers are easier to deal with than you.'

There was a lengthy silence as both contemplated what to say.

Maybe we would be better off back in the office shouting at each other, Cass thought.

The drinks arrived and Finnegan took a long swig of hers before sighing. 'You and I need to start again.'

'I agree,' Cass said, given the lack of sensible alternative responses.

'We'll both have to settle down.'

Settle down? I'm not a fucking horse.

'Let me start,' Finnegan continued. 'And then, if you think I'm being straight with you, you tell me about the school. Agreed?'

'Yes.'

'Noel Ryan is a functional alcoholic, functional being the key word. He can get through a day's work without having a drink. At night, he gets hammered, and has the pride to do so alone, in his home, and not cause the force difficulties by doing so in pubs around town.'

'That's good of him.'

'Yes, it is,' Finnegan said, ignoring Cass's sarcasm. 'Before he was a functioning alcoholic, Noel was one of the best police officers I knew. Open to new techniques and methods. Compassionate to crime victims before the force ever learned the true meaning of the word. Before he was a functioning alcoholic, he was also married. His wife suffered a fatal stroke about four years ago, and he has struggled ever since. But there is a long list of people – in the force, among the public – who owe a lot to Noel, and I'm one of them. He has two years left to pension, and he's terrified of the void that comes after. So I'm going to ensure he sees out his full time with us even if that's all I can do. Understood?'

It was a factual summary. But for the first time, Cass realised that Finnegan had some capacity for compassion herself somewhere within that sub-zero persona.

'I didn't know some of that detail.'

'Didn't you ask your father about us before you started?'

'I don't ask him about colleagues I serve with. I want to form my own opinions free of any histories he might have with individuals.'

'Typically stubborn and stupid,' Finnegan said. 'Your father was – is – an excellent judge of character. Whereas you, you're having a hard time seeing straight.'

'Excuse me?'

'You took against Noel Ryan and took a shine to Liam Devine. You wouldn't be the first.'

'"Shine" is massively overstating it. Devine's been generous with his time, helped me settle in. No more than that.'

'Yeah, he likes them a bit younger than you, all right.'

'Meaning?'

But she knew full well what it meant.

'Like I said, I'm being frank with you,' Finnegan said. 'He chases young ones around town. Turns up at the nightclubs in plain clothes saying he's checking to ensure no minors are on the premises. The managers give him free entry and I've had a couple of reports now that he's left on more than one occasion with company. Wife stays at home minding the children, he goes around getting his rocks off. Oldest story in the book.'

This was the real reason Finnegan had wanted to speak away from the station, Cass realised.

'It sounds indefensible. But if he's off duty…?'

'He uses one of the patrol cars for intimate relations, under the guise of dropping the girls home.'

'Does his wife know?'

'I don't think so. Although knowing Devine, I'd say he has a lot of previous.'

'How young?'

'Seventeen to twenty-one, by the sounds of it.'

He ensures they meet the legal age of consent. I want to be sick.

'So what the hell are you doing sending him into Saint Al's, or any school for that matter? And why send me with him?'

'Because whispers will get me precisely nowhere in a disciplinary process. I need proof. Did you get any?'

'You knew he'd hit up a girl in there?'

'Of course not. I thought he'd be careful enough to avoid any impression he's interested in minors.'

'Then why bother standing down Noel Ryan and sending me in his place?'

'Noel said Devine was making a lot of innuendo and he didn't think it was a good idea for two men to undertake the visit. He was getting increasingly uncomfortable. I agreed Devine was more likely to behave himself with you around. I didn't think he would be stupid enough to actually hit on someone in front of you. So – did he?'

'He handed one of the students a slip of paper right at the end, when he was talking to her one-to-one and thought nobody was looking. He seemed briefly embarrassed, but told me it was just a book recommendation. I didn't see what was on the paper, so I'm in no position to confirm or contest.'

'But you think it was something else?'

'A phone number probably. Or email address or something.'

'What a fucking mess. I wish *I* was closer to retirement.'

'What are you going to do?'

'I'd knee him in the fucking balls if I could. But nobody's made a complaint. I'm dealing in whispers and what-ifs. I'll give him an unofficial warning. Let him know I'm watching him like a fucking hawk.'

It briefly crossed Cass's mind that such a course of action would make it obvious to Devine that she'd reported events at the school. It would no doubt make life suddenly uncomfortable in the station. But so be it. If she had her way, she'd knee him in the balls too.

I think this is the first time I've agreed with Finnegan on just about anything.

'Now, satisfied?'

'About what?'

'That I'm being straight with you?'

'Yes. Not that you have to prove yourself to me.'

'I know I don't have to prove myself to you. I wouldn't fucking dream of giving one of my direct reports that pleasure. But I want us to have a better relationship, or at least a working one. So if you've anything else to get off your chest, now's the time.'

'Why did you get me Maisah Sahraoui's mobile number?'

'Because I didn't know Maisah had been moved from Glencale against her wishes.'

'How did it happen?'

'As you thought. Harbour Murphy intervened behind the scenes, thinking he was doing me a favour.'

'Why would he want to do you a favour?'

'Why would any politician want to do a favour for the head of police in their area?'

'Fair point.'

Finnegan lapsed into silence again, took another swig of the G&T, and then said: 'Fuck it… I'm trusting that this will be kept between you and me. He and I have known each other a long time. He knows I share his party's politics, more or less. He's the most popular politician in this county and has a good chance of bringing in a running mate at the next general election. He asked me to run alongside him.'

Cass was stuck for an instant response, and was grateful for the interruption by a waiter, asking them if they wished for more drinks. Finnegan waved him away.

'I said no, in case you're wondering,' she said. 'And I didn't conspire with him to move Maisah. I tore into him over that. Bloody reckless and wrong. To say nothing of the fact that if I want somebody's help, I'll ask for it.'

It explains a lot. She trusted me to share that information. Do I trust her enough in return, given what she has just said? And given Harbour

Murphy's name continues to pop up in the investigation of Nabila Fathi's murder?

There was one way to find out. Slowly, methodically, she brought Finnegan up to speed on the Currency Comptroller developments, the fact that Nabila had sought to exchange damaged banknotes there, and the criminal provenance of the notes. She cited every salient detail, including the fact that Nabila had given her real address – the flat above Harbour Murphy's shop.

Finnegan listened patiently, and then said: 'So what's your working theory?'

'I still don't have one,' Cass replied. 'But depending on what the CCTV footage from the Currency Comptroller shows, I'd like to dig a bit further into Harbour Murphy.'

Finnegan didn't hesitate. 'Fine. But do it discreetly. He's entitled to his good name. More to the point, he gives me a pain in the head every time he rings to vent.'

'I can do discreet.'

'And not a word to anybody about Devine.'

'Understood.'

'I have something in common with your dad, you know.'

'What's that?'

'I'm an excellent judge of character too–'

Christ. Just when I'm beginning to warm to you a little, your arrogance rises to the surface again.

'–and despite our rough start, I know I'm not wrong about you. Keep going.'

It was a curious way to deliver a compliment, but Cass recognised it as genuine. Nonetheless, she couldn't find the capability to form a response. Her parents aside, it felt like the first time somebody had said anything nice to her in a long time – a time during which all she could feel was guilt for her fuck-up of a husband and a child who had been left motherless. To her immense embarrassment, and more so because she was in a public place, she felt herself choking up again. And even though she refused to let a tear escape, Finnegan saw it as clearly as she had seen through Devine.

'You've had a bastard of a time of it,' she said. 'But you're going to work through it. Because sitting at home isn't the answer – not for you. Understood?'

This time Cass had no difficulty nodding in the affirmative.

CHAPTER TWENTY-FOUR

Cass always felt more whole after swimming, capable of seeing the way forward again. Which was why, after refusing Finnegan's offer of a stiff drink – a touch mortified, a touch grateful – she made her way to the pier for a late-evening swim. The last of the daylight had disappeared hours ago, but a full moon cast its spectral spotlight on the water and the converted gaslights on the pier lit a clear path to it. For fifteen glorious minutes, she swam hard until her muscles began to ache, the waves washing away her most agonised thoughts. As she emerged from the water, however, embarrassment swept back in like high tide.

'So I'm not the only crazy in this place.'

Startled, she swung to her left to see Mason Brady zipping up a wetsuit, preparing to enter the water.

If you'd only seen me an hour ago, you'd have thought me crazy for sure. 'How long have you been here?' *I've already dealt today with one asshole of a man I badly misread. I could do without another standing there ogling me.*

'Just arrived. And tempted to ask if you come here often.'

'As you can see, I'm just leaving. Enjoy your swim. And at the risk of sounding hypocritical, it's hazardous to swim alone at night.'

Which to you must sound preposterous given your background.

'Don't leave me alone then,' he said with a smile.

'I'm not your minder, Mr Brady.'

He did that thing again where he held up his hands in surrender, and mouthed the word 'sorry', smiling the whole time. But it was an authentic smile, not mocking, and for the briefest moment, she wondered what his company might be like.

Almost immediately, she heard Finnegan's voice from earlier: *'...you're having a hard time seeing straight.'*

She grabbed her towel and gear tub and made for her car.

———

Under the cover of a changing robe, she slipped off her own wetsuit and water shoes and dressed in old and comfortable sweatpants and hoodie.

She threw the wet gear into the tub, sat into the car, stuck the key in the ignition.

And then changed her mind.

She told herself it was just curiosity to see his form in the water. But in any event, she grabbed a couple of items from the front seat and made her way back down to the pier.

Where Brady was nowhere to be seen.

Alarmed, she scanned the water again – and then saw him break to the surface at a buoy about two hundred metres from the shore.

She watched in silent admiration as he swam back in – Brady was fast and fluid in the water – but puzzled at his technique, which seemed a mongrel mix of different styles. At regular intervals, he dove under using a breaststroke kick, but when he surfaced to breathe, turned into a sideways front crawl, seemingly arcing just one arm through the water. She hadn't seen anything like it before, and studied the motion in fascination.

'I guess you're a little crazier than I am,' she said as he emerged from the water.

He smiled again, took a few seconds to bring his breathing under control, and said: 'Maybe we just share passions for the right things.'

'What kind of stroke was that?'

'They teach it in the military. Goes by the thoroughly original name of "combat stroke".'

'Won't win any medals for style.'

'The Olympics weren't really what the instructors had in mind.'

'There's a concept behind it?'

'Stay under the water where you can and then go side profile when you can't – smaller target. Or something like that.'

'You ever need to use it?'

'I never silently swam ashore with a knife between my teeth to launch an invasion, if that's what you mean.'

'That's a relief – one less catastrophic US war to worry about.'

'Very droll. And you?'

'Me?'

'Why do you swim alone at night?'

'Beats being at the station counting the paperclips.'

'Nice of you to come back to make sure I was safe.'

'Actually I came back because I was a bit abrupt earlier. Figured the least I could do was return the offer of coffee. I have a flask and a sandwich if you're happy to share.'

'That's very kind of you.'

She poured him a cup and handed it to him together with half the sandwich.

This is the strangest day I've had in quite some time, she thought.

'Sláinte,' he said, raising the cup.

'Cheers,' she said, raising the flask in return.

They ate and drank in what seemed like comfortable enough silence for a few moments.

'Late summer is the best time to swim the coast at night,' she said. 'Plankton light up the sea like neon. There's some technical term for it I can't remember.'

'Sounds awesome.'

'You can't really see it from here because of the streetlights. You've got to wander beyond the pier and down the coastline a little. You get to know the spots.'

'Maybe you'll show me some time.'

'Yeah, if policing doesn't work out, maybe I'll be a tour guide.'

'Seriously, you like your job – being a cop here?'

'I do. Although I worked in Dublin up to recently – a different experience to here.'

'Reassigned?'

'Personal reasons,' she said. 'What about you? Did you like the military? Or is "like" the wrong word?'

'Not at all. I was proud to serve and it was a tough call to leave.'

'Why did you?'

'Other things I wanted to do in life.'

Above the sound of the water lapping the shore, the sound of raucous music was carrying from somewhere in the town. Cass knew she was using vague and flippant answers to keep up a wall. Part of her wished she could be more honest. He was easy to talk to, easy to be with. And she sensed he was itching for company too.

'Burnout,' he said suddenly. 'That was the real reason.'

'You saw some things?'

He smiled. 'My turn to say thanks for the coffee–'

'I didn't mean to–'

'–and suggest we continue this somewhere warmer. Let me buy you a burger and a beer.'

'Second time today I've been offered a drink and had to decline–'

'I get it – you're not allowed–'

'–but you can buy me the burger.'

———

Desiring privacy, she suggested eating not in Glencale, but in Scariff, the next town over, on the other side of the Loop. Less likely to be seen or recognised there, she thought.

He chose the venue, and they drove there separately, giving each other the opportunity to back out. Neither did. She liked his choice. The Rookery – better known as Rook's – was a small family-run hotel and its bar offered exceptionally good food at reasonable prices. Additionally, staff wouldn't be snobby about their ultra-casual clothing.

They were shown to a booth near the window, but Cass didn't fancy being on show for passers-by and asked for a less conspicuous table instead.

After perusing the menus, Brady did indeed order a hamburger and truffle fries but Cass knew the seafood was Rook's speciality and so opted for mussels and pomme frites. To drink, he requested a non-alcoholic beer while she chose an equally unexciting mineral water.

Morbidly, she wondered what her ex-husband would plump for had he been here. The drinks list would have been consulted first, with champagne to start and a decent white to follow. Lobster for sure, and something decadent for dessert, with more wine to wash it down. Coffee as a momentary sop to sobriety, cognac as a digestif. But all of that would effectively comprise one substantial appetiser. The main course would be a half bottle or so of single malt. And if not utterly unconscious by the time he got home, he would hunt for whatever was in the house to round off the night.

In the early years, when things hadn't been as bad, Cass would find a way to cajole him into bed and get some sleep. In the middle years, she left him be but slept fitfully herself, wishing for him to come to bed, knowing the damage he was doing to himself as he consumed more alcohol into the early hours. In the later years, she had learned to ignore him and sleep soundly, but when she came down the next morning, she would find him unconscious on the couch, a bottle spilled or glass smashed, and on three separate occasions, blood from a cut to his hands or arms that needed stitches. She swore every hospital visit would be her last, but of course, afterwards he was puppy-dog contrite and Cass felt duty-bound to try and help him through. Even though she knew she couldn't, which was the worst part of all...

Their drinks came, and Cass determined to banish Hugh from her mind and focus on present company. Even now, she couldn't really tell herself what she was expecting from the evening – only that, after so long alone, it was nice to be here, soothing to have someone to talk to, if only for a short while. Lack of practice meant she'd probably run out of conversation in ten minutes and they'd both be staring at the walls until they could politely make their excuses. But for now, she was content to sit back and enjoy the fleeting, flickering sense of companionship.

For want of something better, Cass told him of her return to her old school earlier that day – omitting Devine's behaviour – and the strange sensation of catching up with her younger self. She realised then how little of interest her life held outside of work. But if Brady noticed, he hid it well – he was a good conversationalist, opening up pockets of discussion on everything from travel to things he'd seen in the news. While none of it was particularly deep or meaningful, they didn't have to struggle for sentences either, to her immense relief. Even better, she laughed a few times.

When the food arrived, there was a natural silence rather than a strained one as they took a few moments to dig in. She couldn't help but notice the enormous amount of salt with which Brady seasoned his food, and it reminded her of something she'd once read: that even though soldiers were much fitter than the average citizen, their mortality rates – once deaths in combat were excluded – were roughly the same because of the excessive amounts of junk food and alcohol they consumed. Presumably a response to stress.

Almost on cue, Brady said: 'So, tell me about policing in Dublin – you said it was a different experience. A tough beat?'

'It had its moments. Drugs in some parts of the city drive as much violence as anywhere else in the world. Which is not to say Glencale is a picnic, but around here, I don't knock on doors wondering whether my stab vest will hold up to a bullet.'

'You guys patrol unarmed, right?'

'For the most part. We have armed support units, obviously, and an emergency response unit similar to your SWAT teams. But the majority of us do our work on a daily basis without recourse to firearms.'

'That is insane. I couldn't imagine doing what you do without being locked and loaded.'

'We have lower rates of gun ownership than the States. Licensing is strict and, by and large, civilians don't carry firearms on their person. The very idea of an open-carry policy would horrify most citizens. So policing is an entirely different proposition here – even if the drugs gangs now have access to arsenals of a small army.'

'That wasn't the reason you left though, right? You said you left Dublin for personal reasons – someone to care for?'

Stick or twist.

'Not exactly. I left Dublin because I got divorced. Wanted a clean break.'

'Jesus,' he said, 'I'm such a frigging dumbass for prying like that.'

No flippancy now. Just a question of how far to swim out.

'No, it's okay. Everyone in Glencale knows anyway, because it made the papers. My husband was – is – an alcoholic. He was a talented writer when we first met – did the art and restaurant reviews for different papers and magazines, had ideas for several books and plays. Always the life and soul of a party, and great fun – at least at first.'

Cass paused to take a sip from her glass, and it suddenly struck her that she couldn't remember Hugh ever drinking water at a dinner table. Not once.

'But over time, he drank more and wrote less – the alcohol dulled his talent, or at least, his willingness to use that talent,' she continued.

'Eventually, everyone stopped hiring him, and he didn't really seem to care. Didn't care about the effects of it on me, either, or what my job was. A handful of times I had the pleasure of being contacted by a colleague to say Hugh had been drunk and disorderly somewhere and thrown in a cell to sleep it off.

'Nothing I tried seemed to help. Even as he deteriorated, the one thing I was sure of was that he would never drive while drunk, because he never had before. Until one day, of course, he did. And ran into a mother and child at a pedestrian crossing. The boy survived; his mother didn't. And that, in short, is how my husband ended up in prison and I ended up back in Glencale.'

'I'm sorry,' Brady said. 'That is fucked up. It must have been so hard for you.'

'A woman lost her life, a child lost his mother, a husband lost his wife – it was never about me.'

'You and your husband – you had no kids yourself?'

'Never thought it would be wise to bring children into that relationship. Alcoholism tends to run in families, or in Irish families at any rate.'

'Families everywhere,' Brady said. 'There's lots of evidence it's a genetic disease.'

'And progressive. The first I really noticed it with Hugh was when he'd start earlier in the day ahead of a night out – the whole day would then become a write-off. Gradually, he needed to keep going the morning after because that's what his system urged him to do. One-day benders became two-day benders. That's the point where you start to despair. Because you realise that, eventually, it will be three, then four, and instead of the person you love being drunk a minority of the time – which you can just about handle – he's drunk the majority of the time, which is unbearable.'

'He knew what he was doing to you?'

'In his way, I guess. Whenever I tried to speak sense into him, encourage him to seek help, he'd say I was becoming "a boring old biddy". There was a note of affection in there somewhere. If he'd hated me, he would have said "bitch".'

'I can see that.'

'You start to lose your own mind, though – that's the odd thing. You begin asking yourself: "Is his behaviour really that erratic or am I just being a miserable, joyless cow?" And you realise the extent to which you're controlling your temper. Day in, day out, trying to be supportive, not callous; to be encouraging, not critical. But it's the hardest thing – or at least, that's what I thought until the accident... Anyway, bet you wish you'd asked me something else. What about you? Ever married? Children?'

'Married once, divorced once, no kids.'

'What happened?'

'She thought every deployment increased the chances of me coming home in a body bag. Couldn't keep doing it.'

'You were in high-risk places? You never said exactly where you served.'

'Anywhere they sent me.'

'Can't be more precise?'

'Think of any major US arena over the last while and I was probably there at some point.'

'Then I guess your wife's concern was understandable, even if it hurt like hell?'

'You would think. She said to me: "We get one chance at life. This can't be mine." Which I should have understood, right? Truth was, I didn't understand it at all. In whatever shithole or shitshow my job got me into, Amy was always what kept me going – the thought of coming home to her.'

'You were angry?'

'I was... motherfucking angry.' It didn't come across aggressively. He said it in a low-key tone, exhaling deeply as if glad to release it.

'Why didn't you just quit – or quit sooner?'

'It wasn't that straightforward.'

'So coming here was to get away from it?'

'That and other things.'

'You mentioned burnout earlier,' she said gently, weary of pushing too hard.

'Poor word selection.'

'But that morning I called to the house – you were having trouble sleeping.'

'Like you said, I guess I saw some things.'

He was searching for a way to continue his story. Cass said nothing, giving him space to figure it out.

'One of our medics said to me once that a surgeon's greatest fear is developing a tremor in his hands. And that, for soldiers, it's a tremor in their heads – the point when a state of heightened and permanent vigilance turns into constant and irrational fear. I realised I was getting to that point, and would be a liability to the guys I served with. So it was time to go do something else. But by the time I saw the light, my divorce papers were in the mail. So I figured it was time to get away. And Ireland came top of the list.'

So we both escaped to Glencale, Cass thought. *But I guess the question is, are we truly starting over here? Or just hiding from our hurt?*

CHAPTER TWENTY-FIVE

In the solitude of Rook's bathroom, Brady felt like head-butting the mirror simply to bring himself back to his senses.

Angry? Motherfucking angry?

Rage was more accurate. He had raged when Amy left him. Was raging still. She walked out at his weakest moment, when he was absolutely broken. Eventually, he had come to see that she had been broken too – by what he endured, by what came after, by what she was expected to cope with going forward.

But still... Rage.

And he'd admitted as much to Kate Cassidy.

That was after already confessing to burnout.

All the meticulous planning – to keep a low profile, say or do nothing of interest, hide his past and his true reasons for being here...

He may have deluded himself that getting closer to Cass was a clever ruse to stay abreast of the police investigation.

But that's all it was – delusion.

He was putting everything at risk.

And for no other reason than the stupidest one of all.

Bit by bit, he was unlocking himself to her.

He knew exactly why.

Brady closed his eyes, could summon the terrors at a moment's notice, the dreadful sensation of steel wool dragging across his face.

His palms became sweaty, and his face flushed as he relived every moment of it.

He could feel the exact point on his wrists where the cable ties had dug in.

The disorientation of the canvas hood over his head.

The urge to vomit from the greasy rag stuffed in his mouth.

The struggle to breathe, the sense of choking.

The moment where he pissed himself knowing there would be no escape.

Being dragged out of the van and dumped onto the ground, blinded by pain, fear rendering him a human wreck.

Hearing the voice of his mother.

'Hush, darling, sleep now.'

Hearing the gun fire.

Through the only sliver of awareness left, realising they'd shot Pitch first.

His turn next...

God, why have you forsaken me?

And then the largest fusillade of gunfire and grenade blasts he'd ever heard in his life.

Bullets crackling and bodies falling.

An agonised cacophony of mutilation and death.

Trying feverishly through the pain to twist away, roll to safety, not knowing in what direction safety lay.

Until a series of hands plucked him from the ground, and ran with him.

And the voice that, like a lifebuoy thrown to a drowning man at sea, was the miracle that dragged him back to the shore of sanity.

An American voice.

Saying three words that brought tears to his eyes every time he thought of them.

'We've got you.'

———

He opened his eyes. Stared at himself in the mirror and despite the haunted reflection, knew he was looking at a fortunate man, one with half his life yet to live. Felt the familiar sense of survivor's guilt that it was Pitch, and not himself, who had been executed. The eternal gratitude to the colleagues who had so selflessly come to his rescue. Imagining what would have happened had they had arrived just thirty seconds later.

He was flown to Landstuhl, the military trauma centre in Germany, for medical repair and rehabilitation. Some weeks later, he returned home to the States, to Amy, physically fragile and mentally smashed. He knew his rage at her subsequent decision to leave him was, in many ways, ill-directed. She had actually wanted to help him through, would have stayed had he been focused solely on recovery, would have held him up when taking every faltering step. What shook her so badly was the fact that Brady had left for his deployment a rational, proportionate man and returned from rehabilitation a cold obsessive, hell-bent on violence.

Don't sleep, can't sleep, the dead haunt you.

PTSD, obsessional, kill or be killed, an eye for an eye.

On the cusp of getting away with murder until Kate Cassidy walks into my life and reminds me of everything I held so close and lost.

Life, love and the chance that a guy might be lucky enough to have both.

I should walk out of here, thank her for a nice evening, and take it no further. But some impulses are too powerful to be controlled.

He had intuited from the beginning that she was hurting too.

Now he knew it to be so.

Two damaged souls colliding with each other.

And he knew the odds favoured this particular collision ending terribly.

PART 2

THE DEAD SLIDE IN AND OUT OF REACH

CHAPTER TWENTY-SIX

C ass woke with a start, nerves jangling from the sound playing almost imperceptibly in her mind: the clang of a church bell in the wind.

She stayed perfectly still for twenty seconds or so and heard nothing, realising it had just been a bad dream.

She was alone in the room, Brady's side of the bed cold. Reaching for her phone, she saw it was a little after four in the morning. Despite the unsettling dream, the isolation of the church and Brady's disappearance, she found herself smiling.

By rights, he should have been sleepy enough: they'd had vigorous sex twice. The first was unfamiliar, fumbling, rushed. The second was less frenetic; without need for words, she showed him some of the things that worked for her until she came. It hardly took a genius to recognise that the spontaneity of the night had probably been unwise. But she was gratified that, for the first night in a long time, she had thought of something other than her ex-husband, a motherless child, or the dead body of Nabila Fathi while drifting off to sleep.

When they'd finished at the restaurant, it was clear to both of them they didn't want to go their separate ways. They opted for his place, as it was closer, and avoided a scenario whereby prying eyes noticed Brady entering or exiting Cass's apartment. Once back at the church, things had escalated quickly.

She realised Brady hadn't been lying about his insomnia. She rose and threw on her hoodie, padding out from the darkness of the curtained bedroom onto the balcony, from where she could see Brady, sitting in an armchair facing the sliding doors, staring out at the grove. Alert but serene, not anxious, not fidgeting. Seemingly unaware of her presence. She padded down the stairs and now he heard her, turning his head and smiling too.

'I hope I didn't wake you.'

She shook her head, preferring not to mention the real reason: being woken by the peals of an imaginary bell.

'Your difficulty sleeping – it's every night?'

'I sleep fine – just from dawn to mid-morning.'

'You try seeing anyone about it – a professional?'

'To say what?' he asked, shrugging. 'I'm a soldier who's afraid of the dark. Which sounds ridiculous, because it is. I've tried the doctors, tried the counsellors and tried the medication. Didn't work. So I'm here, trying to deal with it myself.'

There was a brief silence as Cass contemplated how to respond. *I've been there too,* she wanted to say.

'I've a recurring dream where my old boss says nobody really blames me,' she said eventually.

'But you blame you, right?'

'Every hour of the day.'

———

They went back to bed, eager to have each other anew, to fuck with abandon and drive the demons away.

When she woke again, Cass was alone once more. She showered and dressed, and came down to the kitchen where

Brady had breakfast ready: scrambled eggs and coffee and toasted soda bread.

Not exactly sourdough but not far off, she thought.

They both ate heartily, and Cass complimented the bread, thinking it was homemade.

'Can't take the credit,' Brady said. 'A local woman bakes it, and sells it from Milly Cooper's shop. Milly calls me when there's a fresh batch – better service than Amazon.'

'You get phone coverage up here?' Cass asked. 'I've none on my network.'

'Same here. If she can't get me, she leaves a voicemail.'

She giggled, amused by the strange story: A troubled ex-soldier, coming to Glencale for respite, forming a bond over bread with the local shop-owner. Who always rings him when there's a new delivery. It must tickle him pink – how very twee.

She looked at her phone and realised it was time to go, especially as she would have to drop by her own apartment on the way for her uniform.

A lingering kiss and then she got ready to leave.

'Call me?' he asked.

'See you at the pier,' she said.

CHAPTER TWENTY-SEVEN

Cass was still smiling to herself about Milly Cooper's bread reservation system when she arrived at the station. It took only a moment, however, to sense the frigid temperature inside. Devine was already at his desk when she walked in, and glared at her with barely concealed hatred. She pretended not to notice and simply greeted him as if it were a normal day. There was a grunt in response, and Cass took it that Finnegan had already spoken to him.

I got laid and you got laid into. Good. You're a fucking asshole.

She determined to catch up with Finnegan before end of day to understand exactly what had been said. In such a small station, it would have been preferable not to have enemies. But Cass hadn't been the cause of the fallout; she had witnessed plenty of tension among colleagues over the years, and she wasn't afraid of it. The only thing that mattered, at the end of the day, was that they did their jobs well, as individuals and a collective.

And with that in mind, crack on and let Devine sulk.

She already knew much of her day would be spent revisiting CCTV and driver dashboard footage from the days around the

Bridge Bannon murder. The team had been through a tonne of it already, and there was still more to go.

With the Americans off the pitch as suspects, the burglary gang had returned to the top of the list, while the team still wanted to trace Peter Bannon to be sure they could rule him out of their inquiries.

They thought it likely that the farmer's murderers had been through Glencale at some point for reconnaissance purposes beforehand – a couple of days, a couple of hours, whatever. So the footage, taken from various sources around the town and from a number of drivers who had responded to an appeal, might help. The only problem was, they didn't know exactly for what – or for whom – they were looking.

The burglary gang had always been masked during their raids, so the investigators had descriptions only of their voices, not their faces. It meant they were searching for anything in the haystack of pixels that looked suspicious. It would be a grind of a day, Cass knew. For the shortest of moments, she allowed herself to wallow in the unexpected pleasure of the previous night. It didn't cross her mind to think another day of unexpected developments might be ahead of her.

———

She had almost two hours of fruitless work done when it was time to adjourn for the morning conference. At it, the SIO acknowledged the reality with which they were grappling: with no suspect yet charged, the community would grow increasingly nervous and the media restive. 'Do what you can to allay the fears of any member of the public who expresses their concern to you; don't brush them off,' Kearney said. 'But ignore any reporter who tries to snare you; don't rise to it. Leave them to Sergeant Finnegan and myself.'

The conference concluded on that note. When Cass returned

to her desk, she found registered post awaiting her, and felt a familiar surge of anticipation when she saw the identity of its sender.

Oliver Ashcombe had pledged to dig out all relevant CCTV footage in the Currency Comptroller's possession of Ezme Khaled visiting the public counter and seeking to exchange damaged euro notes.

The same Ezme Khaled who gave the address in Glencale of the flat above Harbour Murphy's shop – the flat where Nabila Fathi had briefly lived.

The envelope contained a single thumb-drive, and Cass didn't waste time trying to circumvent the security protocols on the Garda network. She pulled out her own laptop from her rucksack under the desk, knowing there was no risk attached to it, because the Currency Comptroller would have ensured that the thumb-drive was new and free of malicious software before loading it up with the CCTV.

From her time in Dublin, Cass knew well the precise location of the Comptroller's office on George's Dock at the heart of the city's financial district. While she wasn't familiar with the internals of the building, Ashcombe had told her there were public entrances at the front of the building river-side and at the rear of the building, which led towards the Luas, the light-rail system that connected the financial district to the city centre. There were multiple cameras inside and outside the building, he had said, so she could expect plenty of footage.

But when she opened up the first of three files, she saw that the Comptroller's office had provided a neat clipping service.

Rather than send her the complete footage for the day from each of the relevant cameras, they had selected only the images they thought most relevant.

She started with the first file. On the laptop screen, she could see it was stamped 10 December. Nothing much happened for about ten seconds or so – the footage showed Comptroller staff and visitors in the reception area, going about their business. And then...

The footage was high-quality and clear, and showed a young woman hesitantly enter through the main doors of the building, before being greeted by one of the security guards and directed to the public counter.

She had a scarf around her neck and a rucksack on her shoulder.

Ezme Khaled presumably.

Nabila Fathi definitely.

———

The surge of anticipation was gone, replaced by a profound sadness, because Cass knew she was watching on screen some of Nabila's final hours.

The exchange at the counter tallied with the account Oliver Ashcombe had previously relayed from the Comptroller's records. The 'counter' was technically a transaction window in a wall. Behind the security glass lay an office to which the public had no access. Nabila approached the transaction window, appeared to ask some questions of the teller, and took some notes out of her rucksack, placing them on the window ledge.

The teller popped a form and a pen through the security drawer, and Nabila started completing it. She then furtively scanned her surroundings, as if expecting the security guard to reappear at her shoulder. After a minute, she paused and started fidgeting with the pen and swaying on her feet.

Cass surmised this must have been the breaking point – the question on the form seeking the origin of the money to be exchanged. Nabila continued to stare at the form and fidget... and then shoved the document back into the security drawer, grasped the notes from the ledge, and turned on her heels, hustling towards the rear exit. The teller rose, clearly entreating

Nabila to come back, without success. The security guard was greeting another visitor, and didn't intervene.

The clip ended, and Cass opened the next file. It was from one of the cameras outside the building, showing Nabila approaching the rear entrance and going inside. Cass watched it a few times but nothing obvious jumped out to her. Then she clicked on the final file, which she hoped would be more productive: Nabila hustling from the building.

The camera showed that as she exited the rear doors, her hustle turned into a jog, and, once she was clear of the premises, a full-tilt run. Whatever the circumstances were, Nabila feared something had gone badly wrong and was afraid of being detained, not understanding that the Currency Comptroller staff were not the police, and held no such powers of detention.

At first, it seemed Nabila was running to the Luas stop on George's Dock, which would have made perfect sense. But as Cass watched the footage, Nabila ran past the stop, before turning left onto a side street and out of view, at which point the footage ended. Using Google Maps to double-check, Cass saw that Nabila had turned onto Common Street, which contained mostly retail stores and apartments. But she guessed immediately that Nabila was running to an on-street rendezvous point – it being more likely that someone was parked in a vehicle waiting for her. The instigator of all this – and most likely Nabila's murderer.

Cass now realised she would need a full sweep of the CCTV from all the office premises in that direction, as well as any street footage held by Dublin City Council. She allowed herself one silent scream of frustration, then picked up the phone and started dialling.

Another round of pressure and patience: leaning on the relevant parties to dig out the footage, waiting as it took days to do so. But she was prepared to grind it out, because she could feel the killer was tantalisingly close to her, hidden out of view but just around that corner. The noose was starting to tighten.

———

After making the full suite of necessary calls, Cass switched cases and spent the rest of the morning reviewing CCTV footage related to the Bridge Bannon case. This proved considerably less productive; most of the people she saw on screen she recognised as locals or people with legitimate business in Glencale – truck drivers and so forth. She saw several whom she took to be tourists in new rental cars, but nothing suspicious in their demeanour.

Needle and haystack, she thought, wishing there was an AI solution robust enough to handle this work to the necessary standard. There was no sign of Peter Bannon in the footage, and Cass wondered exactly when he had arrived back in Glencale, and how quickly he had left. Had he known he would be chased across the Atlantic? It seemed that way, if his disappearance was anything to go by. For a brief moment, she wondered if the two Americans – though innocent of the farmer's murder – had actually found Peter Bannon and killed *him.* It would explain their relatively short sojourn in the country. After all, they surely wouldn't have given up so easily if they had been unable to find him, as they claimed.

Just like Nabila Fathi, his body might be lying somewhere and we don't even know it.

The more she thought it through, the more likely she felt that was the case – which made it imperative to trace Peter Bannon's last-known movements.

It was mid-afternoon and the CCTV trawl had yielded nothing more than a stiff neck and a headache. She had missed lunch, thought briefly about ordering a delivery, and then told herself it would be better to leave the station and get some air.

As she walked, she mulled over her new theory. Mason Brady had seen something dangerous enough in the American pair to take their licence plate number and report them once news of Bridge Bannon's murder had broken. Mason Brady, that odd combination of soldier and sap, a man who'd clearly had his fill of violence – presumably inflicting it as well as witnessing it – and yet was so non-threatening to the locals that Milly Cooper was ringing him about bread.

Phone calls and voicemails. A shop-owner at the centre of a small community. Two Americans with sinister intent. Brady walking into the station. Milly picking up the phone. A shop-owner at the centre of a small community. Phone calls and voicemails...

A new question began forming in Cass's mind.

Brady had seen enough in the two Americans to take their licence plate just in case some trouble subsequently arose.

But what had Milly Cooper done?

Nabila Fathi's murderer had remained stubbornly out of view earlier that morning.

But the smoke had suddenly cleared in the Bridge Bannon case and Cass felt a slight chill as she saw in her mind the probable killer.

CHAPTER TWENTY-EIGHT

Sprint up every hill. It will intimidate every rival.

S Brady could remember his beloved high-school cross-country coach shouting his instructions as if it were yesterday. Instructions he'd followed all his life, even when running alone.

But now as he attacked one of the mountain trails near his property, he could feel the familiar effects of his injuries catching up with him. His right knee ached during any extreme bout of exercise, apart from when he was in the water. He couldn't complete a knee curl of any decent weight because the same knee would buckle. His lower back spasmed occasionally, and sometimes the pain would be enough to bring him to a halt. But he always resumed, not because he enjoyed it, but because he had been made and trained this way, and knew the aching satisfaction at the top would be worth the sacrifice.

Kate Cassidy – is she worth the sacrifice?

While serving, he'd been no different to many of his colleagues – he'd do a tour of duty and then, wired from the constant on-edge nature of the job, would return home seeking release. As much booze as his body could tolerate, as much sex as he could find.

Once married, there was no more womanising, but the incessant boozing continued on every homecoming, until a point would come each time where he had adjusted. In the early years, Amy had no issue with that; she knew it was his way of shedding the combat stress and was frequently happy to join him.

But the last tour – the capture, the aftermath – had changed everything. He'd returned home both broken and consumed. And the obsession ultimately won out, bringing him here, to Glencale, which he'd treated as a mission, and acted accordingly. No booze, no women. Drugs only when he needed an edge or needed the edge taken off. A curse of a mission, in other words, and he'd found it incredibly tough to remain disciplined. Doubly so when he was trying to come to terms with losing his wife and to quench the fireworks in his head.

I'd intended to come back, he thought for the thousandth time. *I had something I needed to do – to get out of my system – and it was too black, too malign to tell you. But I was coming back to you once it was done. If only you'd given me the chance...*

He felt abandoned by Amy, even if he knew she would say he had been the one to abandon her.

Cass had endured something similar. He could sense her bitterness towards her ex-husband, just as his own towards Amy was never far from the surface.

Meeting someone in Glencale had been the last thing he expected, the last thing he desired. He wanted no complications, no disruptions, nobody close enough to learn anything about him. Cass had upended that, and he knew already that she interested him far beyond casual sex. Smart – way smarter than him. Tough – she wouldn't allow her vulnerabilities to defeat her. Acerbic – she'd take no shit from anyone. And hot as hell.

All of which was unfortunate, to say the least. Because in a worst-case scenario, letting Cass get too close could be his undoing – and he had no interest in serving a life sentence. It would take a lot to expose him, he knew. But the risk was there.

Which meant, as much as he liked her, it was time to reimpose the self-discipline that had been sorely lacking this last few days. He would have to move to Plan B – and be ruthless about it.

CHAPTER TWENTY-NINE

Cass didn't accuse Milly Cooper of withholding evidence, or potentially affecting a criminal investigation. It would have been ludicrous. If anything, the septuagenarian shopkeeper – sharp as a tack – had simply been doing her neighbourly duty: a form of community watch. Cass just really wished Milly had told one of the team.

The questions at the shop had taken just a few minutes. Once done, Cass emphasised to the shopkeeper that if there ever was a next time – 'God help us there won't be' – every detail, no matter how seemingly small or trivial, might be important. It was the gentlest of admonitions, and Cass followed it with a word of reassurance that the information Milly had just imparted might be of assistance.

Just how much assistance wasn't something Cass could predict. But she was prepared to wager that Milly Cooper's single action had been the unwitting spark that ignited the terrible events. The person who could say for sure was Sarah Delahunty – which was why Cass was now headed in the direction of her farm.

As she drove, she reflected again on the savagery of Bridge Bannon's murder. Violent crime always shook a community and inevitably caused conjecture that social bonds were breaking, that society no longer had 'respect for life'. The opposite was true, Cass knew. Were it possible to trace back over a couple of thousand years the full history of even a small geographic area like the Loop, one would find a litany of gruesome killings, some recorded, many not. There was no shortage of land here that had soaked up blood, and society had simply moved on, as it always did. Even if the media was predictably cranking up the outrage at the pace of the investigation, Bridge Bannon's murder, too, would in time become a footnote. But it would be recorded as detected and solved – Cass had no doubt of that.

The red steel gate of Sarah Delahunty's farm was open as usual and Cass turned in.

That should have told me something in retrospect, Cass thought.

She checked her phone and saw that, as with Brady's place, there was no coverage here. She wasn't concerned: if she needed assistance, she would press the emergency button on her radio, which worked everywhere. In any event, she didn't expect a confrontation.

There were no children in sight this time – clearly still at school. Cass parked next to the paddock and instinctively looked towards the stables, guessing that Sarah might be seeing to the horses. Instead, Cass heard the noise of the kitchen door opening, and turned to see Sarah striding towards her, jangling a set of car keys.

'Hello again,' she said. 'But I have to collect the kids shortly so–'

'It won't take long,' Cass replied. 'I'm sorry for the lack of notice but I was in the area.'

'You have an update?'

'A few more questions, actually, if that's okay.'

Cass could tell it wasn't okay, but Sarah nodded nonetheless. There was no offer to come inside for tea this time, so Cass simply began with what she hoped would sound like an innocuous question. 'The gate below – do you always leave it open?'

Sarah stared at her, clearly unsure what relevance the question had.

'Most of the time. No real reason to close it.'

'Even after your father was attacked?'

'You mean for our own security?'

The penny drops, Cass thought.

'Exactly. As a precaution. I'm sure a lot of households around here would have taken a few extra measures.'

The couple of moments it took Sarah to frame her answer were enough. Cass knew it had never crossed her mind to take additional precautions. There had been no need to.

'We have a dog – no better alarm system. And my husband has a shotgun – licensed of course. Not that he would ever… it's for foxes.'

'You were here the night of your father's murder – that's correct?'

'Yes.'

'And your brother had been staying here for a few days but left before it happened?'

'Yes, but I told you all this last time. And I do really have to get going for the kids–'

'Just a minute or two more. Has Peter contacted you since?'

Sarah fell silent as she deliberated again, and Cass decided it was time to turn the screw.

'Before you answer that, Sarah, let me make something clear: provided we have good reason, we can get a warrant for your phone records, and your husband's phone records if required. We'll work through every phone call you received in the period before and after your father's murder, and I'm pretty sure we'll find a pattern of calls and texts from an unknown number. A burner phone that Peter acquired after landing in Ireland. Correct?'

Sarah said nothing. Cass didn't need her to – not yet. But she would insist on an answer to the next set of questions.

'I've already verified one particular call without needing your phone records. Milly Cooper watches for the welfare of everyone around here. And I realised that when two out-of-place visitors come to her shop looking for your father, she's not going to ignore it if she feels something's not right. She's going to ring someone. Maybe not your father, because she knows he probably won't answer and, even if he did, might not take too kindly to anybody interfering with his business, even someone well-meaning like Milly. So she did the next best thing. She rang you, didn't she?'

'Why ask me if you already know?'

'I'd like to hear you confirm it.'

'Yes, Milly rang me.'

'What did she tell you?'

'More or less what you said. That two Americans had come to the shop, wanting directions to the farm. She didn't say they were suspicious or anything – she didn't have to. She just wanted to make sure we knew.'

'What did you say in response?'

'I thanked her for the call.'

'And what did you do next?'

'Nothing.'

'Nothing?'

Silence again. Cass had been here before, had seen several people in the same position as Sarah now, knowing she was effectively walking a tightrope and a wrong step could be catastrophic.

What will Sarah do? Tell the truth or lie?

'Let me tell what I think you did, and we can run through it formally at the station later. When Milly rang, you knew instantly that the Americans had come for Peter, not your father. You knew Peter had come home to escape trouble. But the trouble had followed him. So you did what any sister would do – you immediately warned Peter. And you didn't have to ring him – because he was still here, wasn't he?'

'I really do have to collect the children,' Sarah said, her voice suddenly shaky. 'Maybe I can–'

'When the full suite of forensics are in, they're going to tell the tale as clear as day, Sarah. And if you continue to withhold vital information from us, it will increase the likelihood of you being charged as an accessory to murder. So think of your kids now, not Peter – he can stand on his own two feet. I asked you this the last time, and I'm going to once more, and please don't make the mistake of lying to me: Where is your brother?'

Sarah turned her head in the direction of her car, which was parked closer to the house, as if wishing to make a run for it.

'You'll be going straight to the station if you don't tell me, Sarah. Where is Peter?'

Cass heard the movement behind her a fraction too late to respond. Her head was wrenched back by someone grabbing a fistful of her hair in one hand and using the other to slide a knife across her throat.

'I'm right fucking here, bitch.'

CHAPTER THIRTY

S arah screamed in fright, and began imploring her brother to let Cass go. But Peter Bannon was not about to yield his grip and roared at his sister to shut up. Cass felt the pressure of the knife at her throat and had the sense not to struggle just yet: any misstep on her part now would be fatal.

Instead, she kept her hands gripped on the arm which Bannon was using to hold the knife. Her body was trembling but her mind had already moved beyond the physical shock and registered the quivering in Bannon's knife arm. He was panicking, not sure what to do or how to get out of his predicament. He had killed once already; was he on edge enough to kill again? Was he stupid enough to slit her throat?

Sarah kept pleading, trying to pacify her brother, inching closer to him as she did so.

Cass closed her eyes briefly and knew this was supposed to be the moment where her life flashed before her eyes, or she made her reconciliations, or some such shit.

But all she could think of was Devine's description and hear his mocking voice saying it.

Skinny runt who didn't have the father's size, strength or sneakiness.

Maybe, but he'd found enough within him to take out his father.

Absurdly, in that moment, she thought of her ex-husband deservedly languishing in a prison cell, and visualised shoving Bannon head first to join him.

Time to test Devine's proposition.

But as Cass prepared to do so, Sarah decided likewise, and drove at her brother. Bannon took a step back, his grip on Cass loosening just a fraction, and she took her chance.

Releasing her right hand from his arm, she drove her elbow back as hard as she could into Bannon's midriff, and felt his grip at her hair and neck release as his stomach folded and lungs expelled air. Without pause, she rammed her heel back into his shin, resulting in a howl of pain, then caught his knife arm again with both hands and pitched forward, using his sudden lack of balance to throw him cleanly over her back. As he fell to the ground, she raised her right boot and stamped as hard as she could on his groin. Bannon crumpled up in a foetal position and Sarah fell on him, punching and screaming. Cass had to haul her aside before dropping to her knees, pinning Bannon to the ground. He was a beaten docket and offered no resistance as she handcuffed him. As she explained why she was arresting him, he started weeping.

Now I have to be polite to this weak-willed prick when I should beat the living shit out of him, she thought.

She finished the formalities, and then lifted Bannon to his feet. Sarah was now sobbing uncontrollably too.

Cass felt a tinge of sympathy for her, but not much more than that. She had to get her own trembling under control, and the easiest way of doing so was by focusing on the practicalities. Others could offer emotional support later.

'Sarah,' she said, 'I'm radioing for assistance now and you'll have to stay here, in my sight, until my colleagues arrive. You need to ring your husband or somebody else who can collect the children.'

CHAPTER THIRTY-ONE

The dumbest of things, but as Cass sat in the ambulance getting the once-over from a friendly medical technician, she cursed the fact that Devine, of all people, had popped into her head in the middle of the showdown.

The ambulance doors were open, and amid the hubbub of activity on the farm, she could see Kearney and Finnegan deep in discussion near the stables.

'I'm good to go now?' Cass asked impatiently.

The medical examination had been Finnegan's idea – she'd insisted on it – but aside from a thin red mark on her throat, Cass had no other physical injuries. The technician applied some ointment but she declined the offer of a bandage. He expressed his concern about delayed shock; she brushed it aside. Sure, she was a little shaken, but not enough that she needed to cut work. The risk of assault was an everyday reality of the job; she never quite got comfortable with it, but would never allow it to intimidate her. As for Peter Bannon, a runt like him wasn't going to haunt her dreams. If anything, she thought with grim amusement, she might haunt his.

The technician eventually relented. Cass thanked him and

stepped down from the ambulance, Noel Ryan approaching as she did so. 'Your father's been on through the station. Couldn't get you on mobile. Wants to know you're okay.'

Evidentially, Ted Cassidy's contacts in the station were still top-notch.

'Could you get a message to him that I'm fine, and that I'll call him later?'

'No problem.'

Cass was grateful, for the only people to whom she wanted to speak right now were Kearney and Finnegan, principally because of the Criminal Law Act and what it stipulated about accessories.

The SIO had, as per his style, organised the team meticulously, focused on ensuring every last detail was handled correctly to minimise the risk of an unsuccessful prosecution. It was a common assumption that once the killer was identified, the rest was merely formalities. This was the peril on which many an investigation had foundered: a warrant was wrongly executed, interview rights were breached, paperwork was misfiled or overlooked. From her perch on the ambulance, Cass had again been impressed at the manner in which Kearney drilled the troops, guarding against sloppiness at this critical stage. But as she approached him, he broke into a grin and she recognised in it the pleasure of success. This case had been wrapped up in weeks rather than months; despite the fact that the media had started to foment, Kearney's superiors would be pleased.

'You need to fill us in,' he said, 'but before that, tell me how you're doing.'

'I'm fine,' she said, for what felt like the hundredth time in the previous hour. But she'd had practice: it had been her stock answer in the wake of Hugh's car crash, too. 'I wanted to speak to you about Sarah Delahunty.'

'Let's go back a step. You did admirably today but I need to know the precise sequence – exactly how you made the connections.'

'It was a lucky break,' Cass said. 'No more than that.'

Finnegan muttered something under her breath. For the first time, Cass realised that her superior might not be as pleased as Kearney, although she couldn't think why that might be the case. But there was nothing for it but to plough on.

'I was looking back over the interview notes for Milly Cooper. We know that even the most truthful witnesses occasionally leave something out – if they were trying to help someone else, if they were embarrassed about something they did themselves, or just by mistake, right? So it struck me that perhaps Milly had omitted something. Two dodgy Americans come into her store looking for Bridge Bannon. What does she do when they leave?'

'She calls someone,' Kearney said.

'Exactly. She confirmed to me that she rang Sarah. Just to make her aware. Milly didn't know that the Americans had sinister intent; she just didn't like the look of them. The next question was what Sarah did with the knowledge. She had already confirmed to us that her brother had stayed a few days with her, but left before the murder. My guess was that Peter Bannon was still here that day, and she immediately realised that the Americans were after him, not their father. So she warned Peter.'

'If that was the case, why didn't Bannon just make a run for it? Why risk going to his father's farm?'

'It's pure conjecture on my part from here, but I'm sure the questioning will reveal some version of this: I think he went to the farm initially to carry out surveillance, see exactly who was after him. He had stolen money opportunistically from a mob gang in the States, which was why he fled. I don't think he expected to be chased home, but the money was enough that the gang had to send a message. Maybe he saw the Americans, maybe he didn't, but either way, he knew he had a target on his back if he couldn't make good. He also knew his father hated banks, hated authority, and kept large amounts of cash at home. My guess is that he pleaded with his father for cash to dig himself out of trouble, Bridge Bannon refused, and Peter tried to beat it out of him. And went too far.'

'And the bleach?' Kearney asked.

'A sloppy attempt to cover his tracks, to give the impression it was the work of professionals. He knew his father's farm; knew where he could find some.'

'Well, as you said, let's see what he says under questioning,' Kearney replied. 'But you've convinced me. Again – good work.' He patted her on the shoulder, and then left to speak with other members of the team before Cass got a chance to say another word.

'You're really okay?' Finnegan said.

'Fine,' Cass replied automatically.

'Then what in God's name were you at, coming up here alone?'

'I honestly didn't think Peter Bannon was still here. I assumed he fled immediately after the murder.'

'You really didn't think he was here? You weren't on some fucking glory hunt or kamikaze mission?'

'No. Once I confirmed Milly had warned Sarah, I just wanted to confront Sarah with that information.'

'You should have spoken to Kearney, sought authorisation. Sought backup, for Christ's sake.'

'Like I said, I didn't think I was walking into a dangerous situation.'

'I've enough problems on my team without someone intent on suicidal solo runs.'

'I swear to you, it wasn't like that.'

Finnegan said nothing but did that peculiar sucking noise with her teeth again.

'About Sarah–' Cass started.

'She's on her way to the station. She'll be cautioned and charged there.'

'That's just the thing. She played no hand, act or part in what her brother did today. She tried to help me.'

'But she played her part in covering up the murder. The law is pretty clear on that.'

The Criminal Law Act. Section seven, subsection two. Cass practically knew it by heart. On a strict reading, Sarah Delahunty was an accessory after the fact of murder. The act further stipulated sanction of up to ten years in prison.

Cass's sympathy for Sarah had been limited to begin with. But then she saw her make the agonised call to her husband, unable to speak the names of her kids without sobbing, and imploring her husband to tell them she loved them.

'The law is pretty clear on lots of things,' Cass said. 'But the Director of Public Prosecutions will decide whether or not to proceed to trial based on our report.'

'And our report will be factual, as it always is.'

'And in every report we emphasise the facts that matter to us and underplay others. Sarah had no role in this. Her father was a bastard and her brother damaged goods. She thought she was helping her brother by warning him, and had no idea what it would lead to. And when push came to shove today, she ran to help me. Is the report going to state that?'

Cass knew she was pushing it, knew she was at risk of shattering the fragile accommodation she and Finnegan had reached with each other. But that mattered less to her right now.

I can't see these kids lose their mother too.

Finnegan stared at her for what felt like an eternity. 'I'll speak to Kearney,' she said eventually. 'But the next time you get an idea like this, you speak to me. Understood?'

———

Cass resisted all offers of a lift home and instead drove herself in the same squad car in which she had arrived. She hadn't anticipated Finnegan's anger and was torn between being irritated by it and understanding it – Cass genuinely hadn't anticipated Peter Bannon's presence; Finnegan feared she had come close to losing an officer.

As Cass left the farm, she remembered her previous exit from the property, the trigger and the tears, and told herself if she ever so much as drove past this place again, it would be too soon. Though of course, she'd have to do so if she wanted to visit Mason Brady – the church was just a mile or so further up the road.

But for tonight, at least, and maybe for a few days more, she would insist on him coming to her.

CHAPTER THIRTY-TWO

'You went to arrest the guy on your own?'

'Jesus,' Cass said, 'I've already gone through this once today with my boss. And a second time with my dad in the last hour. I wasn't going there to arrest him – I thought he was long gone. I went to speak to his sister.'

'But you went there unarmed, with no backup?'

Brady was shaking his head, more in wonderment than anything else. But it was just as exasperating to Cass as Finnegan's earlier interrogation. At least her father had understood and focused on her well-being: he may not have wanted her to join the force, but once she did, he never once called into question her ability to handle the job.

'You're incredible,' Brady said. 'You and your colleagues. I'm not blowing smoke up your ass. You couldn't have paid me to set foot on that farm without a weapon, a team and a tactical plan.'

'Yeah, well, we like to leave suspects alive and buildings standing when we're finished.'

'Enough already with the constant deflection. Take the compliment – I mean it.'

He was trying, and she knew it, and so contained her instinct to explode at him. She hadn't exactly brought her best self to this evening either. She wanted some food, some wine, and to fuck hard for an hour and forget everything else for a while. But she was on edge, thinking of Sarah Delahunty in the station, wishing she could do more for her. And to top it off, there was a slight tremor in her hand every time she picked up her glass. 'I'm sorry,' she said. 'I'm just finding it hard to tune out of the day's events.'

'Tell me what's most on your mind.'

That was more to her liking. Not making an assumption that the memory of being held at knifepoint was preying on her. Offering an invite to speak about things if she wanted to. She had given him only the bare bones of her day, given her inability to discuss case detail. But they had their killer now, and she felt she could trust him enough to say a bit more, explaining the role Sarah Delahunty had played and the effort she had made to assist Cass when attacked.

'A good attorney, character references, testimony from you – maybe she avoids serving time?' Brady said.

'I hope. She wanted nothing to do with her father and never intended for him to be murdered. The rest is all chicken-shit.'

'Unless it had been a colleague and not you.'

'Meaning what?'

'Would you feel the same way if it was one of your colleagues who'd gone to the farm today and been attacked? Your life was put at risk. She was at least partly responsible for that. Maybe she should answer for it.'

It was a perspective she hadn't considered. Chances were if it had been a colleague held at knifepoint – even the odious Devine – Cass would have wanted to beat the shit out of Peter Bannon *and* Sarah Delahunty.

'Not my place,' Brady continued, 'and maybe I'm way out of line here. But seems to me you're trying to prevent another family being ripped apart when you're no more responsible for this woman's conduct than you were for your husband's. Sarah Delahunty had agency. The chips will fall as they may for her.'

'Tell that to her kids tonight.'

———

Brady noticed her hands tremble when she lifted the glass: of course he did. But he wasn't being patronising: he did admire her raw courage.

He wanted to tell her of his own trauma: being captured, coming close to execution. He wanted to tell her that after being rescued, he was unable to speak for an hour or more. The medics initially thought his jaw had been broken until an examination and X-rays told them it wasn't; he simply couldn't unclench his teeth from the shock. Could see and hear everything around him, could gesture but not speak. Couldn't ask what had happened. Couldn't ask for Pitch. Couldn't answer questions about where he felt pain. Couldn't thank his colleagues for saving his life. Couldn't fucking open his mouth.

That's what shock could do. And it scarred him, scrambled his mind – warped it, according to his ex-wife. The physical injuries healed in time but his mind didn't. If he was being truthful with himself, he never holistically recovered, was never fit enough to return to the job. Whereas Cass… tremor or not, he had no doubt she would return to work tomorrow morning – and do her job. Incredible wasn't doing her justice.

It hurt him to imagine ever having to hurt this formidable woman. The last thing he wanted to do was even consider it.

Which was ironic, considering he'd scouted her apartment some days previously – just as a precaution, more than anything. He didn't go in – he'd been trained to blow doors open, not pick locks, and he had no idea what type of security measures she had. But he'd studied the apartment building and its surrounds – to know exactly where she lived, and relevant entry and exit points, in case he ever needed that information. But now she'd invited him in, and he could see everything he needed to know.

———

She woke in the middle of the night, bile rising in her throat. Brady's side of the bed was empty and she registered the low hum of the television in the living room as she rushed for the en suite. She just about made it to vomit into the sink. Delayed shock.

She heard Brady rise and reached back to lock the bathroom door, not wanting him – not wanting anyone – to see her like this. She clenched her teeth and wished it were Peter Bannon in the living room right now. She'd drag him in here and drown him in the fucking tub.

CHAPTER THIRTY-THREE

The joy of being a grunt in a murder investigation, Cass knew, was that you never had to deal with journalists. An aggressive media placed additional strain on a team trying to solve a case. Demanding answers, obtaining inside information, publishing misleading stories, either through mistake or malice, and exacerbating fears in a community.

On the other hand, skilled senior officers could also manipulate the media to their advantage, driving required information into the public domain at the right time. From the clippings in the Nabila Fathi case, Cass guessed that the media coverage, eventually focusing as it did on the failure to catch the killer, had placed unwelcome pressure on Finnegan, though she had never said anything. The coverage in the Bannon case would turn into a different beast entirely now that a suspect was in custody. There was a solid chance that suspect would be charged and brought to court later in the day.

So Cass wasn't surprised as she approached the station to see one of the local journalists, Con Hart, waiting outside with a photographer.

What did surprise her was Hart nudging the photographer

who turned towards Cass, raised his camera, and started snapping.

'Kate, a quick word?'

'Why the hell are you taking photos of me?'

Hart nudged the photographer again, this time for him to cease, and beckoned Cass aside to speak privately.

She didn't know him particularly well, but he had a reputation as an accurate, fair-minded reporter who, because of his reliability, also doubled up as a stringer for the nationals. That ensured just enough credence to hear him out.

'I'm listening but not commenting. Got it?'

'Got it. I heard last night about the circumstances of the arrest: that you went up to Sarah Delahunty's farm alone. That you didn't notify your superiors and that it might have been in breach of procedure–'

What the absolute fuck? No leaks on the team until the moment the suspect is arrested, and then somebody makes a ham-fisted attempt to undermine the investigation?

'Gets your facts straight,' she replied. 'Speak to Kearney or Finnegan.'

'I've no interest in embarrassing you or your colleagues by asking about this in front of other journalists. And the lawyers can hammer out the finer points as to whether the arrest was valid or not.'

'Of course it was fucking valid,' Cass snapped.

'I don't doubt you. The way I see it, there's a much more interesting angle: Hero cop single-handedly disarms and captures suspect. I want to write *that* story, with a picture. The nationals will snap it up, and it will give you serious profile. So give me a couple of quotes and we're laughing.'

No thanks – that's the kind of profile that can kill a career. Colleagues looking at you suspiciously wondering whether you're a bandit – stealing credit from the team.

'No interest, sorry. This is a team investigation, a team effort. And it's ongoing.'

'You know I can write the piece anyway, with or without your cooperation.'

'Print some crap like that and I'm sure the people inside will think twice about cooperating with you in future.'

'I'm making a genuine offer here. My source wasn't half as willing to give you credit – wanted me to run a very different kind of story.'

'Tell me who your source was and I'll happily put them straight.'

She ended the discussion and entered the station, brooding on the fact she now clearly had an enemy within, Devine being the obvious candidate.

———

She made Finnegan aware of the journalist's proposed angle, just to ensure there would be no surprises at the media briefing. Finnegan was suitably pissed about the leak, and Cass knew she would pursue it. She also knew it would almost certainly be an exercise in futility, once one counted the sheer number of people on-site the previous day, any of whom could have spoken to Con Hart. Finnegan inquired a little less gruffly about her welfare; Cass told her she was fine – again – and went back to her desk. Where, an hour later, she got her second surprise of the day: a phone call from Maisah Sahraoui.

'I am glad you caught the gentleman's murderer.'

'We have a person in custody, Maisah, that's all. Nobody's been convicted of anything yet.'

'But it is important for the community, no? When one of your own people is murdered?'

It didn't take a genius to see what Maisah was insinuating, and Cass didn't like it.

'I'm not quite sure what you mean by "your own people", Maisah. If you mean "Irish", let me assure you we make no distinction between victims – every case is a priority.'

'Yes, but the murder of a white Irish gentleman must be solved. There is no question about this. People care about him. But not as much for Nabila.'

If you only knew how few people cared for him.

'That's not the case, Maisah.'

'White Irish gentleman – case solved in no time. African refugee woman – more than one year – nothing.'

'I understand your pain, Maisah, and I understand your frustration. But not every case is the same. Some take longer to solve. It's not for want of effort. Everyone here – all of my colleagues – want to find the person who did this to Nabila.'

'I want to believe that this is true.'

This was the point to avoid guarantees at all cost. It would only hurt more if the investigation progressed no further. Cass knew better than to give one...

But she also had no intention of failing Nabila Fathi.

'I'll show you it is true, Maisah.'

CHAPTER THIRTY-FOUR

A week of arrivals and departures followed. The first to come was a seasonal bout of snow – the thinnest of coatings but enough to give the children some fun and cause a handful of minor traffic mishaps. Peter Bannon departed to Cork Prison, to remain in custody until his trial. Sarah Delahunty – much to Cass's relief – arrived home, the Director of Public Prosecutions deciding there was neither sufficient evidence nor any public interest in bringing her to trial. Cass made a ham-fisted attempt to thank Finnegan but should have known better. Finnegan dismissed her with a curt, 'We submitted facts, not feelings. The DPP took their own decision.'

The curtness was mild compared to the fury which Finnegan unleashed on the team over the leak. She thundered about the treachery of someone giving the media sensitive information that could have undermined the investigation. She made clear she had it on excellent authority – which sounded a lot like the journalist himself – that the source of the leak came from within the station. And she stressed that if it reoccurred, she would summon the force's newly established anti-corruption unit from HQ to root out the guilty party.

Nobody came forward to confess; but there were no more leaks in the days that followed.

There was one further arrival towards the end of the week: the CCTV footage which Cass had requested from Dublin City Council.

————

As she queued the footage, it occurred to her that the Currency Comptroller was within walking distance of the national parliament. Like most rural politicians, Harbour Murphy spent three days of every week in Dublin attending the Dáil. She figured that, unlike some parliamentarians who opted for hotel stays, Harbour Murphy probably owned a place in the capital – which would give him a fair amount of privacy.

Someone had been waiting for Nabila to emerge from the Currency Comptroller the last day she was known to be alive – Cass was certain of it.

Harbour Murphy could easily have been in Dublin for official reasons the same day.

Her profound dislike of him aside, did she really think he was capable of being involved in something so nefarious that it had led to murder?

Old instincts slowly returning.

What were her instincts telling her now?

That he was an asshole, with an invisible hand in all sorts of schemes and scams.

But she couldn't see him for the murderer, or even the orchestrator of it.

————

Within twenty minutes, she knew for sure. It wasn't Harbour Murphy: it was someone new, unknown.

Cass couldn't help reflect on how much easier the search would have been if the force had blanket, rather than partial, CCTV across the country.

Under law, the force could establish CCTV schemes in new areas for the detection of crime only, not mass surveillance. This was the government's idea of a joke: the force didn't have the resources for mass surveillance even if it wanted it, which it didn't. What it did want was good coverage. What it had was CCTV in the main cities and some – but not all – of the bigger towns. Even in the cities, the CCTV wasn't all-pervasive – it was confined to certain areas. If the CCTV network had covered every street, Cass would have had relevant footage much quicker.

And would have been staring at the face of the suspect much sooner, because the city council CCTV footage showed exactly what Cass had been seeking: Nabila Fathi running up George's Dock and turning left onto Common Street before sitting into a small red car parked next to a vacant lot. The licence plate was clearly visible.

And so was the driver.

————

I've got this bastard now.

Cass ran a licence plate check and fed the image of the driver into the facial recognition system to determine if he had priors or was a suspect in any other crimes.

Nabila Fathi tried to exchange damaged banknotes in the Currency Comptroller, probably at this guy's behest, possibly in return for a promised fee or possibly under threat.

The facial recognition system produced no match. But the licence plate database returned a hit.

It went wrong in the Currency Comptroller when Nabila was asked to identify herself and account for the origins of the money.

The car was a Toyota Yaris, eighteen years old. The plate was genuine, which didn't surprise her, because any half-enterprising criminal knew the Garda Traffic Corps used an automated number plate recognition system which ran plates against the database and detected false ones. Rather than help evade detection, a false plate increased the risk of it.

In fright, Nabila gave a false name but her real address – possibly thinking that if she left the money behind for the Comptroller to process, a genuine address would be the only way of getting it back. Or maybe it was just a mistake borne from anxiety.

The Toyota was registered to one Charles Desmond, with an address in Boyne, County Meath. Cass didn't need to obtain a picture of Charles Desmond to know he was not the man behind the wheel of the car.

Nabila was spooked when she returned to the car, and that in turn spooked the driver, particularly when he realised she had given her real address. If any inquiries ensued, the authorities would have the means to trace Nabila – and then trace him.

According to his date of birth, Desmond was seventy-two years of age.

So he decided to kill her, not in Dublin, but in more familiar territory – Glencale. Where he knew somewhere isolated to ditch her body.

The driver of the car was at least a couple of decades younger and olive-skinned – Cass guessed of Middle Eastern or North African descent. He had a neatly trimmed beard which slightly aged an otherwise cherubic, trustworthy face. The average person might have said this was not the face of a killer. Neither Cass nor any of her colleagues would make any such predictions, knowing how little appearances counted for anything.

The killer was smart enough to take her phone, to erase any messages between them. But he never searched her bag – possibly too jumpy by that point to worry about anything other than the phone and fleeing the crime scene – and that was his mistake.

A fellow asylum-seeker surely, Cass thought – that must have been the connection with Nabila. If he had arrived at an Irish port or airport and sought asylum, he would have been registered by her colleagues in the Garda National Immigration Bureau – with details such as name, date of birth, marital status, address and – crucially, photograph and fingerprints – all collected. The fingerprints in turn would have been fed into Eurodac, the EU's biometric database containing fingerprints of all asylum applicants over the age of fourteen. She fed the photo into the relevant database and ran another search. She felt certain it would yield another hit.

It didn't.

So all she could say with certainty right now was that the driver was not Charles Desmond (nor, for that matter, Harbour Murphy), that the licence plate was genuine, and that the car had not been reported stolen. Enough, still, to give her a number of threads to pull.

It's supposition but I'm along the right track. Either this guy killed Nabila, or there was another party involved – an orchestrator, a ringleader – who did it.

She would also run the Toyota through every piece of footage she could get her hands on. Could she build a record of the journey the driver and Nabila took that day, through motorway CCTV and toll records and similar data? And more recently, had the car been seen around Glencale? Did, say, staff in any of the petrol stations recognise it? Had it been in for servicing at any mechanics?

More pertinently, did anybody in town recognise the driver?

I've got this bastard now. Just one final push, and I've got him.

CHAPTER THIRTY-FIVE

Cass pulled the first thread, ensuring an unpleasant surprise for Charles Desmond, the seventy-two-year-old churchgoing widower of Boyne, County Meath, who wasn't used to getting official phone calls from members of An Garda Síochána.

Yes, the Toyota had once been his, but he was no longer the owner because he had sold it, signing all the necessary paperwork.

Sold it to who?

Well, the Toyota had failed the National Car Test and, because of its age and low residual value, Charles Desmond felt it wasn't worth the investment to remedy the problems. He'd been preparing to bring it to a scrapyard when he saw one of those "cash for cars" posters around town. He rang the number on the poster and the cash-for-cars people couldn't have been nicer or more professional. They arrived in a tow truck, asked Charles to sign some paperwork in the relevant places, gave him a one-pager in return confirming that the vehicle would be scrapped for parts, and gave him 300 euro in cash. No waiting around for a cheque to clear. So, you see, he was no longer the legal owner…

Until Cass informed him that in fact he was, and that the cash-for-cars people had probably been running a scam, selling unroadworthy cars like Charles' Toyota for quick profit to people who couldn't afford anything better and didn't ask too many questions about provenance.

'But, but, but,' spluttered Charles, 'they gave me a form.'

'Yes,' Cass said, 'please do search for it, and if you can find it – and the mobile number you originally rang – contact me asap with the details.'

Charles Desmond would, no doubt, have diligently retained the paperwork. But it would be a dead end for sure. The form would have been faked, the mobile number long since out of service, the fraudsters untraceable for all intents and purposes. She was not going to locate her suspect this way.

So time to go another route.

———

'Is this him?' Maisah asked.

Cass had contacted her in advance to say she would be sending through a photo and would be grateful for Maisah's help in identifying the person.

'He knew Nabila and we think he can help us with our inquiries. That's all right now. So – do you recognise him?'

Maisah studied the photo in silence for a few moments. But when she answered, it was categorical. 'No, I do not know him. You do not have his name?'

'We're working on it.'

'I will show this picture to my friends, to Nabila's friends. Maybe one of us recognises him for you.'

Cass knew she should retain control of the search, ensure it was handled in the correct way. But she also saw Maisah would reach relevant people much more quickly than she could.

'Okay, but no posting the image on social media or anything like that. And you tell your friends the same, you understand?'

Maisah confirmed that she did.

———

Cass then left the station, having lined up two specific meetings. She had to drive a distance to the first one: Harbour Murphy was doing a constituency clinic in one of the neighbouring towns and had begrudgingly consented to make time for her, but only if she came to him. She was happy to. Unlike Maisah, whom she trusted, Cass didn't want to send the politician the photo. Nor did she wish to speak to him about the matter by phone. She wanted to witness his reaction to the photo, because it was sure to be telling one way or the other.

The venue for the constituency clinic was a small, drab community hall – a secretary was sitting at a folding table near the entrance, registering those who came in, taking initial details of their query, and asking them to take one of the stacking chairs laid out in a row alongside the wall until the great man was free. At the opposite end of the hall stood a makeshift office – a couple of curtain screens erected to give an illusion of privacy around another folding table and chairs. From here, Harbour Murphy held court and presumably solved all manner of local ailments and disputes.

The secretary, young and friendly, welcomed Cass and told her the politician was just finishing with a constituent. After ten minutes of waiting, Cass's patience was wearing thin and she was giving the secretary venomous looks.

'I'm sorry,' the secretary said, 'but he does insist we never disturb him when he's with someone.'

'It's extremely urgent,' Cass replied, 'so I'd appreciate if you could interrupt him and tell him it can't wait. Now.'

Reluctantly, the secretary rose and walked to the far end of the hall, disappearing behind the screens. There was just enough distance to ensure discussions in the makeshift office couldn't be made out distinctly. When the secretary re-emerged, she walked briskly back to Cass and said: 'He's almost done.'

He fucking will be when I'm through with him, the arrogant prick.

The noise of chairs scraping on the floor signalled the meeting was finally over, and Murphy appeared, arm around an elderly constituent, providing assurance on some matter. As the constituent left, Murphy ostentatiously turned to the handful of people in the queue and said: 'Would you mind if I spoke with Officer Cassidy first? She tells me she has *extremely* urgent business to attend to.'

There were murmurs of assent, and then Murphy beckoned Cass behind the screens. 'I'm sorry to delay you. But you know how it is.'

'Every vote counts, I'm sure.'

'You know the old saying about constituency clinics? A third of people want you to do something impossible, a third want you to do something illegal, and the rest are just fucking lonely.'

He guffawed at his own joke. Cass ignored it and passed a copy of the CCTV image across the desk.

'Do you recognise this man?'

'Should I? What's he got to do with anything?'

'Nabila Fathi. We believe this man can help us with our inquiries.'

'You think this is the bastard who killed her?'

'I didn't say that. Do you recognise him?'

He, too, looked long and hard at the photo, just as Maisah had appeared to on the earlier phone call with Cass. But it produced the same result – Harbour Murphy shook his head and said: 'Doesn't ring a bell.'

She had been scrutinising him for any tell-tale flicker of recognition or hesitancy. There was none.

Time to accept the inevitable, she thought. *He's an arrogant, conniving, selfish bollocks but there's not a shred of evidence to suggest he's connected with any of this.*

'Why did you think I might have known him?'

'Two reasons. I thought perhaps he'd been into your shop to see Nabila. And more generally, I thought if anybody in town would recognise a face, it would be you.'

'Can I keep this and show it around? Maybe my staff might remember him.'

'Not right now. I'll take care of your staff. But if you think of anything…'

'That poor girl. I hope to Christ this is a breakthrough. Anything I can do to help – anything at all…'

Harbour Murphy, the privately educated son of a millionaire farmer, all these years deliberately adopting a thick country accent and a cute-hoor shtick to give the locals the impression he was one of their own.

Well, he *was* a cute hoor, adding millions to the family wealth at his constituents' expense.

But the funny thing was, behind the contrived accent, Cass felt he was actually being genuine for once.

———

Her second stop was the direct provision centre back in Glencale. Because the suspect was not on the database of asylum-seekers, it meant he was unlikely to have resided in the centre. Still, it was surely plausible that he had visited the centre or was known to people there. Hence, she spent a couple of hours showing the suspect's photo to residents and staff. It proved another futile exercise.

Her third and final destination for the day was Harbour Murphy's supermarket, where she asked the staff if they recognised the man in the picture. Once again, a dead end.

Back at the station, Cass felt a touch deflated, if not yet

defeated. There were further avenues to pursue, and she knew better than to expect instant results, but still, just when a result had seemed so close...

She called a halt shortly after six – early by her standards – and went home to change, as she had agreed to call to Brady's place later that evening. The fact that Sarah Delahunty was where she belonged – at home with her family – meant Cass was much more comfortable about the prospect of passing her farm.

She was taking a quick shower when her mobile rang. Rang again, and rang a third time.

It was Maisah, and she had some news.

CHAPTER THIRTY-SIX

As a rule, Brady tried to be judicious in his questions about Cass's job, so as to avoid raising any suspicions. So when she rang to cancel, he didn't pry.

'Something's come up at work,' she said, offering no further explanation.

'Tomorrow night instead?'

'I'll let you know.'

Short and to the point. They did their best talking in the dark, after first exhausting each other physically – and it suited him fine. Her too, he thought. More transactional than a commitment.

Now he had the evening unexpectedly free. Back in the States, he would have called some of the guys, gone for a few beers, seen if he could find enticing trouble.

But he had been scrupulous in doing the opposite since arriving in Ireland. So no trip into the town tonight, no entertainment, just himself and his ghosts. And another long yawning chasm of exhaustion until daybreak when he could finally sleep...

Better off staying in the void.

She's a risk to me.

A risk I'll have to mitigate if things go wrong.

So why am I disappointed not to be seeing her?

Which, he suddenly realised, was entirely the wrong question to ask.

Why had she actually cancelled? What was the 'something' that had come up at work?

He'd learned in their short time together that she didn't talk about any aspect of live police business – she'd only discussed the Bridge Bannon case with him once satisfied that Peter Bannon was in custody and about to be charged. So even if he'd asked, she wouldn't have told him.

But what if he was the 'something'?

Is that why she couldn't visit?

Has she unearthed something?

Is she onto me?

Have I entrenched my enemy at the heart of my terrain?

Transactional? This is a fucking trapeze act.

High-wire insanity.

But maybe that was the point, he thought. His fragile mind, his obsessional mind, the lust for settlement, the willingness to kill, the desire to kill, the decision to run new, avoidable risk.

Maybe I am just insane. But nobody is locking me up. They can come for me but they'll never corner me.

CHAPTER THIRTY-SEVEN

Maisah had gold for Cass: a name, and a last-known address. Maisah had shared the suspect's photograph with everyone she could think of, and one of her friends had eventually responded in the positive: yes, she knew this person, and yes, she had an idea where he could be found. And how did she know him? She was Libyan, had been based in Glencale while awaiting a decision on her asylum application, and had been approached by the suspect, a fellow Libyan, to help him exchange some banknotes. She had said no... and as a result, was still alive.

A name: Akeem Issa. An address: an old farmhouse a couple of miles north of the town.

We're coming for you, Akeem.

And when we catch you–

God give me the strength not to wring your fucking neck.

But first things first: procedure and basic fact-checking. A search of all relevant databases for the suspect, now that she had a name. A search of the property register for the owner of the farmhouse.

Akeem Issa was not known to the Guards or the border authorities, and didn't have a passport or public identity number registered in his name. So, it was either a false identity or he had arrived illegally in Europe and, from there, to Ireland.

The property search showed the farmhouse, known as Muckanish House, was owned by a married couple with a London address. They weren't registered as landlords, so perhaps Issa was squatting on the property. Either way, that could be ascertained later. Over a late call that night, she discussed it with Finnegan, and they swiftly agreed the core facts: Issa was suspected of an arrestable offence, could be present on the property, and was possibly armed. No need to wait for a warrant. As soon as dawn broke, they would be good to go.

———

Preservation of life wasn't the immediate priority one would associate with the armed support unit, Cass thought the following morning, as she watched them run through their final checks.

Among the weapons carried by the unit members were the Heckler & Koch MP7 submachine gun – capable of penetrating multiple layers of Kevlar from 200 metres – and the Sig Sauer P226, the official sidearm used by the US Navy Seals.

But preservation of life was indeed the unit's number one objective – protecting their unarmed colleagues in high-risk operations, and seeking to de-escalate violent situations while minimising risk to civilian life. In recognition of the broad range of emergencies they found themselves responding to, they carried less lethal weapons too, such as tasers, and each member was trained as an emergency first responder.

After Cass's unexpected and potentially fatal run-in with Peter Bannon, Finnegan wasn't taking any chances. The armed support unit would be on hand, ready to escalate or de-escalate as appropriate – the rest would depend on the suspect.

'Safety first, speed second,' Finnegan had ordered a short time earlier. 'We believe this individual has killed at least once. We've got no line of sight on what weapons he may have in his possession. So no one moves until we're ready to move, and we make damn sure none of us gets hurt.'

Cass would have liked a weapon too, her baton and pepper spray seeming incredibly insufficient for what they were about to undertake. Maybe Brady was getting into her head with his locked-and-loaded bullshit. Akeem Issa didn't look particularly threatening or thuggish in the images they had of him, but Cass had no doubt he had murdered Nabila Fathi. And not out of sudden, uncontrollable rage, but in a calm, premeditated way, which made him considerably more dangerous.

As they departed the station in convoy, she felt edgy. It wasn't from the memory of Peter Bannon's attack, for she had refused to linger on it. It was simply the standard feeling when embarking on any potentially treacherous operation. She'd done a tonne of them during her years in Dublin – drug raids mostly – and the feeling at the outset was always the same. A metallic taste of fear; never knowing who, or what, was behind the door. Knowing from the litany of colleagues' experiences the number of things that could go wrong, sometimes catastrophically so. Having no other choice but to trust that her training would get her – and the team – through it unscathed.

It didn't pay to be imaginative in this line of work.

———

But intuition, on the other hand…

She knew on first sight the raid would be a bust. Muckanish House stood on about three acres, bounded in the distance by a wall of sitka spruce forestry to the rear.

The foul smell and brown streaks of a dribble bar told them that slurry had been spread on the land in recent days. But the farmhouse, by contrast, smacked of disuse. A squashed, low-ceilinged, whitewashed affair, it was old, dilapidated and overgrown. Planks had been hammered across the doors and windows in lieu of the smashed glass. A handful of tiles were missing from the roof, no doubt the casualties of winter. A small shed made of timber and corrugated iron was listing to one side. They took nothing for granted, completing thorough reconnaissance before executing their approach. But once they moved, it took mere minutes to confirm what a glance had already told her: nobody home.

The armed support unit was stood down while the local team worked diligently for a further hour picking through the house and shed and bagging what they could as potential forensic evidence. The shed was empty bar a rusting bucket and a few empty, tattered, animal feed bags.

The inside of the house was in better shape than outward appearances suggested: although damp and mould had spread, the walls and floorboards were structurally intact; the kitchen had an old cooker and fridge which still looked usable had the electricity been running; there was a wood stove in the small living room, and beside it, a stack of logs covered in cobwebs.

Upstairs, two small bedrooms, one of which had a filthy, water-stained mattress in a corner; and a bathroom, in which the taps still ran in the cracked sink. Not remotely comfortable, but habitable if you were an illegal immigrant in need of a place to squat, she thought.

The odd thing was, apart from the mattress and the timber logs, there wasn't a sign otherwise of someone spending time here. No rotting leftovers in the fridge, no sign of a jar of coffee or tinned foods, no towels or toilet paper, no sheets or blankets. Still, they'd check the obvious places for prints – the fridge door, stove and toilet handles – and run what tests they could on the mattress.

But it was a minimal yield. If Akeem Issa had been here, he was long since gone, and his car too. As she exited the house and removed her gloves and shoe covers, she exhaled in frustration, the edginess long since gone and replaced by profound disappointment.

There were just four of them left on-site: herself; Devine and Noel Ryan, who were packing the last of the gear into one car; and Bruton, a new recruit at the station, who had decided to walk the perimeter to conduct one final check and was due to drive back in the other car with Cass.

Devine heard her approach, turned, and began clapping slowly. 'Good job. Complete fucking waste of manpower and money.'

'Somewhere else you'd prefer to be, Devine? Back at the school maybe?'

His face contorted in anger. 'No wonder your husband went off the rails, married to a bitch like you.'

She started towards him, ready to swing, only for Ryan to step between them. 'Cop the fuck on, the pair of ye. Concentrate on your jobs, for fuck's sake.'

Cass stood her ground. Devine stepped back, raised his hands in mock concession, and sniggered again. 'Good man, Noel, keep that one in line. She needs a bit of handling.'

It took a superhuman effort not to take the bait. She thought longingly of the tasers carried by the armed support members, and wished she had one now. She'd willingly shoot fifty thousand volts into Devine. She'd aim low, too, for extra satisfaction.

As Devine got into the car and started it, Ryan said – loud enough for him to hear – 'Never mind that ignorant fucker.'

'I've better things to spend my time thinking about,' Cass replied.

But Devine had struck a nerve: the operation had produced

nothing. That was her abiding thought as she stuffed the last of her own gear into the boot, and slammed it shut.

Which was when she heard Bruton shouting in the distance. The new recruit was racing across the slurried field, oblivious in his excitement to the splatters of shit on his uniform.

He'd found the car.

CHAPTER THIRTY-EIGHT

The slurry-spreader turned up at the station the following morning decidedly worse for wear. Wally White had been at a wedding the night before, he explained apologetically to Cass, which explained in turn his hangover and failure to return voice messages until a short time earlier. Cass had seen him arrive at the station in a hideous, red, seven-year-old BMW which, even if bought second-hand, must have still cost a fair packet for someone in his mid-twenties.

He'd been dumb enough to drive, despite clearly having drink in his system. And the stupidity wasn't a one-off: Cass had seen his record – separate prosecutions for dangerous driving and possession of a small quantity of cannabis, escaping with fines both times. She decided to make him aware he was on perilous ground before pursuing his relationship with Akeem Issa.

'You didn't notice the missed calls last night, Wally?'

'Sure, the wedding – the music was loud, like, and I was trying to enjoy myself.'

'Whose wedding was it?'

'Nathan Broderick – one of the lads from school.'

'And you had a few drinks?'

'A few pints, yeah, and a few rounds – you know the way.'

'You still under the influence now, Wally?'

'God no,' he said, squirming as if his foolishness had only occurred to him. 'Had the big fry-up for breakfast. And pints of coffee.'

'You'd pass a breathalyser then for us, would you?'

Strike one. He looked queasy now, and Cass knew he wouldn't be putting up much resistance.

'Tell you what, let's leave that aside for now. Tell us about Akeem Issa – how did you first meet him?'

'I needed a few lads to do a few days' work for me – Aki was one of them.'

'Aki – not Akeem?'

'That's what I knew him as.'

'And you hired him as casual labour?'

'Yeah, stuff you'd need a few bodies for.'

'How?'

'Whatcha mean?'

'How did you first meet him, get connected to him?'

'A mate who works the boats knew a few lads always looking for a bit of work. Aki was one of them.'

'How did you contact him?'

'I got a mobile for him.'

'Still have it?'

Wally flicked through his phone and called out a number. Cass recognised it as the number which Nabila Fathi had dialled several times in the run-up to and on the likely day of her death. She also knew the phone was a dead end, long since out of service, with no registered owner. None of which she'd be telling the idiot sitting across from her.

'And all this was when exactly?'

'Dunno – maybe a year ago, maybe a bit more.'

'You'd have records you could check though, right? Payslips and the like?'

Strike two.

'Well,' he stammered, 'it was casual labour, like, just a few odd jobs, so I paid the lads a day's rate. A good day's rate – fair, like.'

'In cash, you mean?'

'Yeah.'

'I'm not sure Revenue would be too impressed to hear that, Wally.'

'I'm behind a bit at the moment, but I'll sort it all.'

'What caused you to fall behind?'

'The farm's a fucking bitc–' He stopped and corrected himself. 'The farm's hard going. Should walk away from it and get a proper job.'

'You inherited it from your father?'

'Yeah.'

'But Muckanish House and the land around it – that's not yours?'

'I lease that.'

'But that's all in cash too, right?'

Cass knew as much already, having spoken to the London couple who owned the property and who reluctantly admitted they weren't registered as landlords because they had never declared the money. Cass had often thought the size of the black economy in rural Ireland was seriously underestimated, and this one small chain of events was reinforcing her view.

'Yeah.'

'You're a great man for the books, Wally.'

'Always struggled with 'em in school.'

'What was the deal with Akeem – Aki?'

'He did a week's work for me and then asked if I knew anywhere cheap he could stay. We struck a deal – he'd do a bit more work for me for free – a couple of days a week – and could have Muckanish as a roof over his head.'

'So you got free labour and he got a shithole to sleep in?'

'He was glad of it. He'd been sleeping in his car, like.'

'Still though. Worked out grand for you.'

'I'm smashed,' he said, a forlorn note in his voice. 'Between the farm, the fucking crypto thing I did, and the horses. Can barely keep up the payments on my car.'

Cass had to suppress the urge to laugh. Wally looked broken but she couldn't find a trace of sympathy for him. Crypto and the bookies, for fuck's sake. And then trying to take advantage of others to make up for his financial misadventures.

'When did the arrangement start?'

'Like I said, the week after I met him. About a year ago, something like that.'

'And when did it stop?'

'It didn't. He just took off.'

'When?'

'A few months ago. He was there for the shearing – fucking handy too, he was – that was in May. And then the hay at the end of July. So some time after that – about August, I'd say.'

'Did he tell you he was leaving?'

'Not a word. Just took off.'

'When did you last speak to him?'

'Can't remember – when we were finishing the hay, I suppose.'

'You didn't try ringing him when he left?'

'Sure, the house was empty. Completely cleaned out. I just reckoned he'd moved on, like.'

'Was he in any trouble that you were aware of? Anything he was running from?'

'Nothing – honest.'

'And you never had any trouble with him? The two of you never argued, fought?'

'Christ no – not at all.'

'But I'm sure you'd tell us if you knew anything important, right?'

'For sure. One hundred per cent, like. What did he do anyway?'

'We think he can help us with a case we're investigating. We'd like to speak to him.'

'The mobile maybe–'

'Yes, we'll try that. How come you didn't report the car?'

'The car?'

'The car was abandoned and burned out in the forestry behind Muckanish. Why didn't you report it?'

'I never saw it,' he said. 'Swear to God – on my mother's life – didn't even realise the car was there.'

Even though the forestry was quite thin, she was inclined to believe him, for three reasons. Firstly, Akeem had made a decent job of hiding the car, driving it into a clearing that offered good cover from most angles. Secondly, no one around here gave smoke plumes in the fields and mountains a second thought – some farmer was always burning something, whether it was gorse or other green waste. Thirdly, it was clear to her that Wally wouldn't have given the forest a second thought whenever he was at Muckanish, because the forestry was not part of the lease. Cute enough to look after his own interests, but utterly oblivious to the wider world around him. So she could accept his ignorance about the car. But there was something odd about it – the dumping of it, the timing – that she couldn't quite put her finger on.

The hypothesis was that Akeem Issa had, for whatever reason, decided to flee Glencale, and knowing the car was a forensic risk, burnt it out. Perhaps he had some reason to believe the police were about to catch up with him, although from Cass's review of the case file, she couldn't imagine what that could have been, given he hadn't been on the radar of the original investigation team.

Additionally, Nabila had been killed in December and her body found in March. Yet if Wally was correct, Issa was still in

Glencale in August. Why had he been seemingly relaxed enough to stay in Glencale immediately after Nabila's murder, and again after her body had been found and the investigation launched, only to get rattled suddenly in August? There was nothing in the case file – absolutely nothing – to indicate anything of importance happening in the investigation that month.

Then again, perhaps Issa had been supremely confident that he had got away with murder, made his own decision to move on from Glencale, and simply abandoned the car where it was most convenient to do so, with no witnesses and as little forensic evidence as possible. Maybe it was that simple.

But she knew she was making one of the oldest mistakes in the book: assuming that a murderer acted logically at all times and looking for consistent reasoning. Erratic behaviour was much more likely in a case like this. So maybe there was no good explanation for Issa's behaviour other than – for whatever reason – he had decided to leave.

But how to find him now?

And it was then she wondered if he was even still in Ireland. He'd found his way into the country illegally – what if he had exited the country in the same way? She'd be chasing a ghost.

———

She was still at her desk a little after 8pm, double-checking that they had initiated all possible search avenues, when Brady rang. Cass hadn't given him a second thought all day, but was pleased nonetheless to see his name flash up.

'Burger and a beer?' he said.

'That's what I like about you – your foreplay.'

'I know what a working girl needs.'

'I think you'll find that's pejorative.'

'I think I need a dictionary to keep up with you.'

'You need more than a dictionary, my friend.'

'I'm in town – I'll pick you up.'

'In your banger fit for a prince.'

'Banger?'

'Irish term – never mind,' she said.

She wondered, briefly, whether she should stay at work. But the forensics on the car, even though being rushed to the top of the list, wouldn't be available until the following day, and didn't offer good prospects in any event. And she was certain that she and the team had triggered all the correct actions to try and locate the suspect.

Maybe a couple of drinks would help trigger some unconventional step she could take.

'Give me fifteen minutes to change.'

CHAPTER THIRTY-NINE

In the final years of her marriage, Cass had barely touched alcohol. It was hard not to think of that time now as she savoured a third glass of wine, knowing the man across the table would consume nothing more than a non-alcoholic beer, retain full control of his faculties, and look after her if the need arose. Not that it would. Cass couldn't remember the last time *she* had lost control, and wasn't going to start now. But still, it was comforting to think she maybe could, if she wished.

————

She insisted on his place when they finished their food, and so, he sat behind the wheel of his 'banger' – she'd eventually explained what it meant – and drove them out of Glencale, towards his temporary home.

He was glad he had reached out to her earlier – not least because it put an end to his own anxiety as to why she had cancelled on him two nights previously and what she'd been up to in the interim.

He now knew she had simply been working a case –

nothing she would discuss with him, but clearly nothing to do with him either. His worries had been overplayed; his temporary home could remain home for a while longer. He drove contented in that knowledge. Cass, too, seemed contented. They had, he thought, reached this stage at astonishing speed, and if pushed to explain why, he wasn't sure he'd have an answer.

————

She had never been one for drifting off to sleep in someone's warm embrace. She didn't need to be held after sex, preferring her own side of the bed, unencumbered by unnecessary contact. Brady had been around the block enough to get this instantly.

Still, she found herself touched that, despite the fact he never slept at night, he would wait for her to drift off before he rose from the bed. There was something sweet in the gesture from a man who, in different circumstances, would be capable of lethal violence.

She didn't know what to make of his irregular sleeping habit: she sensed he had witnessed – or suffered – greater trauma in his military career than he had so far been prepared to detail. She doubted whether he actually got sufficient sleep in the mornings to make up for the loss at nights. The constant shadow under his eyes was a giveaway in that respect. And yet he functioned, and he endured. A part of her yearned to help him, but she hadn't been able to help Hugh, and didn't know where to start with Brady.

————

He didn't want her – didn't want anybody – to witness the effects. Roaring himself awake from the nightmare, momentarily petrified by the dark, sensing the steel-wool-like scraping of the hood against his face, tasting the bile and vomit in his mouth, hearing the crack of the gun.

Or waking in silent tears, tortured in a different way, because Pitch had come to him in his sleep, pleading for help to be rescued from Hades.

There was no chance Brady would allow Cass to hear his screams or see his tears. It was his agony to deal with, and his alone, no matter their companionable silences, their frenzied coupling, the sense that beneath their casual fling, something deeper was forming. Perhaps because they were both suffering, even if they worked not to show it. He feared the night, when sleep would unleash a flood of subconscious horrors.

Whereas her nightmares came during the day, when a random sight or sound could trigger shaming memories of the devastation wreaked by her husband.

Day or night, peace was an abstract concept for both of them.

———

A distant alarm, a spectre, somewhere in the recess of her mind. Hard to reach, to comprehend, but persistent; an omen. A ticking clock, counting down to catastrophe. No, not a clock. A bell. The fucking bell, swinging softly in the wind again and sounding its ominous warning.

She woke with a start, her heart pounding. No bell, because there wasn't one. She closed her eyes and took a moment to settle herself, taking deep and steady breaths. And then realised, to her absolute astonishment, she could actually hear something else, something closer and decidedly less supernatural: the gentle and steady breathing of Brady, lying next to her, solidly asleep.

CHAPTER FORTY

She lay still for a few minutes, not wanting to wake him. The bell she had already dismissed to the back of her mind; instead, she felt oddly settled, as if someone somehow had applied salve to the raw and twisted knot she'd been carrying around in her stomach for so long. She found herself smiling at the syncopated beat of his sleep – each bar of gentle breathing interrupted by the off-beat of a single snore. It felt as if, after a long winter in which she had feared the freezing sea, she had finally plucked up the courage to plunge in again and surprised herself by how quickly her body and mind adjusted. Equilibrium, or something like it.

She sensed it was close to daybreak, and satisfied that he was still out cold, risked reaching for her phone on the bedside table to check the time: 5.45am, which might as well have been midnight in the tundra for all the light on offer. The room was pitch black, and in the Loop's winter solitude, there would be no hint of daybreak for another couple of hours yet.

Cass slipped out of bed, pulled on his T-shirt, and padded as silently as she could across the wooden floor, gently pulling out the door behind her. Now, she could safely flick on the torch function on her phone, slip across the balcony and down the stairs.

It was a misnomer to think the countryside offered true silence at night: the metallic bark of a fallow deer or curse-like scream of a fox was enough to send a shiver down the spine of anyone unfamiliar with the orchestral range of rural life. But Brady, she knew, would be hardwired to be alert for human threats: a creaking floorboard, wheels on gravel, the tinkle of smashing glass. Hence, she took care on the stairs to minimise creaks. When she got to the ground floor, she heard nothing but silence from the balcony.

She felt like coffee but knew the machine would be too loud. There was a distinct chill in the air – Brady had an oil-fired heating system but, rather than use the timer, simply clicked it on whenever he wanted heat. Much like the coffee, turning it on wasn't an option, as the system produced a loud initial clanking when powering up that would wake him for sure. So she grabbed a herringbone throw from the sofa and went to the chair where Brady usually sat at night, staring out at the trees beyond, perhaps waiting for his own shadow, his own spectre – whatever it was that haunted his dreams – to emerge.

After a few moments, she ditched the amateur psychology and switched her thoughts to Nabila Fathi, and the missing Libyan. Was there, she wondered, the slightest chance that Akeem Issa was still in the country? The previous day, despondency had driven her to assume he was long since gone. But Nabila's murder very publicly remained unsolved; might he just have moved to another region of the country, reducing the risk to himself while satisfied that he was unlikely to be caught?

Once more, she went over every step they had taken to trace him, and asked herself what more they could do. Nothing sprang to mind, and to counteract her frustration, she started from scratch, asking herself what she would do if suddenly new to this case. She would start with the file, read it from top to bottom, make her own notes, check to see if the original team had missed anything – just as she had done when Finnegan assigned her the case. So now, she tried to recreate the case file from memory – not word-for-word, given she wasn't, sadly, the possessor of a photographic memory – but simply the core facts and most salient details. Was there anything in those that could possibly hint at an alternative location, a hideout, for Issa?

After twenty minutes or so running the case over in her mind, she admitted defeat. In her recall, there was nothing to suggest Issa's current location. She gave an involuntary shiver and realised she was extremely cold; the thin throw was more stylish accessory than creature comfort. Even if she did crank on the heating system, it would take a good twenty minutes to warm up the place, and there still wasn't a murmur from the bedroom. A thick blanket would be a better bet, but she didn't want to risk the stairs again, and wondered if Brady kept a spare one in the chancel, the one part of the church she'd only seen from the doorway when he was giving her the guided tour.

That glimpse had been enough to know it was not a second bedroom, as she had originally assumed, but a storage place for him, where he kept spare clothes and furniture, tools and utensils, and various bric-a-brac. She found herself wondering idly whether they used the term 'bric-a-brac' in the States as she picked up her phone, flicked on the torch function again, and padded to the chancel, depressing the handle and pushing the door open as softly as she could.

She scanned the room with the torchlight for any sign of a blanket. There was none, but she spotted a long parka which would do just as well. It came down to her ankles, was too big at the sleeves, and cool to the touch when she slipped it on. Wonderfully, though, it began to work its magic almost immediately and she felt snug and comfortable.

Out of curiosity, she scanned her torch across the rest of the room and began to study some of the items in more detail. A small number of books, mostly on military tactics and strategy, a couple more on American sports – he hadn't struck her as a great reader. The boxes of spare clothes she had seen the first day, and on a bench, a toolbox, a hammer, and an array of power tools. On top of a washing machine, some detergent and other cleaning materials, including a bottle of bleach, which made her think of Peter Bannon and briefly shudder again, not at the memory of the attack on her, but of the brutality he had inflicted on his father.

She scanned again and saw a packed rucksack in one corner, presumably a holdover from his military days. Less IKEA catalogue in here, she thought: the random assortment of stuff spoke more truly to his personality, although still no photos or any other kind of obvious personal memento in sight. Still, who was she to talk, with her apartment of unpacked boxes? Perhaps his were all buried in the rucksack or one of the boxes, or sitting in his ex-wife's basement or shed back in the States. She turned towards the door and saw, on the back of it, a dartboard used for target practice. Not with darts evidently, but a large hunting knife, rammed into the centre of the board, holding a piece of paper in place.

And then she froze, equilibrium shattered, as if powerful hands were shoving her head under the water.

It wasn't a piece of paper.

It was a piece of pure cotton fibre, measuring one hundred and forty seven millimetres by seventy-seven millimetres, coloured predominantly in green and white hues.

A 100-euro banknote, with the familiar signs of damage, as if an animal had chewed the edges, or someone had burned it with a lighter.

Caused by a flooded vault and ham-fisted attempts to clean it.

With a sickening clarity, Cass suddenly saw it all, the bell ringing like crazy in her mind.

The money for the renovation of the church. The military

service in unspecified parts of the world. The many, many mysteries about his background.

Brady had been in Benghazi, and was the source of the notes, Issa his intermediary. Issa in turn had found his own intermediary – Nabila – only for things to go seriously wrong.

And Brady had killed them both to wash away all links to him.

CHAPTER FORTY-ONE

She stood, paralysed in fear, her legs feeling like they had been encased in concrete. Fight or flight: Peter Bannon hadn't given her a choice – his attack had been sudden, and her response had been instantaneous. But this was different: she *knew* she was in the presence of a killer – and a professional one at that.

Her own professional instincts were screaming at her to call for backup and run. Establish a perimeter and get the hell behind it. But there was no phone coverage here, she didn't have her radio, and she would need a car to get a safe distance, a car she didn't have, given Brady had driven the night before. If her flight options seemed limited, fight was a non-runner. Confronting him would be lunacy – she would be no match for his basic strength, to say nothing of his close combat skills. He would snap her neck in an instant. Her best option, her only one, was deception: pretend there was nothing wrong, hope her body would stop trembling and that her voice would hold steady.

She jumped at a sudden creak, her heart a ball of explosive threatening to blow a hole in her chest. She strained her ears but heard nothing further except for the rustle of trees outside.

It was all she could do not to dash for the front door and try to cover on foot the mile or two to the nearest property. Instead, she tried to steady her breathing and her nerves, steeling herself to execute the only way out.

One step at a time, and quietly as possible.

She checked to ensure her phone was on silent and switched off the torchlight, given the camera couldn't run while it was on. Then she stepped closer to the dartboard to take a picture of the banknote pinned to it. She turned on the flash, conscious of the risk she was running, and quickly snapped a shot. She cursed as the room lit up momentarily, as if a bolt of lightning had struck. She cursed again when she saw the poor quality of the photo, so she risked one more, with much the same result. She adjusted the settings on the phone, more in hope than conviction, and tried a final shot. The outcome was slightly better; it would do. For a moment, she considered removing the note for DNA purposes, but just as quickly discounted the idea, knowing it would alert Brady to the fact she was onto him. Safer to leave it where it was, and try to find something else with his DNA – something he would not notice missing or, if he did, attribute it to being lost.

Photo secured, she turned her thoughts to her next objective: a weapon, in case the worst materialised. She picked up the hammer from the bench and made to leave the room. Then, realising it would be inexplicable if he saw her holding it, she returned the hammer to its place. She selected a medium-length screwdriver instead, and slipped it into the deep right-hand pocket of the parka.

The parka was bulky and would be awkward to fight in, she knew. It would make sense to slip it off and be less restricted in her movements. But she would then have nowhere to hide her weapon, and besides, the coat offered some semblance of an excuse. A truthful one: she had been cold, she'd gone looking for a blanket, she'd found the parka.

She slipped back out of the room and towards the kitchen

counter, thankful that on the ground floor at least, Brady had installed tiles. Still no noise from the balcony, still no hint of daybreak. She left the torch off. A few moments ago, she had been cursing the unwanted illumination. Now she returned to cursing the darkness, but her eyes were beginning to adjust.

She knew what she needed: Brady kept a roll of freezer bags on a shelf. She still couldn't make out everything, so she put her hand out and moved it at a snail's pace across the items on the shelf, taking care not to knock anything, until she felt the roll of plastic. She peeled two of the bags from the roll as quietly as she could, and then went towards the sink, where Brady had left some of the utensils he had used the previous night. Using one bag as a makeshift glove, she picked up a fork Brady had used and placed it in the other.

She knew it was suboptimal: the force used paper bags as standard for the collection of such items, given that plastic could allow moisture to gather which would interfere with the sample. But like the photo of the banknote, the freezer bag would just have to suffice. She knew in any event there was little prospect this would amount to a legitimate taking of a sample, but she didn't care about that right now. She cared only about having confirmation. She popped the bag containing the fork into the left-hand pocket of the parka, then went to remove the makeshift glove from her right hand.

And that was precisely the point when the lights came on.

CHAPTER FORTY-TWO

C ass jumped with fright as she saw, reflected in the window over the sink, Brady on the balcony, stationary and staring intently at her. As she turned to face him, she stuffed the second plastic bag into the same left-hand pocket as the fork, while raising her right hand to her chest in an attempt at distraction.

'You startled me.'

He was wearing sweatpants and bare-chested, showing off the same impressively chiselled arms that, just a few hours earlier, had held her so gently in bed. Now, she thought they would be used to kill her unless she somehow managed to persuade him nothing was out of the ordinary. He remained impassive, his facial expression impenetrable except for his eyes: they had switched again, like that first day she'd spotted him, and it chilled her to the bone. Was his face the last thing Nabila had seen, Akeem Issa had seen?

'I couldn't sleep,' she said. 'Didn't want to wake you and thought there might be a blanket in the spare room. Found this instead – hope you don't mind.'

There's a quiver in my voice – can he hear it?

Can he sense my fear, smell it? He was trained to detect weakness, after all.

Is he standing there plotting how to kill me?

'It looks better on you than me,' Brady said at last, a tight smile forming. 'Come back to bed and you can take it off again.'

She put her right hand into the sleeve of the parka and felt the screwdriver. Touched the tip and told herself she would drive it into his ribs if necessary.

'I'd love nothing better, but I have to get to work early. Got a lot on.'

'I'll grab a shower and drive you.'

My nerves won't take this much longer. I have to escape.

'Maybe you want to try and get more sleep. Now that – you know – you managed a few hours already with no interruption. I could take your car and drop it back to you later?'

He didn't respond immediately, as if she'd presented him with a puzzle, the pieces of which he was trying to work through.

'I was totally knocked out,' he said eventually. 'First time in a long time.'

'I'm glad. You needed it. I hope it's the start of a better pattern for you.' *I hope to get the fuck out of here in the next few minutes.*

'You really won't come back to bed?'

'I wore you out last night. You need to get your energy back. And I need to get to work.'

That smile again, and a slight, almost imperceptible nod. An acceptance that she would leave? Or an assurance to himself that he had things figured out?

Despite the warmth of the parka, she was shaking.

'Okay, you know where the keys are... But you'd better come up for your clothes.'

He turned and walked back into the bedroom, out of Cass's view.

CHAPTER FORTY-THREE

Wild fucking horses wouldn't drag me upstairs and into that bedroom.

Beneath the parka, she wore only panties and his T-shirt. But Brady's car keys were on the kitchen table, her handbag was on one of the kitchen stools, and her boots were near the church door where she'd kicked them off the previous evening.

Get the fuck out of here while you're still breathing.

It would look bizarre fleeing like this. But then, she'd never have to explain it. She was only ever coming back to this house to arrest him for murder.

From her position, she could see the bedroom lights go out.

He was playing her at her own game – deception – and she wasn't going to fall for it. But she wondered what would happen when he heard her unlatch the door and run for the car...

No point second-guessing. Just have the screwdriver in hand and be prepared to use it.

Nerves ablaze, she grabbed the keys and her handbag, before locating her boots and pulling them on. Keys in one hand, screwdriver in the other, she opened the church door as gently as she could.

The only way he could have left the bedroom without me seeing him is through the window, and I would have heard the noise.

A sensor triggered as she opened the door, bathing her and the front of the church in light.

Sitting duck. Run, you stupid cow, run.

The distance to the car was less than forty yards but seemed like a mile.

Hard and fast with the screwdriver if he emerges from the shadows.

Aim for every soft spot on his body, and keep going.

Maim enough to subdue him...

Don't be a fool.

If he emerges from the shadows, I won't know until it's too late.

Even if by some miracle I see him coming, he wouldn't subdue.

My life or his.

Run, for fuck's sake, just run.

Cass launched into a sprint, simultaneously pressing the fob key to unlock the car. The crunch of gravel beneath her feet felt as loud as cymbals crashing, but to her eternal relief, she saw the familiar flash of hazard lights, confirming the car was open. It took her about six and a half seconds to cover the ground, glancing from side to side as she ran. The sensor light went off and returned the driveway to darkness as she yanked the car door open, slid the key in the ignition, and prayed that the battered wreck would start.

It did, without hesitation.

She hammered down the handbrake, yanked the gearstick into reverse, and jammed on the accelerator. Wheels spraying gravel, the car lurched back, and the sensor light came back on.

Cass glanced in the rear-view mirror, and jumped again at what she saw.

Brady was standing in the doorway, hands in pockets, seemingly unperturbed... as if this was all part of a plan.

She shunted the car into first, put her foot to the floor, and sped out onto the road.

———

She drove on autopilot, and it took a few minutes before her nerves settled enough to allow her to take in her surroundings, and her speed.

She was on the main road back to Glencale, travelling at more than eighty miles per hour.

And when she clocked her speed, something else dawned on her: the ease with which the battered wreck was responding to her touch.

She pressed further on the accelerator, and the car picked up pace without protest.

Brady had hidden it in plain sight. The dishevelled exterior was just a disguise: the car engine was clearly fine-tuned for high performance. For high-speed getaway… Or high-speed pursuit.

She shivered as she thought of what she had just escaped.

CHAPTER FORTY-FOUR

She knows.

He remembered elite unit training, the sleep deprivation, the food deprivation... and the hallucinations he'd suffered after one particularly hellish twenty hours in the mountains. He'd thought a fellow soldier was reaching into his chest to pluck out his organs but was so overcome by exhaustion that he put up no defence, unmoved and uncaring when, through blurred vision, he saw his colleague hold up something brown and palm-sized: his liver.

It was only some time later, when the sugars had somehow helped bring him back from the edge, that he realised his colleague had simply reached into Brady's uniform to take a packet of M&M's with which he then fed to him to try and keep Brady going.

Brady had never forgotten the hallucination or the apathy it provoked in him despite believing he was under attack...

So it was natural to ask himself whether he was hallucinating as he saw Cass remove the freezer bag from her hand and stuff it into her pocket.

But he knew he wasn't.

I don't know how she knows, but she knows...

She must have used the bag as a glove to pick something up – something of mine – a hair, maybe, or something I touched, like a knife. A sample.

Did she know all along, and deceive me? Get close to me to get the evidence she needed?

No: she surely would have planned it better than this. She's standing barefoot at the sink in my fucking coat, for Christ's sake...

Which told him, oddly enough, that it was better to wait. Draw breath, take what was most needed – time – and think.

So he bluffed, and made his entreaty to her to come back to bed.

And when she said no, citing the need to get to work, he made his offer to drive her.

He didn't expect Cass to suggest that she would borrow his car. That would complicate his plans. But it seemed best to say yes, to pretend there was no issue, to seem utterly relaxed about it all.

Cass was trying the same bluff, but unsuccessfully: her face was white with fear.

What gave me away?

I hid every trace. There is nothing in the house – nothing – that could be used against me.

I didn't use the shotgun to kill, and there's no way she found it – it's too well hidden.

She got the coat from the spare room.

Nothing there but tools, a knife, my backpack. The backpack that's fully packed – clothes, toiletries, passport, minor sums of money – as a precaution.

Indicative of nothing by itself. Certainly not indicative that its owner is a killer.

But somehow, she's figured it out.

She knows.

And if he had even the slightest doubt, the manner in which she fled the house would have dispelled it.

Leaving her clothes behind, ramming the car into reverse, before taking off like a bullet from a gun, absolutely terrified.

If he were an innocent man, he would have thought her insane.

But he wasn't, he'd been reckless – and it was time for Plan B.

CHAPTER FORTY-FIVE

What had she really seen? What could she actually prove? By the time she'd reached the station, Cass had driven through a hurricane of emotions.

Relief – simply to have escaped in one piece. Rage – at the thought of how Nabila had died. Self-recrimination – for getting so close to Brady and not seeing him for what he really was. Anxiety – desperate to ensure his immediate arrest, but unsure how to effect it, given the circumstantial nature of the evidence. Irritation – for giving into her fears and fleeing when she should have taken him into custody there and then. And doubt – the worst of all, tracing inexorably through her veins, telling her she was suffering from delusion. The further away from Brady she got, the greater the doubt she felt...

It was, after all, the first unspoken rule of any case: don't go all in on a witness. Memory could be faulty, and an uncertain witness's testimony in court could be torn apart by the defence. What a person saw and what they remembered seeing... well, it was like the image a person had of themselves versus how they were actually seen by others: the gap could be the size of the Grand Canyon.

So what did I really see? What can I actually prove?

One damaged banknote.

The damage looked identical to that on the notes found in Nabila's rucksack.

That was the sum total.

What had the Currency Comptroller said in relation to the Benghazi notes?

They started showing up around Europe, individuals walking into central banks across different member states and trying to exchange the damaged notes for new ones. Both in small and large quantities. Including in Ireland.

Which meant the notes were in circulation – even if limited circulation.

It was entirely possible – if not exactly plausible – that Brady's possession of one such note was entirely coincidental...

I spent time in the guy's company and slept with him, for fuck's sake. We were good with each other, good for each other. We were building something and it felt reassuring – promising – for both of us. There was a touch of reticence on both our parts but no hint of subterfuge in it – not one.

Besides, why would he even risk associating with a police officer if he had murdered two people? Unless this was an act of subterfuge from the start. To find out what the police knew. To determine whether he had cause to worry or was on safe ground. That day outside the station: maybe it wasn't accidental that we encountered each other. Maybe he had researched me and knew everything about me and waited until I appeared. Maybe I was just an easy mark.

But he's not that fucking good, nobody is. And could my antennae be so lousy that I wouldn't have spotted something was amiss?

I saw a damaged banknote.

And can't prove anything right now.

So process what I do have until I can prove something.

―――――

What she had to process consisted of a blurry photograph and the fork she had taken from Brady's kitchen.

The station was mercifully quiet when she arrived – just the overnight duty officer, who was on a call which spared Cass the need for small talk, although she noticed his querying look at her unusual choice of clothing. She changed back into the uniform she had discarded with so much relish the night before – it seemed like a lifetime ago now – and took the time to make a strong coffee before sitting at her desk to plot her way through the next steps.

Generally speaking, a person's property was inviolable, and could only be searched with a warrant. But there were, of course, exceptions. The law had been amended a few years back to recognise that, occasionally, a member of the force could find themselves invited somewhere in which they then saw an item which they believed to be evidence of a crime. In such circumstances, they were legally entitled to seize and retain the item.

Cass had been invited onto Brady's property – she hadn't been trespassing. But in her haste to avoid detection, she felt sure she'd made what was, in retrospect, a clear mistake. The note was the potential evidence linking Brady to a crime – that was the item she should have seized, and would have had legal cover to do so. By contrast, the law did not envisage taking a random item unconnected to a potential crime for the purposes of a DNA sample. Cass felt fairly sure a court would view the DNA sample as illegally procured – if it even got as far as a court.

So what to do? It had seemed so clear-cut in the church. But now? Just all-pervasive doubt again. Her instinct was to seek advice from Finnegan, but she couldn't countenance telling her the extent to which she'd got involved with a person she now suspected of murder. Nor did she want to tell Finnegan about the manner in which she'd taken the DNA sample from the house, or lost her bottle and failed to arrest him on the spot.

Get over yourself. Nabila is dead, Akeem Issa is most probably dead too, I know their likely murderer, and I'm sitting here worrying about Finnegan? Yes, because she really will think I'm a basket case, unmoored, unprofessional, unworthy of the job – a job I know I want to keep doing now.

But there was no way around it – all roads led back to her superior. Finnegan already harboured suspicions that Cass was prone to solo runs – the episode with Peter Bannon being the prime example. Even if it were true – and Cass didn't believe it to be so – this was too significant to keep from her.

Besides, my fucking judgement is shot. I couldn't see Brady for what he was. This needs a grown-up in charge now, someone actually capable of rational perception.

Lost in thought, she was startled by the ping of her phone. She saw immediately it was from Brady, and after a moment's hesitation, clicked open the message.

> Dinner 2nite? I'll collect car then – can get lift in.
> Kill 2 birds with 1 stone.

Her instant reaction was one of cautious welcome: this would give her the day, which might even give her a route to get legal clearance to search Brady's car.

But why was he acting so normally? Could it really be that he saw nothing erratic in her behaviour a few hours earlier, or had bought her pretence?

And then she read the message again.

Kill 2 birds with 1 stone.

Was it some coded declaration?

Was he taunting her?

Whatever this was, better to keep the pretence going. Seized with anger, she texted him back as seemingly normal as she could.

> Sounds good. I'll book somewhere.

Somewhere public. Somewhere safe. With a fucking posse ready to arrest you, you treacherous murdering bastard.

CHAPTER FORTY-SIX

Cass didn't expect an FBI agent's work ethic to stretch to being awake at 4am. But she figured Nicole Wilson would have her phone within reach and, more importantly, would answer, despite the five-hour time difference between their respective locations.

She was correct: Wilson answered, groggy and distinctly unamused. 'Please tell me it's a goddamn emergency.'

'It is. The guy I asked you about – Mason Brady?'

'What's he done?'

'He may have committed two murders.'

'May have? Cass, you're ringing me at this hour with a suspicion?'

Yes, I caught my 'may have' too. Because I'm going hot and cold. I know what my head is telling me – I saw the evidence with my own eyes. But I can't reconcile what he's done with the person I spent time with. He's a treacherous murdering bastard. Maybe.

'I know you can't tell me much,' she said. 'I just need an answer to a single question.'

'Cass–'

'Did he serve in Benghazi? That's all I need to know. He did, right? He did a stint there. Just confirm that much for me.'

'I'm not confirming any goddamn thing.'

'He's a double murder suspect, Nicole. One of the victims was twenty-four. She'd just been granted refugee status. Could finally see a better life ahead of her. Someone hit her, strangled her and dumped her body in the woods.'

There was a groan as Wilson processed what she'd been told. Cass looked at the clock and thought, not for the first time, that while Nabila's killer would get a mandatory life sentence, they'd technically become eligible for parole in twelve. Nobody could give Nabila her life back; Cass failed to see why her killer should eventually get his back. And then, as sometimes happened, she felt a twinge of guilt as she thought about her ex-husband in prison. She hated him, she thought he'd got off lightly, and yet, she'd known him long enough to know what seven nights in prison would do to him, let alone seven years...

'You know I'm not unsympathetic, Cass,' Wilson said suddenly. 'But why the hell does Benghazi have anything to do with two homicides in Ireland?'

Cass explained about Nabila Fathi, Akeem Issa, the damaged banknotes and what she'd seen pinned to Brady's dartboard. 'Brady being in Benghazi is the link to Issa and Nabila,' she added.

There was a long pause, before Wilson said: 'Could just be a coincidence.'

'Thank you,' Cass replied, feeling a flood of relief to have a link finally confirmed. 'I won't bother you again with this unless I have proof.'

'I didn't tell you anything. And Cass?'

'Yes?'

'If you do get proof, don't hesitate to call – even at 4am.'

———

Cass had decided she needed something else before going to Finnegan. And in the short time available to her, she had two ideas. Nicole Wilson had been the first. Fiona Mitchell was the second.

Absurdly, Cass looked over her shoulder as she made the short walk from the station to the estate agent. For sure, Brady could have already made his way into town somehow, but he wasn't going to attack her on a public street in daylight.

Having received an advance call from Cass, Mitchell was at the door when she arrived, and ushered her through the pleasant and airy reception area and open-plan office into a considerably more cramped rear room, with boxes of brochures and associated paperwork piled at either side of a well-worn desk bearing a laptop and decades of coffee cup rings. *Her father's desk probably,* Cass thought.

Like her, Fiona Mitchell had gone into the family business, before assuming full control of the estate agency when her father had died a few years previously. She was well liked around town, professional and fair to deal with; her honesty helping the firm gradually overcome her father's cut-throat reputation.

Cass declined the offer of tea or coffee and got straight to the point, explaining that she was looking for some background information – confidentially of course – on Brady's purchase of the church.

'We're off the record?' Mitchell asked.

'Yes, just background queries at this point.'

'Well, there was nothing unusual about it, if that's what you're asking. It was a cash deal–'

'He paid outright in cash – no mortgage?'

'Yes, but that's pretty common these days. You've got your standard portion of first-time buyers or families trading up who need mortgages or refinancing. And then you've got a portion of people who've got a bit of savings or proper wealth, looking for a new home or a holiday home in a nice part of the world. Looking for a bit of isolation and privacy in some cases. We see a lot of those buyers in Glencale, do good business because of them, particularly on higher-end properties. Brady's purchase was nothing out of the ordinary.'

'And where did the cash come from – do you remember?'

'Well, he didn't walk in with a suitcase, if that's what you're asking,' Mitchell said, laughing. But then she saw the look on Cass's face. 'We have guidance against that kind of thing, to prevent money laundering,' she added.

'So the money came through a normal route?'

'US bank account, I recall. But no hiccups on any of the bank transfers.'

'Did anything else strike you about him?'

'I can't say anything did. He was pleasant to do business with.'

'Did you have any more contact with him after the sale was completed?'

'Yes, he asked for recommendations for tradespeople – electricians and plumbers. I gave him the names of the guys we work with.'

'He needed certification, right?'

'Yes. And then he asked us out a couple of months ago to take shots.'

'Shots?'

'For these,' she said, holding up a brochure. 'Listings. He was talking about moving to Dublin, doing a course, that kind of thing.'

'He's selling?'

'Well, no. He hasn't asked us to list the place. Just said if he did buy in Dublin, he'd need a quick sale here.'

———

She rang Maisah Sahraoui on her way back to the station. But Nabila's friend had never heard of Mason Brady, and didn't recognise the photo of him which Cass had pulled from the passport system a short time earlier.

'What has this man got to do with Nabila's murder?' Maisah asked. 'I thought Akeem Issa was the murderer.'

'I'm just closing off loose ends,' Cass replied.

———

At the station, her instinct was to find Finnegan and confess to the fuck-up she'd made of everything. There were no circumstances in which the force would accept as reasonable the fact that an officer had been involved with a murder suspect – even if suspicions had formed only after the relationship had begun. To say nothing of the fact that the same officer had form, in the shape of a criminal ex-husband in prison for manslaughter. It was so surreal she wasn't even quite sure Finnegan would believe it, even if Cass at last now felt she had enough with which to go to her. But as she walked towards her office, intent on laying out chapter and verse even if she incurred Finnegan's excoriating judgement, she was interrupted by Noel Ryan.

'The boss doesn't want disruptions,' he said. 'There's been some news.'

He pointed to the kitchenette, adding, 'Let's talk there.' When he was sure they were alone, he continued. 'Devine has been suspended. The ACU are investigating.'

The anti-corruption unit; Cass's stomach lurched. 'Because of what happened in the school? It looked iffy but it was hardly proof...'

'Relax. Finnegan knew his ways. She quizzed him about it, he refused to say a word, she gave him an unofficial warning. And then she went investigating.'

'Investigating?'

'She'd heard the names of a couple of girls around town who he'd preyed on. Both seventeen. In one of the squad cars, for fuck's sake. One of them said she's in love with him; the other was traumatised by the way he used her. Finnegan handled them sensitively and with care. And then she called the ACU. He's fucked – and rightly so.'

'I can barely believe it.'

'It's a lot to take in, and when word gets out – because it always does in a small town – we'll no doubt see more girls coming forward. Plus, Finnegan thinks he may have had his wife under coercive control.'

'You knew this: it was you who flagged him to Finnegan.'

'I've seen Devine's type before.'

And what does that say of me? I didn't see through him until the evidence was in front of my face. And the same with Brady.

While all the time failing to see the decency in Ryan, because I applied my wreck of a personal life to his – and judged him accordingly.

Finnegan has one catastrophe of an internal matter on her hands in Devine, and now I'm going to give her another. Maybe there's a way of fixing this first.

'Noel, I could do with your help tonight on something a bit… extracurricular.'

'I'm not at my best in the evenings. I'd only embarrass you.'

'I've done that all by myself, believe me. Fucked things up entirely.'

She could tell he didn't want to hear it, didn't want to be dragged in. But against his better instincts, he said: 'Tell me.'

'I've been seeing someone – Mason Brady, the American from–'

'The Bridge Bannon case. The fella up in the old church in the Loop.'

'Yes. I had no reason to suspect anything when I hooked up with him. But now… I think he may have form.'

'Form for what, exactly? Drugs? Theft?'

Had she imagined it all? Was her judgement so shot that she had conjured up a preposterous scenario? What did she know for sure?

251

'Murder, possibly.'

Cass didn't think it was possible for somebody of Ryan's permanently flushed complexion to go so pale.

'Bring him in for questioning, for fuck's sake.'

'I don't think I have enough yet.'

'Tell me what you do have.'

She did – releasing a torrent of words, feeling a great rush of relief to be confiding in someone.

When she was done, he said: 'You need to tell Finnegan – now – regardless of when you started the relationship, regardless of how you lifted that sample. Forget all that. Just tell her.'

'I will after tonight – I just want to prove to myself first that I'm not going all sorts of crazy.'

'We're all fucking crazy to do this job,' he muttered. 'So what exactly is your plan?'

'I don't have one yet... but I'd value having someone there in my corner.'

He shook his head, as if silently cursing the naivety of youth. 'Where and when?'

'Somewhere public, around eight. You'd be at a discreet distance, observing. Just in case anything goes wrong.'

'And if it does?'

'We'll take him,' she said.

'You look at me and mistake me for GI Joe or something?'

Despite the stress, or maybe because of it, the absurdity of the reference made Cass laugh.

'You're not the crazy one,' Ryan continued. 'I'm the fucking mentaller to go along with this.' But his thin lips had creased into the trace of a smile.

CHAPTER FORTY-SEVEN

The rain started mid-afternoon, shortly after Cass had texted Brady with a time and place. Glencale House seemed an obvious venue. The appearance of privacy, sufficient nooks to allow Ryan to find a discreet spot and observe at a distance.

Brady texted back immediately:

> Am stepping up in the world. Off 2 buy dinner jacket...

In the interests of pretending all was fine, she sent him a smiling face emoji.

Then she turned back to building her case against him. But it was difficult to swat away thoughts of the impending showdown. Would he have the balls to sit there and pretend nothing was wrong? Or would he, by any miniscule chance, have disregarded her behaviour that morning? Be oblivious to the fact that he was a suspect?

A peal of thunder, a squall of rain in response: serve, return. The timber windows in the old station rattled. It was dark outside by 5pm. As she had done a dozen times already that day, she considered sending off the DNA sample and seeking expedited processing. But again she held back, knowing it had potential to backfire.

Motive: Why did she keep asking herself about motive? Most of her colleagues considered motive utterly secondary in an investigation: gather what actual evidence was available first and see where it pointed. If it led to a suspect, and it was decisive, then motive barely mattered – until court at least, where the prosecution and the defence could argue about *mens rea*, intent or lack of it. So why did she keep returning to motive? Especially when, on the face of it, the motive was abundantly clear: murder to hide the source of illicit money, presumably a lot of it.

But why go to such lengths? Why not just leave the jurisdiction, and leave any investigators chasing straws in the wind? *Was* there something else she was missing? Drugs or other criminal activity besides the money itself?

Her attention was broken by a colleague landing a gear-bag on a desk as he arrived for the night-shift.

It made her think of Devine, and whether he would leave his personal things in the station until the anti-corruption investigation was finished, or sneak in some night – or stroll in bold as brass in daytime – to collect the stuff.

As she watched her colleague unzip the gear-bag and remove food containers to store in the fridge, it hit her.

The church in catalogue perfection.

Completely devoid of mementoes, of personality.

The packed bag in the spare room.

The estate agent's photos taken as a precaution.

The deceptively fast car.

Brady was a man ready to run at a moment's notice.

With dismay, she saw his calm demeanour that morning, and his subsequent text messages, for what they were: a sham.

He was already running – nothing surer.

Without a second's hesitation, she grabbed Brady's car keys from the desk and dashed for the door.

CHAPTER FORTY-EIGHT

An extendable baton and a can of pepper spray – it had seemed insufficient when hunting Akeem Issa and seemed even more insufficient now. But Cass pushed the concern to the back of her mind. She had to know.

She thought of Nabila's lonely death in the Loop, and shivered. In her rush, she'd left behind her radio, meaning no ability to summon emergency assistance if required. But given the distance from the station to the old church, it wouldn't arrive on time anyway. She dialled Ryan on her mobile. When it went to voicemail, she hung up and dialled him again. And got precisely the same result. She phoned the station and left a message for Ryan to contact her asap.

She threw Brady's car into the corners and pushed it to its limits on the straights. The car shook in the wind as the storm took full hold.

Motive: if she hadn't spent so much time futilely obsessing about motive, she might have seen through his deception sooner.

But that was just an excuse, she knew. Her real failure had been leaving the church when she should have arrested Brady on the spot. It was a failure borne from fear. She wouldn't allow it to get in the way a second time.

The heat in the car was on full blast but as she took the familiar turn-off to climb towards the church, she shivered again. She would be entirely alone up there, disoriented by the dark, deafened by the storm.

Then she thought of the church bell pealing its haunting omen in her sleep, and she shivered a third time.

She pressed on the accelerator.

CHAPTER FORTY-NINE

The car wheels crunched once more as she drove across the gravel, the headlights illuminating the seemingly deserted church.

He's gone. Just as I thought...

So why am I shaking uncontrollably?

She pulled the car to a halt, rain drumming off the roof. She fished in his glove department for a torch and was relieved to find one. It meant she had to choose whether she held her steel baton or pepper spray in her free hand. The storm made the pepper spray redundant, she figured – the wind would blow it everywhere if she had to use it outdoors, maybe even back in her own face.

So the baton.

She exited slowly, acutely aware he would already have the upper hand if somewhere on the property.

Wind whipped against the trees and drove a deluge of rain into her face, forcing her to scrunch up her eyes. Her fist locked on the baton, her heart hammering, she took a couple of steps cautiously across the drive, scanning from side to side with the torch.

And then she shrieked as the drive was suddenly bathed in light.

The fucking sensor light; she had forgotten.

She remained stationary, allowing her heart to settle, watching for any signs of motion.

Nothing.

She resumed her approach, cautious as before, reaching the front door and trying the handle. Locked. Using the torch, she scanned the front windows. All shut. Still no sign of movement.

She felt a touch more certain that she was alone. But the eeriness of this place in the storm, its murderous history, the bell clanging furiously in her mind, wouldn't allow her settle.

She walked to the rear of the property, and shivered again as her torch swept across the small graveyard. How Brady had spent his nights awake here was beyond her. But then, perhaps that spoke to a psychopathic tendency he had hidden effectively.

She ran the torchlight over the rear windows and sliding doors: same result. All locked, no sign of life. She had no desire to step into the church, but knew her search was incomplete if she didn't.

She swung her baton hard against one of the doors, but it had little impact against the tempered glass. She scanned the ground for something more effective and saw a loose brick by the graveyard gate. It took three attempts, but eventually the brick shattered the glass and triggered a house alarm. Gingerly, she stepped into the church, wet boots scrunching on broken glass.

She found a switch to flick on the light. The open-plan kitchen and living area were empty as she already knew. The door of the spare room was closed. She walked slowly towards it, imagining Brady leaping from somewhere at any second, the noise of the alarm doing nothing to settle her nerves.

As she grasped the handle, the wind died down for a brief moment. It was just enough to hear the sound of an approaching car.

CHAPTER FIFTY

Cass ran out of the church and took cover behind the gable wall furthest from the drive, enabling her to observe the imminent arrival. It couldn't be a random visitor, not up here, in this weather, on this night. Brady must have access to a second vehicle, would see his own car parked outside, and would know she was somewhere on the property. Her fist white from gripping the baton, she concentrated on steadying her breathing and preparing for the violence that was sure to come…

And then, to her astonishment, she heard the short wail of a siren, a warning shot to those who needed it to cease and desist.

Relief flooded through her veins. The sensor light flicked on again as Cass ran back across the drive to greet Finnegan and Ryan.

'You're okay?' Ryan had to shout to be heard above the wind.

'Fine,' Cass said, 'but he's not here.'

'You're sure?'

'Pretty much.'

'Let's make it certain.'

Finnegan first radioed base and gave instructions to deal with the alarm company. Then the three of them conducted a proper sweep of the church and graveyard, during which the alarm stopped squalling. The sweep yielded nothing.

They returned to the squad car, and Finnegan signalled Cass to get into the back.

'Now,' she said, a distinct edge evident in her voice, 'would you care to tell me what the fuck is going on?'

———

It felt oddly fitting to Cass that she was sitting where a suspect normally would. She had a case to answer, after all, and the time for silence was gone.

She positioned herself in the middle of the back seat, to have eye contact with Finnegan who had turned sideways in hers to glare at Cass. Ryan sat looking straight ahead, watching the rain beat against the windows; he would play no part in the inquisition. But before she answered Finnegan's first question, she had one of her own.

'How did you know I was here?'

'Noel got your message to call him and guessed where you'd gone,' Finnegan said. 'He came to me – as you should have done – and said he was worried you were about to do something stupid.'

'"Dangerous",' Ryan interjected. '"Something dangerous" is what I said.'

'Same bloody thing,' Finnegan snapped. 'Get on with it.'

'Some of this you already know. Bear with me on the repetition and on the gaps,' Cass began.

'In 2017, during the Libyan Civil War, about 160 million euro was lifted clean from a branch of the central bank by one of the factions involved. Other currencies were also taken – Libyan dinar, US dollars – but for our purposes, the euro are what matters.

'Mason Brady served with the US military in Benghazi around this time – doing what, I don't know. But he was there – that much, I've confirmed,' she continued.

'The euro notes were damaged by flooding in the bank vault. The faction who lifted the notes later attempted to use a cleaning agent to undo the damage, but only made it worse. This made the notes difficult to offload, difficult to use in everyday transactions, because businesses would be reluctant to take them. And it created a second problem: it made the notes very recognisable when people tried to exchange them for new notes in central banks across Europe.

'In 2016, a year before the bank raid, Nabila Fathi arrived in Ireland from Egypt seeking asylum. While her application was being considered, she was housed in the direct provision centre here in Glencale.

'At some point in more recent years, a Libyan, Akeem Issa, made his way into this country, but this time illegally. We have no record of his entry or exit, and he was never captured in the European system.

'In December 2020, CCTV captured Nabila trying to exchange some of the Libyan notes in the Currency Comptroller in Dublin. Separate CCTV footage showed her getting into a car nearby the Comptroller's offices driven by Issa.

'Shortly after her return to Glencale, Nabila was murdered and her body dumped. But her killer made a mistake. She had tucked a couple of the euro notes into a hidden compartment in her rucksack, maybe as payment, maybe as security, and the killer didn't realise this. He was concerned only about her phone, thinking that was the only item that would tie him to Nabila. But the notes were what enabled us to trace her movements to the Currency Comptroller, and subsequently to the footage of her getting in the car with Issa.'

Now the next part of the chronological sequence is January 2021, when my husband gets into a car drunk and ploughs through a pedestrian crossing, killing a mother and injuring her child. But let's sail right past that one.

'Finally, Mason Brady arrived in Ireland. He bought this place with cash in Glencale and started renovating it. Records show he arrived after Nabila's death but before the discovery of her body. But I think he may have been in the country longer – somehow had a route to get in and out.

'Nabila's body is found in March 2021. Meanwhile, Issa is keeping a very low profile. He has an arrangement to stay in a ramshackle farmhouse a few miles outside the town – and then disappears completely sometime in the summer. We find his burnt-out car – the car Nabila had last been seen in – but not him.

'And then Brady. He restores this place. He also keeps a low profile, but seems to be liked by those who encounter him. Courteous, helpful.

'We get to this year. Bridge Bannon is murdered a couple of miles down the road from here. Brady voluntarily comes to the station, and gives a witness statement about his two fellow compatriots. You know that part of the story.'

Now the awkward bit.

'At an appropriate point when it was clear Brady had no involvement in the Bannon murder, he and I… begin seeing each other.'

And grow increasingly fond of each other, or so I thought. But I'll omit that too.

'Last night, I stayed here. I didn't sleep well, and in the early hours of the morning, went looking for an extra blanket in the spare room when I saw something. Brady had pinned to a dartboard in the spare room one of the damaged banknotes: the same notes that Nabila had in her rucksack, the same notes lifted from the central bank in Benghazi.

'That's everything I know. The rest is conjecture. But it looks to me like Mason Brady killed Nabila Fathi and then killed Akeem Issa.'

'Why?' Finnegan asked.

'The money. I thought originally that Issa must have been the source of the damaged notes, smuggling them with him into Europe, and onto Ireland. I thought it was probably a small amount, maybe a few thousand. But now I think Brady was the one who smuggled out the money – maybe a lot of it. It would have been easy for him to do so. He finishes his tour of duty, he's honourably discharged from the military, allows some time to pass to avoid suspicion, and then lands in Ireland with some kind of plan to start changing the notes. But it's not as straightforward as it seemed originally. So he somehow makes contact with Issa and Nabila. The December run to the Currency Comptroller was a trial, I think. And when it didn't work out, Brady realised he had a series of problems – illicit money that he couldn't launder, and two people who could trace that money back to him.'

'But this heist in Libya – it was by one of the tribal factions, right? So how did Brady come across the money?'

'I don't know,' Cass said. 'Maybe his team conducted a raid at some point, discovered a quantity of the notes, and kept it to themselves – I can only guess.'

'Forensics on Issa's car?'

'Working on them as we speak but I wouldn't hold my breath.'

'And if we conducted a forensic sweep on this place,' Finnegan said, waving her hand in the direction of the church, 'we're going to find your DNA everywhere, right?'

'Yes,' Cass said, with a twinge of embarrassment, recognising – despite their dysfunctional relationship – the extent to which she was silently seeking Finnegan's approval.

'Tell me exactly what happened here overnight.'

'When I saw the note, I got scared. I left the house, taking Brady's car. But before I left, I took a kitchen fork with his DNA on it. At some point, he saw me in the kitchen, maybe even bagging the fork. Either way, he knew I was acting strangely. But he pretended to ignore it, and let me leave. So I fled.

'He then sent me a message saying hold onto the car and that he would meet me in Glencale tonight. I was wobbling already, wondering if I was seeing things that weren't there. And I fell for the ruse. It gave him time to escape. He was on permanent standby to evacuate at a moment's notice – but I was blind to it. And when it eventually dawned on me this evening, I knew I had to get out here.'

Finnegan sucked her teeth, the by now familiar tic when she was contemplating something. 'Why did he kill them so far apart?' she asked. 'Nabila in December but Issa months later? Why stay here so long after killing them? And why keep the note on display?'

'It would have been stupid to commit two murders in a short period of time – he spaced them out to ensure less chance of detection. For all we know, he and Issa may have agreed that Nabila had to die, but Issa may not have expected anything to happen to him. As for time, I think Brady stayed here precisely to ensure he wasn't under suspicion, and when no one came knocking on his door, maybe figured he was out of the woods and decided to stay a bit longer. That's my best guess. As for the note – he had no way of knowing we had found identical notes among Nabila's possessions. That information was kept from the media and never leaked. So Brady had no way of knowing we had linked Nabila's murder to the notes… What do you think?'

'I think you're reading a lot into a single banknote pinned to a dartboard.'

None of the three spoke for a few moments, the only sounds the wind and rain continuing to hurtle incessantly against the car. Eventually, Finnegan looked at Ryan and said: 'What do you think?'

'It's circumstantial but can't be coincidence. The note at the very least suggests all three of them were in contact at some point. Cass has enough to get a warrant for this place and we can bulletin the ports and airports. But we can't use the DNA exhibit she took.'

Finnegan turned her face away from them and towards the church, as if weighing a decision. 'Noel, you start the ball rolling tonight. Bulletin, warrant – the works. I want Brady held for questioning and I want to be drinking my breakfast coffee inside this fucking place tomorrow morning. Cassidy, you've nothing more to do with this unless I tell you, understood?'

'But I'm central to this,' she protested.

'And that's exactly the problem. Central to it in ways that, frankly, make this a bit of a mess. So now that you've notified me, we're going to follow every fucking last line of procedure from this point, understood?'

I fucking hate when she says that. 'Understood,' she said reluctantly.

'Good. And that fork you lifted from his kitchen – you can't be sure if he saw you or not?'

'No. Possibly – probably.'

'Then if anyone ever asks, it was for self-defence, not to take his DNA. Got it?'

'Yes,' she said, in the absence of a better answer.

'Last thing. You're not going home tonight, not until we know where this guy is. We'll pay for a room at the Glencale. Ryan will be in the room next door. No ifs, no buts.'

'That's not necessary. I think we're bett–'

'I'm not asking you for a view on what's necessary or not.'

In the rear-view mirror, Cass caught Ryan looking back and giving her a slight shake of the head. *Don't challenge her. Accept it.*

Somehow, it shook Cass from the unyielding tunnel vision of her pursuit, and she was suddenly quite moved. Finnegan considered her a basket case, Ryan owed her nothing, and yet both had raced to be at her side in a moment of potential danger.

'Understood,' she said softly. 'And thank you for your concern.'

'Don't get carried away,' Finnegan replied. 'Room service is on yourself. Don't think I'm going to feed you too.'

CHAPTER FIFTY-ONE

R yan drove them back into town, Finnegan contacting colleagues and executing orders along the way, including to set up the national alert. Despite her thoughts being squarely on Brady, Cass couldn't help notice the slight twitching in Ryan's hands on the steering wheel.

She felt a surge of sympathy for him, and asked herself why she felt so little for her ex-husband, and knew the answer: because she had been generalising, lumping Ryan in the same category as Hugh, when they were nothing alike. If she could find a way to apologise to Ryan without being intrusive or patronising, she would. They took her back briefly to her apartment to pack an overnight bag, and then to the station, where she provided Ryan with a fuller debrief. Then she was cut loose, with directions from Finnegan to stick to the hotel and get some rest.

I'd get more peace of mind if I could work the case, she thought.

Upon check-in at Glencale House, the friendly receptionist began to list the various amenities and services the hotel had to offer, including the pool and spa. Politely, Cass cut him short, saying she was familiar with the hotel. In fact, she realised that in all the time she'd lived in Glencale – originally and upon return – she'd only ever visited the bar and restaurant, and never actually stayed there.

Her mind drifted back to childhood visits to the hotel, and the afternoon teas. A part of her wished she was back there, with her mother for company and madeleines on demand; instead she was alone in an expensive hotel room, a personal and professional failure without an anchoring point in her life apart from the job.

She cursed her self-pity, took the card key and made her way to her room. They'd given her a small suite – Finnegan's doing or the hotel's, it wasn't quite clear – and even in her weary state, Cass could acknowledge its elegance, if not appreciate it. Carved mahogany four-poster bed and furniture, plush carpet and thick curtains, a welcoming array of fresh fruit, artisan chocolates and mineral water, and numerous other small touches.

If the suite was old-school luxury, the bathroom was modern chic. Its centrepiece was a freestanding bath which, to Cass's eye, looked the size of a small dinner table. She ignored it all, slipped off her shoes, and lay on the bed, running through every interaction with Brady she could remember, asking herself how she had got things so terribly wrong.

———

She woke to the sound of a strange ringtone, and realised it was the hotel phone rather than her mobile.

Groggy, and surprised that she had fallen asleep, she fumbled for the receiver.

'Noel?' she asked, assuming her colleague had some update.

'No, it's me.'

She sat bolt upright, terrified that he had somehow tracked her. 'How did you know I was here?'

'I didn't. I rang the restaurant – we were supposed to be

meeting there, remember? They checked with the front desk who put me through to your room.'

'Where the hell are you?'

'In transit.'

'In another county or another country?'

'It all looks the same to a soldier.'

She looked at the time: just after 9pm. She had been dozing for less than fifteen minutes. All told, fifteen hours had passed since she had fled the church in his car.

Not sure how he arranged transport, but assuming he had some kind of a backup plan – a second car stashed somewhere, a rental, whatever – two hours give or take from his place to the nearest airport, or four hours to Dublin airport which offered more frequent routes. An hour to fly to London; two hours to Paris, Amsterdam and Frankfurt; any number of options from one of those hubs. Or he could have flown direct from Dublin or Shannon to the States – seven or eight hours to New York or Washington – but he would have needed good fortune with flight times. So, best bet: he's still in Europe somewhere.

She fumbled with her mobile until she found the voice memo function, pressed record, and held it as close as she could to the receiver. She remembered her plan from earlier in the day – to come at Brady sideways rather than with a full-on frontal assault.

'I like what you did with the car.'

'Old military trick. Take a – what was your word? – "banger" that blends in and fine-tune it to within an inch of its life. Less conspicuous than the armoured Cadillacs and diplomatic vehicles. Much safer to travel in.'

'A trick you used in Benghazi?'

The interrogation proper has started, he thought, *and she's recording it for sure. Now we're in combat with each other.* 'Here and there. I guessed you probably had my records. You seemed to understand what I'd been through, even though I couldn't–' *Tell you,* he thought. *I couldn't tell you precise details of what I'd suffered – and where it happened – because it would have potentially exposed me.*

'What *you'd* been through?' Cass said through gritted teeth. *Is this fucking guy for real? He kills two people and is still looking for sympathy for whatever personal trauma he suffered? He's going to use that as an excuse to justify what he did? Theft and murder?*

Brady stayed silent, and Cass remembered his composure when giving a statement in the station on the first day they'd met.

'Tell me how you picked Nabila.'

'Nabila?'

'You're going all coy on me now?'

'I've told you more than I've told anyone for years.'

'A woman's murder is a pretty big omission.'

'You're talking about that unsolved case from last year?'

'Yes, I'm talking about Nabila Fathi, the twenty-four-year-old woman brutally murdered and dumped in woodland in the Loop. An area which you're intimately familiar with.'

'And you think I murdered her?'

'You're going to tell me you didn't?'

'I arrived in Ireland after she was killed, just in case you have your timeline wrong.'

'A convenience we'll be examining closely.'

'That's why you got close to me? Because you had me as a suspect?'

'You're reinventing history, my friend. You deliberately drew me in to try and get close to the investigation. I see that now.'

'I didn't even know you were investigating that fucking case! I know nothing about the woman.'

'Nabila,' Cass said.

A stand-off ensued: Cass thinking furiously whether she had any avenue to trace the call in real-time and realising with frustration she hadn't; Brady wondering how to answer clearly without implicating himself and struggling to see a route through.

'I didn't kill Nabila,' he said eventually. 'I was aware of her murder, of course – who in Glencale wasn't? But I had nothing to do with it.'

'Either Akeem Issa killed her or you did, but either way, it amounts to the same thing. You were in league. We've got his car, the same car in which Nabila travelled the day she tried to exchange money for the two of you. The forensics will tell us the rest.'

'What money?'

'The money we found in Nabila's rucksack,' Cass replied irritably. 'Two notes from a batch you know all about – damaged by flooding in a bank vault in Benghazi.'

Now he finally knew what had frightened Cass earlier that morning in the church. Jesus H Christ, what were the chances? The media reports about the dead woman's murder had never mentioned the discovery of notes. The cops had done a good job of safeguarding that crucial bit of information.

'And Nabila tried to exchange it somewhere?' he asked, while trying to piece the rest of the puzzle together in his mind.

'You know she did. In the Currency Comptroller in Dublin in December 2020. Staff there asked her for details and she panicked and fled. And you or Issa killed her for it.'

He had convinced himself there was nothing in the church to link back to what he'd done. But of course, there was, because he'd kept one trophy, a souvenir, a testament to completion of a very personal mission: he'd kept the note. Not thinking for one moment that anybody would ever realise the significance of that trophy but him.

'I was in Benghazi, and I did know Akeem Issa,' he relented. 'You're right about that much but wrong about everything else. I never knew, met or had any connection to Nabila, and I wasn't involved in her murder.'

Cass held back, waiting to see if Brady would continue. Brady appeared willing to do so.

'One of the warlords carried off millions from the central bank in Benghazi – but that much I assume you know already.

My unit was tasked with supporting intelligence-led efforts to recover the money. God knows why, given the country had bigger problems. But we had our orders.

'We got a tip-off one day about a portion of the money being moved from Benghazi for dispersal to tribal allies in another region. So we moved immediately to see if we could intercept it.

'But the hostiles had their own tip-off. Long story short, we were supposed to ambush them but they ended up ambushing us. Two of us were taken hostage. Having realised what happened, headquarters sent a separate unit to extricate us. They rescued me but were too late for Pitch.'

'Pitch?'

'Stewart Shapiro. Pitch was what we called him cos he had a lousy throwing arm in the pick-up games at base. To think we ever laughed about anything… Anyway, they were too late for him. I had a few broken bones but the mental damage was much worse. Everything I told you about that is true. I came home, sought help, couldn't heal, then tried to do it my own way.'

'And Akeem Issa?'

'He was our translator.'

Cass's mind was whirring, trying to assemble the picture he was painting.

'Now do you understand?' he asked.

Yes, I see it now, and I think I believe him.

'So you suspected Issa provided the tip-off that led to your ambush. He was rewarded with some of the money from the bank raid – easy to do, because the gang had more of it than they possibly knew what to do with – and he sought a route out of Libya. Issa was the one who came to Ireland with the money. You came to Ireland hunting Issa.'

This is the point where mental reservation resumes, Brady told himself.

'I came to Ireland to rest and recuperate. What Issa was doing here, I've no idea.'

'But you found him and killed him – as an act of revenge?'

'I found peace here. If Akeem Issa found trouble, that's his problem.'

You believed this would be the chief route to recovery, Cass thought, *executing the person who had betrayed your unit, got your colleague killed. You thought this would settle the night-time screams in your head, disperse the shadows at your shoulder. You took that note from Issa's body and pinned it to that dartboard to say: 'Mission accomplished.'*

'The note was proof of kill, wasn't it?'

'As far as I know, a note's just a unit of currency.'

'Did you know Issa had killed Nabila?'

'I didn't make that leap. She was Egyptian, right, not Libyan? And from what the papers had reported, it seemed like some kind of sexual assault that had ended in murder. The papers mentioned nothing about a Libyan suspect, or banknotes, or anything like that.' *I didn't make that leap,* Brady thought, *because I'm just a soldier executing a mission, not a detective. I've the physical capability to kill, but not the deductive capacity to have figured out that connection.*

Whatever mental scarring he suffered, Cass thought, *it didn't impact on his ability to track his target halfway across the world and kill him while leaving no traces. And then remaining cool enough to hide in plain sight for months on end. His mental acuity must be off the charts. He was miles ahead of me – of everyone.*

'You know we're getting a warrant to search the church, right? We'll do a forensic sweep of your car while we're at it. We'll put out a European arrest warrant. And Ireland has an extradition agreement with the States. We're going to hunt you in the same way you hunted Issa.'

'Then you'll be wasting your time. Akeem Issa killed Nabila and I didn't – you know that now. What else have you got? You don't even know Issa is dead – you don't have a body. So you have nothing to charge me with.'

'I'll find something to charge you with.'

'You'll find nothing in the church, apart from a shotgun which, I'll confess, is unlicensed but, as ballistics will demonstrate, hasn't been fired in a long time. Other than that, you have possession of a stolen euro banknote, the theft of which I had nothing to do with. What's the punishment for being in possession of an unlicensed, unused shotgun and a single stolen note? I'll send you a cheque to cover the fines, because I'm a good citizen.'

He laughed, but not cruelly, almost as if inviting her to see the funny side too. But she was in no mood to.

'If you're such a good citizen, why did you run this morning?'

'I needed a change of scenery.'

'The church – it was your penance, right? A way of seeking absolution? You kill Issa, and in return you renovate an old church – you figure you've balanced the ledger.'

'You're stretching, Cass. If you weighed the sins of Issa and mine, I'm pretty confident God would be on my side.'

'You're an asshole, Brady. And I will find Akeem Issa's body.'

'Best of luck with that. A guy like him? Could be anywhere now. Back in Libya for all you know.'

'I won't let this go.'

'I know you won't, Cass. That's what we have in common – we don't let things go.'

'We have nothing in common.'

'I don't know about that. We both blamed ourselves for things in our lives that weren't our fault. And we tried to make amends in our own way.'

'Your idea of making amends is pretty fucking sick and twisted.'

'Akeem Issa was fucking sick and twisted, Cass,' he said, voice rising for the first time. 'He got Pitch killed. He killed Nabila. Who knows what other evil shit he was part of? Believe me when

I say I'm not going to lose a moment worrying about Akeem Issa's fate.'

Because you know exactly how he met his fate, she thought. *You burnt his car in one place to eliminate forensic traces and disposed of his body in another to make it look like Issa had vanished.*

I nearly lost it there for a moment, he thought. *But the worst part of all, I've lost her.* 'I'm going to miss you,' he said, sounding suddenly subdued.

'Don't worry – I'll find you.' *I'm not going to yield a fucking inch to you.*

He ignored her hostility, and instead made another attempt at bridging the gap between them. 'You know now you've nothing to fear from me?'

When her colleagues in the station listened later to this curiously intimate section of the recording, they counted a full fifteen seconds of dead space before Cass answered.

'Yes,' she said, 'but you need to tell me where I can find Akeem Issa's body.'

'Goodbye Cass,' he said, and hung up.

CHAPTER FIFTY-TWO

S he slept as if in a fever, tossing, sweating and hearing the church bell swinging in the wind. She saw her ex-husband driving their old car, mounting a footpath and ploughing into a faceless soldier whose fatigues bore the name tag 'Pitch'. She saw Hugh in a prison corridor, defeated and decrepit, oblivious as Mason Brady slid alongside him with a shank, ready to wreak revenge for his friend. She saw Nabila race across the corridor to intervene, but arriving too late.

She woke up roaring at Brady to stop.

And when the terror in her chest subsided, she realised she knew where the body of Akeem Issa was.

She shuddered deeply at the thought of it.

———

'You want me to do what?' The tone of Finnegan's reply was sufficient warning, but just for good measure, there was visual warning too in the shape of her puce face.

'I know it sounds off the wall,' Cass persisted, 'but I'm certain that's where Brady buried the body.'

'Christ, give me strength. You don't even know there is a body! We're searching Brady's place from top to bottom already and there isn't the remotest hint that he was involved in a murder. We haven't even found the bloody shotgun he told you about.'

'You heard the recording.'

'And there's nothing on it that amounts to anything near a confession.'

'Jesus, Nuala, he never was going to confess – he knew I'd be recording the call!' She surprised herself by using Finnegan's first name. But it seemed to serve in some odd way as a circuit breaker.

Finnegan sighed deeply, before lowering her decibel level. 'Listen, everything you say makes sense from one perspective. But I'm already searching his property on the flimsiest of evidence. I have no basis for an arrest warrant and even less to press charges. And now you want me to dig up a graveyard too?'

'Where better to dispose of a body?'

'Why leave a burnt-out car at one side of town and take the risk of driving the body to the Loop to bury it? It makes no sense.'

'It does if you want people to think Issa just took off and burnt out his own car.'

'And maybe that's exactly what happened.'

'Cleaning up that graveyard was part of Brady's plan. If anybody saw freshly disturbed ground where he'd interred Issa, he could just point to the wider work he'd done renovating the graveyard. Nobody would question it. Nobody would think he'd added a body to those already buried there.'

'Do you know how fucking awkward it is to get permission for that kind of thing? And there's no keeping it quiet, especially if we're wrong. There'd be uproar.'

'Do you think I'm wrong?'

'I think I'd be better off ignoring you and leaving that fucking place and its ghosts undisturbed.'

'It could be closure for Nabila, for Maisah.'

'If I do it, it won't be because you fucking guilt me into it.'

'I'm not trying to. I'm just trying to do my job.'

'You'll have me in a fucking grave if you keep this up.'

CHAPTER FIFTY-THREE

A few days later at first light, Cass stood alongside an unexpected visitor and watched as a specialist Garda team, assisted by a local authority crew and observed by an environmental health officer, got the search of the small graveyard under way.

Nicole Wilson had flown in from the States to witness the exhumation, after Cass had fully detailed what she knew about Brady. Wilson, dressed in plain-clothes so as not to attract interest, was now explaining the reasons why.

'One of DC's most esteemed citizens is a former army ranger who founded his own private military company. No global battlefield too ugly for his contractors. Adored by the Pentagon, donates to Republicans and Democrats, rakes in the cash – you get the picture,' she said.

'After things went to shit in Afghanistan and Iraq, he saw a lot of his company guys – as well as former army colleagues – come home in body bags. The rumour is he started putting up funds and logistical support for ex-soldiers seeking to avenge fallen comrades. A paramilitary hit squad, in other words, still prosecuting old wars. Tracing ghosts.'

'Rumour?' Cass interjected. 'Surely it would take you guys no time to bust open something like that.'

'It's not really our beef. More for the CIA, who could detect and shut it down in a heartbeat like you say. But they don't want to know. Not unless something goes wrong somewhere and it lands on their plate.'

'And you reckon Brady was funded by this guy?'

'Makes sense, don't you think? Cos it wasn't just funding Brady required – he also needed live intelligence to find Issa, he needed active escape routes in case anything went wrong, the works. From what you've told me, I struggle to believe one guy could have executed all of that so cleanly without support.'

'So if we get proof, are you going to make it the FBI's business?'

'I don't like what our esteemed DC citizen is doing. It's wrong on every level. But I got to tell you: back home, a lot of folks would sooner pin a medal on Brady than handcuffs for this.'

'You're saying there'll be no appetite to assist us in finding him, or to investigate this company behind him?'

'I've an appetite to assist, and I'm here with the blessing of my immediate bosses to see what you find. I'm just saying, the level of inter-agency appetite might not be so great.'

'There's nothing honourable in what he did.'

'I can safely say not everybody on our side of the Atlantic will see it that way.'

———

As the morning progressed, Cass brought Wilson up to speed on other matters – chiefly Hugh's imprisonment and its causes, their divorce, and more. She also revealed her liaison with Brady. Wilson apologised for being initially circumspect about revealing the contents of Brady's file.

'Until you mentioned Benghazi and the murders, I thought

there was nothing there,' she said. 'He had an admirable record, plenty of commendations, the esteem of colleagues... but this is some pretty cold shit he did over here.'

Cass had little further to add, and a short time later, Wilson returned to the station to check in with her office and make some calls.

In early afternoon, Noel Ryan took Wilson's place standing alongside Cass, observing the search in progress. 'You really think Brady buried the body here, next to where he was living and sleeping?' he asked.

'He wasn't sleeping. Maybe this was part of the reason why.'

'Gives me the jitters even thinking about it.'

'Tell me about it.'

'Are things always this lively around you?'

'I'm starting to think I'm fucking cursed.'

'Dunno. Can think of people in worse positions.'

'Such as?'

'Whoever gets the job of trying to sell this place after all this shit, for starters.'

———

But thirty-six hours later, as she watched the teams conclude their work and pack up their tools, Cass began to think she really was cursed. They had found nothing, only old bones. No recently buried, decomposing body. No bag or bundle of damaged euro notes. Nothing – not even the shotgun Brady admitted was somewhere on the site.

He tried to tell me.

'A guy like him? Could be anywhere now. Back in Libya for all you know...'

I didn't listen.

And now Finnegan will have to answer for all this.

CHAPTER FIFTY-FOUR

There was no neat way to wrap the item, so Cass stuck a gift tag on it instead. She left it in Finnegan's office and then rang Maisah Sahraoui. She explained as best she could, with the information she could make available, what had happened to Nabila. They had finally identified Nabila's murderer; they just wouldn't be able to bring Akeem Issa to justice.

'I don't understand,' Maisah said. 'Why you cannot catch him?'

Because we think someone else caught him first.

'We believe he's dead, Maisah. We understand he became embroiled in a separate dispute, and was killed in recent months.'

'You know this for sure?'

'We are fairly certain of it.'

Maisah began to cry, and Cass waited patiently until the weeping subsided.

'I am sorry again for your loss, Maisah.'

'You know this man who killed Issa? You know him personally?'

'We believe we do,' Cass said cautiously, 'but you'll understand if I can't identify a suspect to you.'

'I don't want his name,' Maisah said. 'I want you to thank him for me.'

Finnegan came out of her office, her face inscrutable, and summoned Cass in the familiar way.

When she walked in, expecting more trouble, Finnegan was holding the nine-iron – and to Cass's surprise, grinning.

'A token – for being such a pain in the ass. And for backing me anyway.'

'I'll back anyone who brings in results. Two murders, two detected.'

'Three murders,' Cass corrected. 'One killer in prison, one killer in the ground, and one on the loose isn't exactly the closure I was hoping for.'

'Maybe the Yanks will see to Brady.'

'Nicole Wilson says not.'

'She'd know, I suppose.'

'It's a travesty if he's not brought to justice.'

'You honestly think that?'

'All murders are equal.'

'Except you and I both know they're not,' Finnegan retorted. 'Akeem Issa targeted, exploited and murdered an innocent and vulnerable young woman. Brady killed a killer, thinking it would make the world a better place.'

'We're suddenly tolerant of eye-for-an-eye bullshit now?'

'You're talking to the woman who beat the shit out of somebody with a golf club.'

'And left him breathing – there's a world of difference.'

'Look, I'm not sanctioning it. I'm just saying, maybe it's not the worst outcome, on balance.'

'Because I compromised myself?'

'Because you cared for him.'

'The only thing I care about now is locking him up.'

'Fair enough. But it's beyond our limited jurisdiction now, in any event.'

Cass nodded her acquiescence and stood to leave. At the door, almost as an afterthought, she said: 'By the way, if you want me to apologise to Harbour Murphy, I will.'

'Why would I want you to apologise to Harbour Murphy?'

'Because I hassled him a bit, thinking he was involved or knew more than he was letting on.'

'That fella always knows more than he lets on. Good to give him a fucking rattle now and again – keep him in line. Don't you dare apologise to him.'

'Fair enough.'

'If you need some time off, by the way, after all of this–'

'Given my choice in men, the less time I have for my personal life, the better.'

'And a serious answer?'

'I had enough time off, don't you think? Really, I'm fine,' Cass said, before adding: 'For now.'

CHAPTER FIFTY-FIVE

A month later, as the first blushes of spring came to Glencale, and the town readied itself for the new season, Cass arrived to work to find a postcard at her desk.

The front of the card showed a coastline dominated by a huge sea stack, and bore a simple greeting: 'Haystack Rock, Cannon Beach – Welcome to Oregon!'

She flipped the card over to see a neatly written message.

Safe harbor. Swimming great. But miss my style critic.

Harbour is spelt with a 'u', you douchebag.

But despite herself, she smiled at his effrontery. And felt an ember of connection, still burning.

In the weeks since his emergency exit, she'd found herself flicking between the instinct to hunt him and the desire for his company. The latter was insanity, unless she told herself she now knew his very worst secret, and could live with it. Could she?

And if so, how was it she couldn't find it within herself to forgive her ex-husband for his unintentional act of killing and yet tolerate Brady's very deliberate act of murder?

She knew the answer to that question but didn't want to admit it to herself, because to do so would be to acknowledge Finnegan was right: some killings we are prepared to tolerate.

Was 'safe harbor' his private joke that he was out of reach, or code to her that he posed no threat?

'You know now you've nothing to fear from me?'

Yes, Cass thought, *I know that now. And I see your come-find-me plea, and as fucked up as this has been – as fucked up as you may be – I know we had something genuine, if only for a moment.*

But coming to find you?

The following day, she continued to think it was insanity.

And the day after that, she thought she just might.

ACKNOWLEDGEMENTS

A teacher returns some corrected essays and gives a small compliment to one student about the potential of his writing; the student will cling to it for years, on bad days and good...

The editor of a community newspaper studies the empty CV of a teenager with no connections and no experience and decides to give enthusiasm a chance...

A senior journalist believes a colleague of his would be a good fit for government and recommends that person to a Cabinet minister seeking a new advisor...

And so on.

There may be individuals who carve out their own path in life unaided, certain they owe nothing to anyone. I'm not one of them. And so, to all those who have taught, guided and supported me - in ways seen and unseen, major and minor - thank you.

In the context of writing generally and this book specifically, I'd like to express my particular gratitude to the following:

To North Monastery school in Cork city, whose teachers have done so much for so many, and in particular Joe Duffy, Hester Forde and the late Jim Turner for building a kid's confidence.

To Cork City Library and librarians everywhere.

To Dr Finola Doyle O'Neill for early career guidance.

To Stephen Flanagan, for two decades of friendship and support, for reading so many drafts and providing so much invaluable insight. To Michael O'Farrell, for the indispensable feedback and encouragement, and to Senan Molony for reading a previous unpublished effort and insisting I could do better.

To Betsy Reavley at Bloodhound Books, for taking a chance

on this book; to Clare Law for the excellent edit; and to Abbie Rutherford, Tara Lyons, Kate Holmes and Hannah Deuce for their work, as well as the design team for the striking cover.

To my wonderful agent, Annakarin Klerfalk of InterSaga Literary Agency – I wouldn't have got to this point without you.

To my parents, John and Eileen, for their unconditional love and values, and to my siblings, for being the best – I love you guys.

To my parents-in-law, Michael and Anne, for being such wonderful people, and always making me feel at home.

And finally, to Danielle, Líadain, Iseult and Síomha – my world would be nothing without you.

A NOTE FROM THE PUBLISHER

Thank you for reading this book. If you enjoyed it please do consider leaving a review on Amazon to help others find it too.

We hate typos. All of our books have been rigorously edited and proofread, but sometimes mistakes do slip through. If you have spotted a typo, please do let us know and we can get it amended within hours.

info@bloodhoundbooks.com

Printed in Great Britain
by Amazon